The Peace Lover

To Peter and Renate
With fond love and
Best Wishes

Ken

Oct. 23, 06

This Novel is a FICTION work. The characters and names are fictional and any resemblance to characters and names living or deceased is purely coincidental.

ISBN: 1-4196-2357-5

To order additional copies, please contact us.
BookSurge, LLC
www.booksurge.com
1-866-308-6235
orders@booksurge.com

The Peace Lover

Kanwal Mathur

Publisher
2006

The Peace Lover

In loving memory of my wonderful parents.

For my great family and friends

My special thanks to Hilde, my wife,for all her support
Also my daughters,Sibyl and Anu
My son-in-law Hicham
My grandson Malik
And a very special thanks to my son,Arun for the encouragement to write on a new Mac PowerBook G4.

Writing is a type of therapy.
I encourage and recommend that people write at least about their lives.
There is a hidden writer in all of us.

Children should be encouraged and taught to write their thoughts,feelings and experiences in a diary and at some time to put it to print.
Children share,and learn from each other,while learning to express themselves freely.

My sincere thanks also to the great team of dedicated professionals at BookSurge Publishing particularly
Nina Brauer,Carolyn Johnson,Thomas Kephart, Melissa Bolton, Julie Burnett and Kendy Sproul.

One

Peter sat at his desk, in what was a poor excuse for an office, in New Brunswick, New Jersey, he shared with two others, who were in and out, though mostly out. He was in a reflective mood and taking stock of his life. It was one of those moments when workload was really not much to speak of and kind of dull, with a dash of repetitiveness thrown in for good measure.

A moment earlier, he had surveyed his work area, glancing at what was an excuse for an office. Well, he had thought, an office of the United States Government Agency, after all, cannot have any semblance to one in the private industry. The costs and expenses had to be tight, considering taxpayer's money and what not, but all the same, this was a shame.

His office in the Green Energy Corporation, down the road in North Brunswick had been simple, neat, and adequate. He had quit his job as The Spare Parts Manager three years ago because the company was being reorganized and that meant he would have had to move to Richmond, Virginia. The thought of moving was not very exciting, considering the new offices would be in some boony town. He had always lived in a city and although New Brunswick, New Jersey was not an exciting place, it was mighty close to New York City, and New Brunswick was home after all.

He had often wished for some international flair in his life as he grew up, especially when he went to Rutgers University, in his hometown. He had come across some foreign students who came from exciting cities in Europe. The exchange student, Rita, had brought some excitement to his otherwise bland life. She was very intelligent but for some reason everything was always better in *Milano, Italia*; her home town. Peter's mom was overjoyed to meet Rita, being Italian and all that, when he invited her for Thanksgiving dinner at home. The brief affair was not meant to be. He saw himself falling for all the whims she had and felt like a slave. She had the terrible habit of generalizing her arguments and felt she knew it all better than anyone in America. She was damn good looking and insisted that Milan had the best-looking girls and the most handsome men in Europe.

Peter's serious exposure to internationalism came when he worked for the Swiss subsidiary of, the Green Energy Company, in North Brunswick. The Swiss company had a number of Europeans, primarily in the management. The Europeans were multilingual and he felt left out, and often hurt, especially during office social events. There were times he tried hard to get friendly with the European inner circle, but each attempt left him disappointed. He had felt pain, much to his chagrin, as they talked down about Americans in the office and at social events. He had very perplexing emotions, wanting to be part of a group and hearing unexplainable derogatory comments about America. Were they just plain jealous, or ignorant, or both? Joe, his wonderful close friend, a buddy from the old schooldays, had commented once that the Europeans he knew suffered from many shades of inferiority complexes. He knew Joe was right, after all, he had two years of psychology, in under graduate at Rutgers. Joe was an admirably smart guy and a true Jersey kid.

Peter was puzzled about his ancestry. His Granddad was from Switzerland but no one talked about him much. He looked handsome and tall man in the only photograph he had occasionally seen in his Grandma's room. In her rare moments, she shared some of her past, about Grandpa, and especially that he was a bit of a playboy. Peter learnt that he was a person, reserved, an introvert, who kept to himself. Granddad had died during one of his rare trips to Switzerland, where he had gone to attend the funeral of his brother; or was it perhaps a cousin? Grandma preferred to change the subject when it came to Grandpa. It always annoyed Peter when that happened, but Grandma remained unflinched. Granddad was called Carl Miller. Grandma was once looking at some of Grandpa's things, which she kept under lock and key, and in a moment of weakness, showed Peter his Swiss driving license. Grandpa's name on the driving license was Karl Mueller, born

January 1, 1910, in Zurich. There was other information about him, but in German and Peter had regretted not paying much attention to foreign languages in school. Surprised at her slipup about Granddad, she had suddenly snatched the license away from Peter. What was so secret about a driver's license?

Grandma was generally very secretive. Peter had overheard her whispering, at times,. to his dad in a strange guttural language. Dad, Hank Miller, had laughed once that his real name was Heinrich Mueller. Dad had some knowledge of Swiss German but he had also inherited a rather secretive personality, though not as bad as Grandma. Peter had heard him talking in what sounded like an Americanized version of Swiss German to some of his German and Swiss friends from the old country. The group would switch to English if Peter happened to enter the room. Were they being polite, he had wondered, or were they just being secretive? After all, the guttural language was Greek to Peter. He was always left with plenty of unanswered questions about the family past and swore, once, to dig into the family's secretive past.

The other thing that irritated Peter was that his Grandma always called him Hans-Peter. All attempts by his mom and dad to remind her that he was called Peter, and not Hans-Peter, fell on deaf ears.

Peter's mom was, thank God, just the opposite. She was gregarious, boisterous, fun loving, and very Italian and more than made up for the shortcomings of his dad's side of the family. She was a Jersey girl of Italian descent. Her parents spoke no English; which made for many delightful, amusing attempts at conversations. Mom's family was immensely large and a lot of fun. Family get-togethers were loud, noisy, and always centered around food. In fact, his mom seemed to spend many an hour in the kitchen. Mom was a great cook, and Peter and his dad both had a bit of a potbelly to show for it. Peter had plenty of family in the New Brunswick area and he enjoyed the frequent impromptu gatherings. He and his mom's family were baseball fans and there was always much ado about baseball teams, at local and national levels, that kept the conversations at high pitch. Peter was a Brooklyn fan, which he kept to himself to avoid a war with the rest of the family, who were Yankee fans. Individuality was not cherished in his Italian family and any attempt at it met with a torrent of unsolicited comments that left him with a sense of guilt. Peter's cousin Jeanie was also considered a black sheep of the family for being an independent loony.

His observations over the years had been that mom's family considered his dad's family as cold Germans. His Grandma kept a safe distance from the 'rowdy gang,' as she frequently referred to the Italian part of the family. Any attempts to reconcile were met with historical barrage of what the Germans and Italians represented. Peter found this strange, because they were all Americans.

Two

Peter had slowly drifted into memory lane, gazing out of the window as if in deep thought about the business at hand. He was suddenly shaken by the voice of Jeremy, his colleague, who informed him that the chief wanted to see him in about an hour.

Peter's desk had a stack of files that needed some working. He had to review the Department of Security, New Brunswick, section reports from the field and computerize updates in a summary format on the events in the field. Lots of paper work was being computerized so that the upper echelon, with the right clearances, could read the latest summary on the field events. Peter's title was "Event Analyst" in the department. His job description bore little resemblance to his real work because of the rapid changes and constant reorganizations in the Agency. His work was mildly interesting and generally flooded with paper work. Some of the event reports were, however, very interesting but written by agents whose writing skills left much to be desired. The handwriting in many cases resembled those in a doctor's prescription, which only a Pharmacist could decipher. He would frequently request clarifications from the field agents, but was usually met with comments that in short said not to bug them and to go jump in the lake. The polite ones usually said that they had no time and they were involved in something very serious that demanded their undivided attention. Peter often worried that serious security matters were not professionally treated. The chief had consoled him by saying that there were not enough hours in the day to run after every sordid detail, unless absolutely necessary. What constituted absolute necessity? Peter had wondered very often. The field agents, he was told, were highly experienced and did not waste time on the trivial details of an event. Peter worried all the same, since he knew, from his experience working for the Green Energy Company, that trouble always lurked in the details.

He had been strongly motivated to work for the Department after 9/11, when all his patriotic feelings overflowed, meshed with a deep concern about the security problems that the nation faced. The multiple Intelligence agencies hesitated in sharing information, which Peter painfully knew was the heart of the problem, compromising the security of the nation.

Peter headed for the chief's office. Chief Andy Macgregor was coming out of a meeting and looked rather worried. The chief was a cool cat, never ruffled by any situation, no matter how complex. He was a Jersey kid after all and a damn good professional, never at a loss about anything except, as Judy, his secretary, would say, when his wife called.

The chief, after exchanging some brief pleasant comments, looked seriously at Peter and said, "Peter, we have been observing you since you joined the Department and have come to the conclusion that you are one of the serious, caring breed of people, who are in short supply.

The Secretary, of the Department of Security, in Washington was creating an elite team of analysts, selected from the various Intelligence Agencies. The elite team would be multitasked and interchangeable with field operatives. Do you follow me?" the chief asked.

Peter acknowledged with a queried look.

"Your background is suitable for such an job," the chief blurted, not waiting for a reaction. Peter wondered what was coming and his pulse increased, but he decided to remain silent and very attentive.

"Does this mean I have to move to Washington?" Peter enquired. The response was a vehement no.

"You will stay here, so I can keep an eye on you." And with a wry look he said, "Maybe you can help us reorganize the department to become an elite group. Know what I mean?"

Peter had always felt a cool chill when people at work, especially his bosses, said, "You know what I mean?" His old buddy Joe told him once that it meant they want to cover their rear. Somehow, it sounded logical.

The chief's parting words were to the affect that the new assignment was a very highly confidential position with top secret clearance requirement and demanded pure and absolute dedication.

Peter walked slowly back to his office, in deep thought.

"Got fired did ya!" Judy said as he passed her desk, which overflowed with paper. He managed a smile in response. What else could he do? After all, he was heading for a top-secret assignment.

Jeremy said nothing as Peter returned to his unappealing desk. His mind was flooded with questions as he attempted to get a grip on himself. In the old days he would have settled back in his chair, lighted up a Kent cigarette, and poured himself a coffee. Now he had to contend with a watery, lukewarm black liquid: so-called coffee. Boy how he missed, a choc-full-of-nuts heavenly coffee. Starbucks, café latte, came close but not quite. Changing times. Oh well, he thought.

Trying to concentrate on the regular work suddenly took on another meaning. Peter read the field reports and felt now he could contribute more to the department instead of being a mere paper pusher. He could have an input in rectifying matters that seemed to fall by the wayside. The bureaucracy at the higher levels would most likely resist, not realizing that affective and efficient security was vital for the reduction in the growing terrorism that plagued the nation and the world. The prospects of a challenge gave an exciting meaning to his life, which was certainly welcome.

The workday was at an end and Peter strolled down the Main Street to catch a bus home.

He walked to his parent's home, instead of his rented, studio apartment, in New Brunswick, which he barely used. His mom was busy as ever and the aroma of fresh marinara sauce that met him at the door meant yummy food.

His mom took one look and said, "Hey Peter what is new? You have a worried look about you." His mom had that certain knack, so nothing ever escaped her, as far as Peter was concerned. Peter had given up long ago about hiding anything from her.

"Maa, looks like I got a promotion," he said, without much thought on the repercussions that followed. Mom went into an orbit, screaming with joy, and started calling the relatives. A couple of minutes later, cousins, uncles, and aunts started pouring into the house, congratulating Peter.

Fortunately, no one asked about the specifics of the promotion, not until Aunt Silvia, who appeared in all her glory, loudly asked what the promotion was and whether or not he would make more money. Not waiting for an answer, as usual, she said, "My Pietro is now 007 Bond, licensed to kill."

She always thought that Peter worked in a cloak and dagger governmental agency. Aunt Silvia's comments sounded ridiculous enough. Those who heard had a hearty laugh which subsided as the inquisitive minds in the midst awaited a response. Peter felt that he was now licensed to lie, to keep the secret, and said, "No promotion to Bond 007, but more money perhaps." That was good enough for the merry gang and the party continued into late hours. Aunty Silvia kept haunting Peter, saying that he was still a bum, not having married, and should get married to her husband's youngest sister, also by the name Silvia. No chance, Peter thought, specially now with the Top-secret assignment.

Three

The chief had called him the next day and reminded him not to talk about the new assignment, which was subject to approval from some higher-ups in Washington. He was told to catch a train at the New Brunswick station to the Union station in DC. His interview had been scheduled for the afternoon. He was instructed to catch the 9:00 p.m. train, the same day, back to New Brunswick. Judy handed a train ticket to Peter and reminded him that the train to D.C. left within two hours.

"Peter Miller," called a voice on the announcement speaker at the station. "Please come to the information desk for a message." Agent Langdom came up to Peter as he approached the information desk, shook hands with him and without much ado escorted him into a waiting van.

There were two agents in the van, who coldly observed him and greeted him with a nod. The van headed to K Street, stopping in front of an unassuming office building.

The office of the Special Intelligence Agency (SIA) of the Department of Security, was on the top floor and the trio were ushered into a conference room. Some overfed Agent types were meeting and looked up to greet the trio, introducing themselves with inaudible voices. After an exchange of nods, they adjourned.

A sharply dressed, executive-looking agent, with a shining badge, entered the conference room. He greeted them as he shook their hands.

He made some inaudible comments, as he poured himself some coffee. "Help yourselves to some coffee. I am John Schaefer, the Director of Operations of the newly formed Special Intelligence Agency," he said.

"Welcome, Mr. Miller, Mr. Townsend, and Mr. Jackson," he continued. "You have been selected to join a very elite group of analysts, as per the Secretary's order 3974, in the fight against terrorism, which is spreading worldwide. The war on terrorism needed a new innovative approach, since the current strategies were barely working and the politicians were making it into a political football. We badly need a solution that will work, and this elite analyst group must come up with a strategy to solve the nightmare."

Schaefer informed them that the elite group, who came from diverse backgrounds, would comprise of nine Analyst Agents located nationwide. The Director would assign tasks to the Agents. The elite group would be expected to develop new strategies on preventive programs. The nine Agents would be located around the country and would report directly to Director Schaefer in Washington DC. Some of the elite Analysts would be required to travel world wide, as directed.

Schaefer emphasized that all nine Analyst agents must remain single, for the next three years; the time estimated by the Secretary to streamline the operations of the Special Intelligence Agency. The selected nine Analyst agents would carry special IDs and cell phones. The Director discouraged them from discussing new strategies with the current Intelligence Agencies, whom he called the "Establishment," so that fresh approaches for combating terrorism are not sabotaged by people resisting changes.

The establishment had become an increasing liability for the administration. A new approach and reorganization of an antiquated system was mandatory to meet the terror threat. The Director was going to give each of the elite analysts a very special high tech telephone, for communicating with each other and the Director only. A special GPS system, in the office of the Director, would keep track of the location of each agent. As a rule, the agents could call each other and the Director at any time, and be prepared to move with deliberate speed when called for action.

Each Analyst Agent would receive an individual training program. The Director's Administrative Secretary, Cathy, would make all arrangements. Only coded written messages were to be used between the Agents and the Director's office.

"Good Luck," were the Director's parting words as he walked out of the meeting.

The three strangers, Townsend, Jackson, and Miller, were now suddenly linked to each other in a secret bond. They walked up to the Director's office and were introduced to Cathy, the Administrative Secretary. The trio fell instantly in love with Cathy.

Peter returned home after midnight. A new chapter in his life had begun, full of hope, challenge, and excitement.

Four

Chief Macgregor was all over Peter the next morning, fishing for information. Peter responded vaguely that the elite group was in its infancy and would take time before it became an efficient group. Peter was careful not to divulge any names or a gist of the briefing he received in Washington DC.

Chief Macgregor slowly tired of the vague responses from Peter and started to lose interest. "Peter, me lad", he said. "I need your desk for a newcomer from the New York office. Why don't you work out of your home or look for another work place? But do stay in touch. Know what I mean? Sorry for rushing you and good luck."

Peter gathered his belongings in the office and the phone rang. It was Judy. "I am sorry you got laid off Peter," she said, in a cute Jersey accent. "I will miss ya, honey!" Peter took a deep sigh of relief that his new job was still a secret.

The window in his office suddenly crashed to the floor with a loud bang. Jeremy stood up and cursed. He said that it was a group of juvenile delinquents who had recently thrown stones at windows in the Public Service Office next door, the other day. There was a commotion as people from the office came in to see what had happened. Peter looked around the room to survey for any collateral damage and his eye caught sight of a sharp hole in the office wall. Jeremy and Jim also saw the hole and upon examining said that it was a bullet hole. Suddenly policemen were all over the building. The detectives looked around the room for evidence and took photos of the bullet hole in the wall. Peter quietly slipped away and kept looking over his shoulder as he caught a bus home.

The special ID phone rang, with Cathy at the other end. "Peter," she said. "Move out of your apartment. You might be in danger. Temporary arrangements have been made for a house located at 201 Lake Drive in North Brunswick, owned by a Secret Service Officer, known in the neighborhood as an Insurance salesman for a Midwestern Insurance company. The home and communications in the house were secure."

Peter went back to his apartment and packed his luggage. He called his mom to inform her that his new job required that he relocate immediately.

He hailed a cab and they went to 201 Lake Drive. Policemen with guns drawn, surrounded the house. The police waved the cab to stay away.

"The occupant has been found dead," said a cop as Peter approached. Peter was surprised but decided not to ask any questions and went back to his parent's home in New Brunswick. His mom was immensely happy and hugged and kissed him as though she hadn't seen him for ages.

The special phone rang again. This time it was Schaefer. "Peter, you may be earmarked by someone who is trying scare tactics. I suspect it is the establishment, who are now wise to you having joined the SIA. We must create a diversion for your safety. Take a few days off work and spread the word that you have quit your new assignment for a job with the Department of Commerce."

Peter was a bit shook-up, but the time with his mom gave him a chance to relax as he prepared himself mentally for the new adventure. His dad seemed quietly worried about what was happening, but remained busy with his routine.

A letter, from the Department of Commerce, arrived after a couple of days, confirming his job with the Statistical group in the New York City branch office. Peter casually waved the letter to his mom and left it on the dining table to make sure the family knew about his new job. Peter also called the old office in New Brunswick and told Jeremy that he had been transferred to the Commerce Department. Jeremy's response startled Peter

"Hey, it is better to be safe than sorry. The detectives suspect that the bullet was meant for someone specific...you perhaps?"

A week went by and Peter worried about what he had gotten into.

Peter followed the directions to the Department of Commerce office near Battery Park, in the City. The New York Office manager, Tom Henley, welcomed him and gave him a small office with a view of the Hudson River. He got an ID which legitimized his work place. It was easy to get lost in the five floor offices. Everyone was busy and Peter knew that New York was a good place to maintain a low profile. Tom Henley, Peter thought, must know something because he never asked any questions, gave no assignments, and offered no comments.

Cathy gave Peter a schedule for the crash training course. All the experts were in the New York state. The next ten days, Peter felt overwhelmed by the various experts, who were veterans in their fields of expertise, no doubt. The workout was very complete, mentally as well as physically, and left Peter drained at times. Peter became awed by know how and the substance in the training courses and the realization that the technology was advancing at a dizzying speed. He felt very confident and ready to take it on and yet had a strange feeling that the technology was in command with a money flag, running the country, pulling the rest of the world kicking and screaming. The trend of humanity, regrettably, was steering towards increased aggression and more conflicts. Human compassion and values were sadly losing out.

Peter saw innumerable applications of technology deployed in the tactical field. He realized the commercial aspects of the technology, which needed a market and sales venue to convert it into money. New tools of combat were being tested in the field. The human being was but a guinea pig and a slave to greed since the start of the industrial revolution. What ever happened to sacred life? Peter wondered.

He could think of several peaceful applications of the new technology, but the experts he met appeared indifferent. The last on the list of trainers, who were all known by ridiculous numbers like Gh792 and so on, to protect their identity, had it all figured out when his parting words were, " Technology that destroys makes big money and increases power, and power rules the world."

Peter could not muster an appropriate response. How could he tell the trainer that he was a peace lover at heart?

Five

Director Schaefer left a message for Peter to meet him in New York City, at the Hilton Hotel on the Avenue of Americas, the next day at 5:00pm.

Schaefer looked Peter over when they met and gave a sign of approval.

"Peter, your ancestry being Swiss," he said. "I want you to tackle and resolve a persistent problem we have with the Swiss weapon manufacturers, who we suspect supply arms, either directly or through channels, to hostile groups and countries. We have assurances from the Swiss government that they are doing everything to keep it under control, but we have our suspicions. Arms are now sold to terrorist groups very often, without the knowledge of governments. The idea is to cut the supply of arms and the funds making their way to the terrorist groups. I know it is a tall order for a first assignment but I have full confidence in you. Remember you are not licensed to kill.Good luck, *mein freund.* "

Cathy, as usual, was on the ball and the next day Peter was on a flight to Zurich. He managed to sleep on the overnight flight out of New York. Peter took a train to the United States Embassy in Bern to get some briefing and to meet his contact in Switzerland, as instructed.

The contact was on home leave so he met with the Intelligence Officer, who gave him a list of the manufacturers and names of some contacts the U.S. used in earlier attempts to resolve the problem. Peter returned to Zurich and checked into Hotel Astor, a short walk from the station on the Weinbergstrasse.

Fall was very much in the air. Peter had a nice view of the city, the lake, and the Alps from his hotel room.

Too early to call it the day, he walked down to the Central and along the river Limmat. The Niederdorf area had a row of friendly looking bars.

He looked across the bar as he ordered a beer and saw Edmund Meirhof from the Green Energy Company, with whom he had worked on a project with Virginia Electric. Edmund saw him and waved with a loud laugh.

"Hey Hans Peter, old buddy. What are you doing here"?

It turned out to be a very pleasant evening, catching up on old times and topping the evening with a *servelat* sausage and delicious *brot.* Peter gave Edmund his business card, which read:

Peter Miller
Development Consultant
United States Department of Commerce
New York, N.Y.

Edmund was impressed with Peter's credentials and repeated it a few times during the conversation. He was envious of Peter for having escaped the corporate turmoil. He gave Peter some sad stories on how the reorganization had devastated some of their old colleagues.

The only contact name from the Embassy, who was responsive, offered to meet with Peter the next day for lunch. Dieter Hopf was an employee of the Swiss Department of Defense, about sixty and looked fit. An ardent skier, he was once a Swiss national ski champion. Dieter held the rank of a Colonel in the Swiss army. He was multilingual and had seen quite a bit of the world, working for the private industrial sector and the Swiss government. He had that air of quiet efficiency about him that impressed Peter from the very first day they met.

Peter recalled how amused he was at the military ranks of some of the Swiss employees when he worked in the Green Energy Company. Military service in Switzerland was compulsory. Some of the Swiss he knew went on to the officer's training program and came up the military ranks. Business had to take a back seat, Peter remembered, because of the minimum three weeks military training courses each year in addition to the ski holidays and the minimum four weeks holidays and Swiss holidays. Peter also remembered how some of his Swiss colleagues at work pulled their military ranks with other Swiss colleagues, when push came to shove.

Dieter explained to Peter, when they met, that the Swiss government was also deeply concerned about the matter but had not made any headway. Some of the council members in the Swiss parliament were not in favor of joining forces with the U.S. because of the media attention in Switzerland, which clobbered the politicians' failed attempts to seek a solution. Dieter arranged a meeting with the Federal Council member in charge of the Defense Department in Bern for the next day.

Dr Hans Hilfiger was pretty much on the ball and promptly accepted Peter's proposal to let a NGO or a private consultant explore a solution. Peter gave Hilfiger his new business card which read:

Peter Miller
Business Consultant

Dr Hilfiger suggested to Peter that he apply for a Swiss passport because of his father's dual (Swiss and U.S.) citizenship. The Swiss passport would come handy for his work in Switzerland.

Dieter was very resourceful and called some of his shady contacts, informing them that he had a potential buyer of weapons.

The meeting with Prof. Doctor Hans Malinofsky was cold to start with, as the well dressed man in his seventies drilled Peter on his credentials, taking notes all the time.

"My son, now settled in the U.S. went to Seton Hall University," Malinofsky said, as if to test Peter, and seemed to relax when Peter said that he was a graduate of the Rutgers University in New Jersey.

The dialogue that ensued revealed that Malinofsky had been a professor in the Warsaw University and had lived in Zug the last ten years as a Research Consultant to Maschinen Fabrik Muehle in Schaffhausen. Malinofsky held impressive patents on armaments. He pulled out some from his briefcase, to show them to Peter. The meeting abruptly ended as Malinofsky excused himself and wishing Peter a nice stay in Switzerland, left the restaurant.

Dieter informed Peter that Malinofsky would check Peter out, and if satisfied, would take Peter to the next phase. Dieter cautioned Peter that patience, nerves of steel, sharp wits, and lots of money was the name of the game. It was now clear to Peter that trust had to be established, like in all business developments.

"By the way," Dieter said, pulling out the Swiss passport. "Here you go. Reliable Swiss efficiency." Peter nodded as he put the passport in his jacket to admire it later in the privacy of his room.

Cathy called. Peter should withdraw funds as needed, through the Intelligence Officer at the US Embassy in Bern. Peter wondered how Cathy knew that Peter was posing as a buyer and would need money.

Several days passed and other attempts to make contact with shady dealers were not successful. Peter decided, on the spur of the moment on Saturday morning after a breakfast of tasty Swiss coffee and croissant, to take a trip to Geneva by train. Peter was surprised that he was able to catch some Swiss German words, but most folks he had met spoke good English. He sat in the smoking section of the train, after buying a Swiss cigar. He remembered how Grandpa loved to smoke them and the whole house stank while mom and grandma complained.

No sooner had he lit the strong tasting swiss cigar, when Malinofsky suddenly appeared in front of him and said, "*Isch noch frei?*" Meaning; is the seat available? Malinofsky was quiet, occasionally glancing at Peter, as he read the *Zuricher Zeitung*. There was, to Peter's amazement, a silent communication with Malinofsky on not to speak first. The coffee and sandwich cart came and Peter took coffee *mit rahm* and a bottle of Henniez water *ohne gaz*. Peter ordered in Swiss German, hoping desperately that the man understood him.

The man responded in English with a kind smile and said *weider lueger*, meaning good bye in Swiss German.

Malinofsky made the first move, as expected by Peter, enquiring about where Peter was going.

"No, I am going to Lausanne today," Malinofsky said, as if to say; you get off at Lausanne too. They both got off at the Lausanne station and walked across to the taxi stand. Malinofsky opened the door and motioned Peter to get in. "To the train station in Blonay,", Molinofsky said, in English. The taxi driver turned around and said that he spoke no English, so Malinofsky gave the direction in French, with ease.

Quite suddenly, Malinofsky turned to Peter and said accusingly, "Who are you? No one in this business ever heard of you. Don't lie, Mr. Peter, or death will be swift when you least expect it because this business does not tolerate imposters."

Peter kept his cool and said that he represented several clients who desperately needed an assortment of RPGs, machine guns, AK47s, and 40 bazookas and that his clients would take all if Malinofsky could deliver.

After a moment of silence Malinofsky said, "Let us see what you can do fast. We have a twenty-foot container that was intercepted during transport to the Swiss military camp. Delivery had to be taken by Monday morning, before the search for the lost container by the Swiss army got serious. The container was on a transport truck, hidden in a large storage facility near here and you can see it now if you agree to take delivery on Monday morning against cash in two suit cases."

"What is in the container?" Peter asked.

"Lots of rapid-fire weapons and RPGs. We do not have a manifest or papers," Malinofsky said.

"If you are for real and need the firepower urgently, you will take it now and we will then be in business," Malinofsky said, with an air of a nasty challenge.

Malinofsky lost no time and directed the taxi driver up the hill near Vevey. The taxi stopped at a storage warehouse, with a big "Condemned" sign.

"The storage facility will be demolished on Monday afternoon," Malinofsky said, as they walked towards the door, which opened as if someone expected them. Peter walked in and among piles of old construction materials saw an army container, locked with the seal of the Swiss army.

Peter walked around the container and said, "We will take the gamble." Surprising himself. "How much?" he asked, sounding like a professional.

"Twenty million Swiss francs, in cash," was the prompt answer.

"Done," said Peter.

There was a look of surprise on the face of Malinofsky and he responded with a sign of thumbs-up.

The taxi pulled in to the station in Lausanne and Malinofsky shook hands with Peter, saying that he would call him in the Hotel Astor on Sunday night to give him the final directions for the pickup.

"Don't play any games, you can be sure we will kill you," were the warning parting words from Malinofsky.

Peter was desperate and nervous at what he had committed to doing. The threat of death was real, if he failed.

Back in his room in Zurich, it was almost midnight. He debated calling Dieter first or Schaefer and decided to call Dieter. Dieter listened to it all and said that he would call back in half an hour. Sure enough, after half an hour on the dot, the phone rang.

"Meet me at the Zurich train station, at the ticket counter number 5, at 9:00am tomorrow," was Dieter's response.

The station on Sunday was busy and Peter made eye contact with Dieter, who motioned for him to follow. They walked up to an office on the first floor of the train station, with an armed guard at the door who saluted Dieter before opening the door. The office room was filled with cigar smoke. There were three military officers, who looked very serious and shook hands with Peter and Dieter.

One of the high ranking military officers rapidly laid out the instructions to Peter.

"The container you saw in Blonay, yesterday, has been moved to a warehouse in Lausanne. We have been tracking it. We are glad you accepted the offer from Malinofsky. Please take down all the instructions from Malinofsky and confirm that the money, in cash, will be in two metal suitcases. We will arrange for you to pick up a rental car tomorrow morning at the rental agency in Central Platz for driving to the warehouse in Lausanne with the suitcases, containing twenty million Swiss francs. You will be accompanied by a rough looking, undercover military policeman, who will stay with you in the hotel tonight, as a bodyguard, and will coordinate the action with us.

As soon as you exchange the rental car, containing the money, with the container truck, drive the container truck to the border at Basel, on the main *autobahn* to Germany. The border police in Basel and Germany will do some checking and allow you to cross into Germany. The border police will instruct the undercover policeman with you, on the drop-off location of the container truck. An unmarked police car will pick you up at the drop-off site and bring you back to the hotel through the back roads, to make sure no one is following you. We suspect, however, that Malinofsky's men will follow your container truck up to the German border."

Peter took a deep breath and prayed to the Lord. It all sounded excitingly simple enough.

Dieter walked back to the train station, main level, with Peter and filled him on some of the details. "The police have been tracking several suspicious individuals and plan to catch the ringleader. We should also meet an official of the Swiss bank in the next days to follow up on the deposit of the money by Malinofsky and his instructions to transfer the twenty million Swiss francs."

Peter walked back to the hotel lobby and hung around to see if he could spot any suspicious characters that may have followed him. He walked up to the check-in counter and thought of changing his room in case he was being watched. He told the clerk that he needed to change his room to the other side of the hotel because of the noise from the street below. "Oh yes," she said, promptly gave him a new key. "You are now registered as Mr. Dieter Mueller. Please leave the hotel in the morning by the front door and a rental car will take you to the rental agency."

She handed him a call message from Dieter, informing him that the undercover policeman was in the adjoining room. The Swiss think of everything, Peter thought.

Malinofsky called late at night, and the bodyguard immediately connected a hearing device as soon as Peter picked up the receiver.

"Mr. Peter," said a muffled voice, not responding when Peter tried to identify the caller. "Meet me tomorrow morning at Esherwys Platz at 10:00am, with the money. You must come in a rental car with the two suitcases, loaded with the money, in the luggage compartment. You drive away in the container truck and we will drive away in your rental car. Report that the rental car has been stolen in Esherwys Platz in the afternoon and not before."

The phone went dead, before Peter could say anything. The undercover policeman indicated that it was too short to get a trace on the call.Peter called the rental car agency to confirm that he would pick up the rental car before 9:00am.

Peter came out of the hotel just before 9:00am and suddenly, as if out of nowhere, Malinofsky appeared and shook Peter's hand, motioning him to walk with him around the corner to the tram stop. There, stood a truck, partially blocking the street with a gray colored container.

"I have to pick up the car, and you told me that we make the exchange at 10:00 am at Escherwyss Platz. And what is with the gray colored container?" Peter protested.

Malinofsky quickly pushed Peter to sit next to the truck driver and crammed himself into the front seat.

"We don't want you to get caught driving a military green colored army container so we painted it commercial grey." They took the short drive to the car rental location, with Peter bewildered about the sudden change in the plans.

The undercover policeman, he had met at night, appeared at the counter of the rental car agency with a grouchy face, wearing Rental Car Overalls, as Peter walked up.

"You were supposed to pick the car up earlier," he said, looking at Peter's driver's license. "So the rental charge rate will be from 8:00am." Peter felt pleasantly stunted at what was taking place and waited while the rental forms were filled out, under the watchful eye of Malinofsky.

"Your luggage was delivered an hour ago. It is too big for the trunk space so you have a van for the same rate," said the undercover policeman as he cursed at the ignorant tourist.

Peter felt a gush of life returning to his body. The van was loaded with the two boxes, just barely.

Malinofsky said, "Mr. Peter, I will come with you in the car."

The Under cover agent screamed at them, "You cannot leave this truck here for more than five minutes, otherwise it will be towed away."

"Yes! Yes! I will be right back, " Peter shouted back, not knowing if that was in the impromtu drama unfolding , as he drove off with Malinofsky.

"Turn left. Now right, and drive in to the parking garage," ordered Malinofsky. Peter, upon being asked to park the van, saw four men and three women, very well dressed, walking towards them.

"Open the rear door of the van and open the boxes," ordered Malinofsky.

Peter found that the boxes were not locked. The four men asked Peter to step back as they examined the stacks of Swiss franc notes in the two boxes, methodically. The women cohorts received instructions in some language totally Greek to Peter and punched keys into what appeared to be some kind of calculators. Peter could see that this team had done this type of work before. They looked at Peter and smiled from time to time. Peter suddenly realized that they were wearing very natural looking facial masks. He wondered whether Malinofsky also wore a mask and what was going to happen next.

There were cars coming in the parking garage but the team kept working and did not draw any attention. It was about half an hour before Malinofsky came up to Peter with a smile.

"Our check of the money is now complete. You may go back and pick up the container truck. My informants tell me that you have a bargain with the type and quality of weapons that are in the Container. How come you work alone?" he said, looking content with himself.

"I prefer it that way, to avoid any confusion. I trust people so I have no cause for concern. My clients are very well organized, which makes my job easier. I do not have to threaten people with death like you did to me. Would you like to come with me to Germany? Otherwise it will be a lonely drive," Peter said, very relaxed.

"So, you take the weapons to Germany? I am indeed very sorry for threatening you and also changing the location of the swap, and I saw that it did not cause any alarm. We have to be very careful in not falling for a trap," said Malinofsky, sounding cautious.

"Yes, and I should hurry, otherwise the container truck will be towed away, which will make my client ferociously angry," Peter said, looking at his watch.

Peter walked away from the Malinofsky gang and took a taxi back to the car rental agency. The undercover policeman was sitting in the driver's seat and looked impatient as he talked to a policeman, who appeared to be giving him a ticket.

Peter drove the truck to Basel, getting lost a couple of times. The border police asked for the papers, which Peter had none. He was asked to step out and led to the office. Peter had no way to communicate since the police tried talking in German and then in French. The truck had canton Vaud license plates. The police was on the phone and after a few minutes a man entered with a stack of papers. A brief discussion ensued. The police gave him and Peter an OK sign and Peter drove the truck to the German police check point, who waved him on. The man carrying the stack of papers was following the truck in an expensive Mercedes and flashed his car lights to get Peter's attention. Peter pulled into a gas station off the autobahn. The man followed him in. He was a private investigator, working for the Swiss police and told him to drive to a Total gas station at the Karlsruhe exit.

"We will leave the container truck there and I will drive you back to the hotel in Zurich," he said.

Dieter woke him next morning and it was off to the meeting with the Swiss bank. Mr. Moore in the bank was informed that they expected the cash money to be deposited in an account opened many years ago by Malinofsky. Most of the large transfers were made to Italy and were monitored by the Italian Intelligence. The new banking laws required lengthy investigations on the source of the funds, etc. The border police at all border crossings were on alert. The money could not leave Switzerland. The money was not marked because the crooks were very sophisticated and would become alarmed. Two ring leaders in the arms trade had been identified in Italy and would be arrested if the twenty million Swiss francs were transferred into their account in Italy.

Peter was greatly relieved, and yet, worried about the consequences if the money slipped out of reach of the Swiss, after all, Malinofsky and his compatriots were professionals. They probably could second guess any plans the Swiss had to trap them in their covert ventures. His name would be mud and the Department would fire him for his innovative ideas that cost the Swiss twenty million Swiss francs. The what-ifs and the consequences of such a failure seemed astronomical to him. He admired the banker's confidence in the plan to arrest the ring leaders but it could all fail if the money slipped out of Switzerland. If, however, the plan succeeded it would only amount to a small success in the interdiction of the sales of weapons to hostile parties. A better plan was needed, urgently.

Peter shared his concerns with Dieter, who smiled and said, "Patience, my friend. Slowly, slowly, catchy monkey."

Six

Schaefer called to review Peter's progress and was updated. He encouraged Peter to find another approach to deal with the problem of weapons ending in the hands of terror cells. Schaefer was encouraged that the major banks had finally started cooperating but there were all those mid to small sized banks who appeared to be out of control.

Peter suggested making Switzerland an example that could be implemented in other countries. Schaefer laughed, "Peter, I really enjoy your idealism. Thank God for visionaries, otherwise there would be no hope for us mortals."

Schaefer reminded Peter that, as a rule most bureaucrats are conservative individuals who shy from making decisions unless either put under the gun or made to hurt where it counts, the pocket. "I am afraid most of the general public behaves the same. Most decision makers in governments are reactive instead of being active. Mediocrity has become the rule instead of being an exception. There is an acute shortage of true leaders. I am sorry, Peter, if I sound too down beat, but please don't be discouraged by my comments," Schaefer said, with a deep sigh.

Peter was used to such lectures in realism; they meant nothing more than a copout to him. Peter decided to invite Dieter for a brain storming session in a quiet Restaurant with private rooms for small groups, which was in the quaint town of Rapperswil at the end of the lake of Zurich.

They began listing what had been done so far and the current government strategy; to curtail the sales of weapons from Switzerland to hostile groups and then follow it with a proposal for a new plan. Dieter smiled and said, "Yes. Yes. American, corporate style. Position Paper."

- All attempts so far were cloak and dagger type. The cost was high and very little to show for it. Dieter estimated the bureaucratic cost per year was around five million Swiss francs.
- The area of interdiction required controlling many agencies, private groups, banks etc. The logistics of getting the cooperation of all was an insurmountable task.
- The Politicians, special interest groups, party politics and affiliations diluted the efforts to get the problem resolved.
- Historically, regimes under a dictatorship or an autocratic head of the state controlled such problems by dealing a severe blow to the enemies of the state.
- Fear factor, implemented as law, generally worked against the enemies of the state. Combating fear with fear had historically worked but the efforts to protect the innocent had been inadequate.
- Most of the rebellions occurred against oppressive regimes that had forced citizens to resort to destructive actions. Revenge often became the rule, banding several groups who shared this destructive approach as a possible solution.
- It had been a very rare happening when a regime sat down with the opposition to negotiate in good faith. The Regimes ended up enforcing their will on the people.
- Poverty, abject poverty in many cases, forced taking up of arms to get the attention of the Rulers/Government.
- There was a failure of Governments all over the world to serve the interest of the destitude.
- There was a failure to provide sound education at grass roots level.
- Corruption, in society, increased the sense of hopelessness in people

The terror groups could be classified as follows:
Freedom fighters
Fighters because of sheer desperation
Fanatics
Severe fanatics
Just plain bad elements in society who destroyed with or without a cause.

Peter and Dieter felt that the list of current status covered the major considerations and observations.

The new Proposal for Switzerland would be:

Invite the Insurgents, publicly, to come for meetings to address their grievances, and their desire to procure weapons to fight for their cause, guaranteeing them safe passage and the nonviolent resolution of their problem with their active cooperation. The progress on the implementation of the solution agreed should be made public and transparent.

Simultaneously meet those Insurgents, privately, who do not wish to address their grievances in public

Insist on resolving the Palestinian, Sudan, and other extremely critical conflicts around the world with the resolve of peace pacts on no more aggressions by the parties in conflict. Switzerland should play the role of the Peace Maker.

A declaration that all and any conflicts must be settled by negotiations.

Illegal possession of any weapon will result in extremely heavy fines. Any weapon legally acquired must be registered, and kept with the local police authorities.

The weapon manufacturers in Switzerland should not be allowed to sell to Private buyers, unless approved by the Police/Government.

The well-known, spiritual value based programs, such as those operated in India and other countries by acclaimed teachers should rehabilitate terrorists, insurgents, and all those held in the jails for offences against the public.

Establish World Human Value Educational Centers, all over the world with particular emphasis in countries where insurgency is a critical problem.

Introduce a Resolution in the United Nations, which should be signed by all nations in the world denouncing that violence shall not be the medium for settling disputes. Special purpose UN offices should be set up to negotiate and resolve disputes. The local UN offices should ensure prompt attention and resolve as a preventive measure.

The performance of each elected government in the world should be monitored and the results made public.

Dieter and Peter looked at the Position Paper again and again and felt a challenge coming on that would be worth putting heart and soul into. Dieter then transmitted the Position Paper to Dr Hilfiger in Bern.

Peter felt that the response could be that the conceptual proposals are too idealistic, but it should be publicly made clear to the opposition that not resolving the growing weapon problems was a cardinal sin and a failure of their sworn duty to the public who elected them.

The adrenalin in Peter was running high. He sat, in the evening, looking over the Herald Tribune in his hotel room. The papers were full of bad news; conflicts, murders, and what have you. Humanity was indeed in a very sad state. His cell phone ringing startled him.

"Hi Peter," came the terribly sweet voice of Cathy. "How is the business of Peace coming along? Schaefer was planning a meeting of the analyst agents to brainstorm on Friday, next week, 9:00am in the K street office."

"Okay by me," he replied.

Dieter called to inform that Dr Hilfiger would meet them the following afternoon at 2:00 pm, in his office to discuss the Position Paper. Peter felt a sense of pride in the quiet efficiency of the Swiss. Dr Hilfiger had planned the meeting on Friday so that the Federal Council members would have the weekend to think over and then prepare for a debate during the Full Council meeting, on the following Wednesday.

Peter went for a morning stroll along Zurich Lake. The air was cool and the walk was energizing. Dieter picked him and they drove to Bern for the meeting with Dr Hilfiger. Peter was mentally prepared for a debate; after all, the solution steps were radically different.

Dr Hilfiger and the meeting participants had read the Position Paper.

"Mr. Miller, what makes you think that your proposal will work?" asked Dr Pouch, one of the Council members from Canton Valais.

There was a moment of silence and Peter spoke, "Gentlemen, Gandhi succeeded in getting the British out of India with a non-violence strategy. We forget that we are all human beings and have created a massive, complicated mess by not adhering to human principals and rights. The world has tried solutions that disregard human values. Just imagine, every day we watch television images of suffering all over the world, and we can switch channels to entertain ourselves with no pain or concern for our fellow human beings. We watch conflicts, destruction, people in pain, every day and we carry on as if we do not give a damn, and feel that it is somebody else's problem. We are immune to the human tragedy. All we see are governments that continue to fail the human cause, as the public at large watches in panic and horror. Let us give peace a chance if we are going to survive. There are very serious problems that face us, including the availability of weapons in the hands of hostile groups and countries with environmental calamity at our door steps. Some leaders talk about economics of trade and employment with no concern to the pain and destruction the illegal arms and weapons, easily available to hostile groups, inflict. We are fueling the fire and not extinguishing it."

Peter's presentation shocked the participants. They had never heard such straight talk. A brief silence gave way to wondering the sanity of Peter. Peter observed ego taking over substance in low toned murmurs. There was no doubt now that the speech was interpreted as a wake up call. Dieter smiled at him with a wink of approval. The next hour the discussion appeared to get louder and at times heated, among the Federal Council members, in Swiss German and at times in French. Peter worried that he was left out, and his attempts to intervene fell by the wayside. Coffee and refreshments were brought in but the discussion stayed uninterrupted. Peter started feeling fatigued from the air of anxiety and concerned that no one appeared to be addressing the contents of the Position Paper.

Dr Hilfiger looked at Dieter and Peter and said that the council needed more discussion time and would continue at the Wednesday Federal Council meeting, next week.

"Good presentation, Mr. Miller. Let us hope for the best," Dr Hilfiger said, with a dry smile. "We will be in touch."

Dieter's impression of the meeting was politely good. He felt good vibes but the Council members were critical since no other country had considered the new approach. Typical reaction of politicians, they do nothing and will not let others do anything either, thought Peter.

Seven

Peter received a call on Saturday, from a man named Breder, who was the Vice President of the Maschinen fabrik in Shaffhausen. He invited Peter for dinner.

Breder was a tall, well dressed, military type, in his late fifties; a man of the world. The Restaurant in Hotel Waldhaus Dolder had an impressive view of the Zurich city and the lake.

Breder expressed concern about Peter's efforts to reduce hostilities. He was alarmed that the outcome of Peter's proposals would seriously affect the bottom line of the Swiss weapons industry. Peter wondered how much Breder knew about his presentation in Bern.

"I don't think so," was the confident answer from Peter.

Breder decided to be frank. "You have proposed that we suppliers refrain from selling to private groups. Thirty percent of our sales are to private groups and we get Swiss government approval before the sale is consummated."

"Do you know where the weapons are used?" asked Peter.

"We do not consider it our business once the client pays and takes delivery. You want to change the way the arms industry does business."

Peter decided not to start a match of argumentative words.

"The spreading of terror in the world is everybody's business. We should pool our brain power to find a solution that does not impact your bottom line." Peter felt that he had touched a nerve with Breder, so he continued, "Would your company, and all the other weapon manufacturers in Switzerland, be interested in diversifying into the space industry to offset the income from sales to private groups? The private weapons buyer should buy through the Swiss Department of Defense. So you would still make sales to the private groups that meet the government's safety criteria. You will in fact be transferring the process of approving, tracing, etc. to the government, and diversify into the space industry, which is a growing and profitable industry."

Breder looked comfortable, "An interesting idea, Mr. Miller. I will discuss it at our next meeting of the Manufacturer's Association, of which I am the President. I will keep you updated and will call you or Mr. Dieter Hopf."

So, that is how Breder reached me, Peter thought. News traveled fast.

Peter was mulling over how the meeting had gone and realized that the weapon manufacturers were not a bad lot. They appeared willing to accommodate, in the interest of public safety, as long as their bottom line was not affected. All the same, Peter wondered about the kind of human beings working in the arms industry world over. It was true that about thirty percent of the world trade was weapons that killed and caused incredible amount of human tragedy.

Alfred Nobel, the founder of dynamite, must have had some trace of human concern, perhaps more like guilt, when he founded the Nobel Prize foundation.

Peter recalled that a person he had met state side, a scientist in the defense industry, had justified it all in that the dynamite was for defense and the construction industry. This person, however, agreed that history reveals that the true nature of human beings is aggressive, if challenged, some more than others, and the sword was mightier than the pen. How sad.

Eight

The meeting room in the K Street office in Washington was small and had a window, which was rare since only the management, or the big honchos, occupied offices with windows. The size of your office was directly proportional to the rank you carried in the department. The field operatives were given cells in a large office room. Why did the guys who did the dirty work have such cramped work places? Peter was pondering as he walked through the maze of offices to the meeting room.

There were six people in the meeting room.

Schaefer entered the room at 9:00 am and quietly sat down at the head of the table. There were some refreshments and a large thermos with coffee with additives on a side table.

Schaefer smiled, after some thought, "Would any one like a coffee or refreshments before we get started?" The six in the room walked over to the refreshment table, making small talk.

"You don't know each other, so why don't you introduce yourselves," Schaefer said, trying to get the meeting started.

Gina Davis, from California; Bud Mullen; Amin Hasan; Mina Fernandez; Fred Hopkins; and Peter Miller.

"I thought it would be helpful for the elite analysts to meet so that we could share the progress. You may take notes and I will prepare a gist of the meeting for the Secretary of the Department of Security. Please be extremely careful with your notes. We live in strange times," Schaefer informed.

"The meeting today will be for each one to report your progress and we will summarize tomorrow, before you return to your assignments. Any questions or comments?"

Mina Fernandez went first. She had a background in the Security Industry, and later worked for the FBI. Her update was an array of the technology in place and being developed to combat terrorism. Some of the high tech systems, Peter heard, were way beyond "big brother is watching."

Gina Davis had worked for the New York Police Department and was down to earth in her narration on increasing police patrol and severe sentences for the terror cells. The intelligence gathering, done by the police, was affective in the past. The NYPD and other police departments around the country were increasingly under pressure for faster responses and interdiction. She was working on improving listening devices that the police were deploying and expected that the results would be encouraging.

Bud Mullen was an Intelligence officer in the Pentagon for many years, and was preparing better coordination on Intelligence between the several agencies. He cited that at least one Intelligence agency had received a warning before every terror attack, but had failed to react promptly because each member of the Intelligence community had preconceived notions on what was a real and an unreal threat. A very severe problem according to Mullen was in the perception and lack of knowledge of the enemy. He was therefore working on educational aspects so the agents would learn about the behavioral psychology of the terrorists.

Amin Hasan gave an angry update about the lack of knowledge in the Intelligence community about not only the Muslim world but also the world at large. Someone who had never been in the field and possessed little or no knowledge of what or how to evaluate the raw data collected, very often did the evaluation. He proposed infiltrating the ranks of the terrorist cells, as had been done in the two world wars and major conflicts. Israel, in his opinion, had a better Intelligence collecting and evaluating system than the United States in spite of the massive resources available. He complained that there were "Too many chiefs and no Indians." The Insurgents, according to Amin, were a select group of rogues in Muslim communities all over the world. These select groups were a menace to all peace loving Muslims, who felt intimidated. The trouble was that very few agents had even bothered to look at the documented evidence, let alone learn Arabic and other Muslim languages. It was crucial to have qualified experienced agents collect and evaluate the data on the Middle East and implement the corrective actions.

This could eliminate at least fifty percent of the intelligence paper pushing personal employed by the Intelligence departments. He estimated that the government had a miniscule percentage of Muslims working on the Muslim terror intelligence networks.

A reflective silence fell on the meeting participants. There was a lot of truth in what Amin said.

Peter started his presentation by agreeing with Amin's observations and recommendations. He then laid out his non-violence strategy that he was testing in Switzerland and asked that the elite analyst group seriously consider the example Gandhi had taught to resolve conflicts. Peter felt that a peaceful strategy that respected human beings would reduce the terror. A new doctrine, a new world order, was the only way out of the increasing human disaster.

Fred Hopkins reported nothing.

The following hours were filled with a healthy, open debate till Schaefer abruptly looked at his watch and said, "It's getting late, lets continue tomorrow. Same time, same place. By the way, because of security reasons, you are all in different hotels. It may be a good idea not to meet socially. We have a problem which I will discuss with you tomorrow."

Peter left the meeting room, wondering what happened to the two analyst agents who met Schaefer with him. He stopped at Cathy's office to check about his return flight to Zurich. She looked very busy and said, "You are booked on the American flight out of JFK on Saturday evening to Zurich. Do pick up your DC—NY ticket tomorrow."

He had just settled down in bed when the special phone rang. It was Schaefer, "Do you know where Gina is?"

"No," came the prompt reply from Peter. Before Peter could enquire, the phone went dead. He wondered if Schaefer thought of Peter as a ladies man. He definitely did not think of himself as one. In fact he always thought that he was shy and reserved when it came to women and his mother had always felt that way too.

Nine

The phone rang at 6:00 am and Cathy said, "Good morning Peter, sorry for the early morning call. The meeting has been moved to the adjacent building, 7th floor of the Justice Department."

Schaefer was in the meeting room talking to Amin and Bud Mullen when Peter walked in.

The meeting started without the usual exchange of greetings. Schaefer lost no time in speaking and looked very worried.

"Gentlemen, we have a serious problem. Three of the elite analysts agents, gone missing a few days ago, were found dead last night. To add to our woes, Mina and Gina are missing as of last night, having not checked into their hotels. Fred Hopkins of the FBI is investigating."

Amin, Bud, and Peter exchanged uncomfortable glances.

A cool chill ran down Peter's spine. He wondered whether the crash of the window and the bullet lodged in the office wall minutes before he left his office in New Brunswick, and the police at the 201-lake drive in North Brunswick where he was asked to stay, were interlinked attempts on his life. He felt a faint urge to call it quits.

The phone rang as Peter was on his way to his hotel. It was Schaefer.

"Peter, I did not want to offer any explanation on the murdered analyst agents at the meeting but I can tell you that we have been able to now locate Gina and Mina. They have handed in their resignations, for personal reasons. The FBI investigation continues on the murders.

The Secretary, as a result, has requested that we continue with the few agents and desist from holding any meetings of the elite agent group, until further notice.

The events have shown how complex and dangerous the terrorism problem of has become. I will call you in Europe when I know some more. Be very careful. Good Luck."

Ten

Peter checked out of the hotel and took a shuttle to Newark. His mom was thrilled to see him but worried that he had lost weight. Peter called chief Macgregor in the New Brunswick office and got an earful that the Department budget was cut, so he was unable to get a replacement for Peter.

He went on to say, "Peter, me lad, our investigation of the bullet lodged in the wall in your office, the day you were leaving, concludes that it must have been earmarked for Jeremy or you. By the way, Jeremy quit."

The unsolicited information from the chief now confirmed Peter's suspicions.

"So what are you doing these days? I had to spread the word in the office that you had been fired because of your secret assignment. You know what I mean?" the chief continued.

"I am doing some statistical work, which is boring at best, but the job pays enough to make ends meet," Peter said, sheepishly.

"I am sorry. I thought the job would be challenge for a bright guy like you. So long and good luck." The chief hung up with what sounded like a chuckle.

Peter's dad sat down next to him in the living room. Kind of rare, Peter thought.

"So where are you working now?" he asked.

"Well, dad, what I am about to tell you must remain strictly confidential between you and me." Peter felt the urge to share his fright.

"But of course, dear" came an unexpected consoling response from his dad.

"I am working in Zurich for the U.S. Government, to try and stop the sale of weapons from Swiss manufacturers to the terrorist cells," Peter said, trying to be brief.

His Dad appeared to go into a shock and then in a deep thought.

Peter decided to get up and get some beer for his dad and for himself.

"Nice to see father and son, communicating," said his mom. " I am cooking a special meal for the three of us."

His dad was collecting his thoughts while Peter took the first sip of beer. There was an eerie silence and they both took several sips of beer before Peter's dad continued the conversation.

"Peter, this is very strange and very frightening. Now let me tell you a bit from our past. It may help you. I tell you in strict confidence. Granddad, before he immigrated to the U.S., worked in Switzerland for the Swiss Weapon Manufacturer's Association. Well, it was a cartel in fact, that coordinated and cooperated to protect each other, so that they did not end up killing each other in competition, for a lack of a better choice of words," He said, with a worried look and continued after a thoughtful pause

"The arms industry as always is very lucrative, as you may have learnt, and everything was and probably still is game. The Swiss government was very aware unofficially, and officially said that the cartels were considered illegal, but took no action.

Grandfather had several meetings with the Ministry of Defense in Bern, keeping the government abreast of the major activities of the arms industry. Granddad, like most Swiss, was secretive by nature. He found himself getting entangled in some business in the Middle East, which resulted in threats to his life. He therefore quit his job, in the interest of the security of his family, and decided to immigrate to the United States. I am sure that Granddad worked for the Swiss Embassy and the U.S. government, as we settled down in New Brunswick. Granddad did not return to Switzerland for many years. He finally retired and decided to take a trip back to Switzerland, when he received the news that his brother, who was in his sixties, had suddenly died of heart failure. Granddad was a very thorough and meticulous man in all what he did. He suspected that his brothers' death had been under strange, dubious circumstances.

We learnt later that the Swiss police had requested his help in the murder investigation of his brother. Granddad ended up staying on for several months in Switzerland.

We believe, as did the Swiss police, that he had found the culprit who had murdered his brother in cold blood. Granddad was found dead the day he was scheduled to return to the United States. The death certificate stated heart failure as the cause of death.

Peter's dad continued, "I have been in pain since Granddad's death, or murder, and must find a closure," he said, with tears running down his cheeks. Father and son silently shared the pain. There were forces in play that seemed beyond their grasp.

The dinner with mom and dad that evening was sober, with lots of small talk. Peter sensed, however, that his mother knew that something strange had happened between father and son, but whatever it was, it had created a loving bond that she had always felt was amiss.

Peter was flying back to Zurich on Saturday. Peter's dad offered to drive him to JFK.

"Please son," his dad said, tearfully. "Be very careful. I love you dearly and now knowing what we know, I am scared, very scared for you. My heart is aching and I want to keep you from going, but I also know that you have Granddad's genes and that you will seek justice. There will be no solution to the hatred in this world as long as there are human beings alive. I really don't want you to go. It is a hopeless cause to save this world." He broke down in tears.

Eleven

The American code sharing flight with Swiss International was full in the economy section of the plane. The check-in agent smiled and gave Peter a wink, handing him a boarding pass in the business class. Wow! Peter felt important and settled down in his seat. The seat next to him was not occupied. Double wow, Peter thought, he could spread out during the overnight flight to Zurich. This called for a double chivas. Peter enjoyed the meal and settled into sleep.

He woke up suddenly by the announcement to fasten the seat belt as the plane had entered some rough weather. He glanced at the seat next to him, which was unoccupied when he fell asleep, and now occupied by someone in deep sleep. Peter went back to sleep and woke up when the lights came on in the cabin and the stewardess smiled, setting up his breakfast tray.

"What would you like, coffee or tea, sir?

"Coffee please," Peter said, trying to wake up.

"I will have coffee also," said the passenger sitting next to Peter.
The voice made Peter turn around. He was speechless and felt a sudden gush of emotions.

"Golly, gosh, Gemini X'mas, Cathy!" Peter gulped, still at a loss for words.

"Good Morning, Peter. Did you get some sleep? Fancy that, we are not only on the same flight but sitting next to each other," Cathy said, with that million dollar smile.

"What a wonderful surprise to wake up to. On a business trip?" Peter asked, after collecting his wildly scattered thoughts.

"Vacation. And a badly needed one too," came her dreamy voice.

"Keep talking, Cathy, please. I don't want to wake up from my dream," Peter said, surprising himself.

"What did you say ?" Cathy reacted as if she did not catch what Peter had said.

"Your first trip to Switzerland, Cathy? " Peter responded, trying to hide his embarrassment.

"No, no, I was born in Switzerland and I love to visit the old country, whenever I can afford it," responded Cathy.

"I love Switzerland but I have seen very little of it," said Peter, trying to keep the conversation going.

"I know, I know," came the reply from Cathy.

Suddenly the airplane hit turbulence, and the pilot announced his apologies that the plane was now diverted to land in Geneva because of bad weather in Zurich. The passengers were given vouchers to take the train to Zurich.

"Fancy that, Peter; we are on the same train together to Zurich," Cathy said, with a mischievous laugh.

"I love it. It will be a nice Sunday trip on the wonderful and comfortable Swiss train," he said, trying his best not to show his enthusiasm.

They both took coffee and *wegli brot* from the refreshment trolley in the train and settled down. Cathy looked at Peter, and as if having read his mind, said, " Sorry, no shop talk, I am on vacation."

"Of course." Peter nodded, in agreement.

Cathy was fluent in Swiss German, French, and Italian. "I learnt it in the primary school, but I feel rusty for the first few days when I come back. My relatives get annoyed at me when I am at a loss for a word. They think I am a show off because I live in the U.S.," she explained

The conversation drifted to the places of attraction to visit in Switzerland. Cathy was very knowledgeable and was a history major, so the verbal guided tour was immensely interesting for Peter.

Difficult as it was for Peter, he decided to be cool as the train pulled up at the station in Zurich. He shook her hand and as a last minute thought, kissed her cheek.

"Peter, we kiss on both the cheeks, in Switzerland, "she said, teasingly.

Peter obliged.

"You would have to give me three kisses, alternately on each cheek, if we had parted company in the French speaking part of Switzerland," Cathy said, with a smile.

Peter obliged again, saying, "What a delicious custom. Is there any part in Switzerland where one kisses four, five, maybe six or more times?"

"Now, let's not get carried away." Cathy blushed.

Cathy and Peter parted company at the Zurich train station. Peter walked away reluctantly. His mind was overflowing with emotions he wanted to share with Cathy.

Peter checked into hotel Ascot, near the Bahnhof Enge, train station in Zurich.

The evening was young and the heavy down pour had stopped. Peter walked to the lake to catch some fresh air and admire the view of the Alps in the horizon.

"It's the foehn and that's why the somewhat eerie but beautiful view. I always get a headache when its foehn," said Prof. Malinofsky, startling Peter."I am happy to see you again Mr. Peter, my friend. I am glad you did not get lost after our episode in Zurich," he added. "By the way, the money count was exact. Thank you.You can't believe the problems we have in collecting the correct sum of money, in spite of the agreement."

Peter kept smiling in response and put his hand on the Professor's shoulder, "Do you have time for a beer "

Malinofsky gave a broad smile and they strolled to the Theater Platz, crossing the bridge over the river Limmat. The restaurant was loud, one of the few area restaurants open on a Sunday. They decided to go to the *servela*t and *bratwuers*t(sausage)grill stand, and walked towards the lake, beer in one hand, and *bratwuerst brot* in the other.

Malinofsky, with a dry smile said, "It is time we go *per du,* I am Hans."

"I am Peter," came the response from Peter, who was versed in some of the Swiss customs.

"The Swiss banks have made it increasingly difficult to process our recent large cash deposit and transfer it to accounts in other banks," said Hans.

Peter responded, showing surprise, "But you must be a well established client in your bank, after all, you have been in business some time. Is that not right?"

"Yes, yes. But the damn Americans are threatening the Swiss Banking industry to stop money laundering, etc. Can you help us, Peter? We can supply you as many arms as you want, not only Swiss made, but also from other countries in Europe. The problem is getting the money in and out of Switzerland, which has been a traditional safe haven. You or your buyer clients must have good connections, to have paid us twenty million Swiss francs in cash."

"Hans, I am a middle man. My clients make all their own arrangements, but I will investigate and get back to you through Dieter."

"Okay, my friend," Hans replied, as Peter waved goodbye.

Dieter was waiting for Peter in the lobby when he returned to the hotel. Peter updated him on the impromptu meeting with the Professor.

"Dieter, something puzzles me. How did you know where to find me? You must have a great tracking system. I also wonder how the professor knew about my whereabouts?"

Peter enquired.

"The Swiss government Intelligence unit is hooked up with that of the United States, but it is very selective. Only selected personnel, like yourself, are tracked with the special telephone you carry, for protection and security. Schaefer is aware and his department is one of the U.S. intelligence units that reciprocate the favor on selected Swiss agents working in the United States on joint U.S/Swiss programs. I have extended a limited courtesy to people like the Professor for monitoring his activities, in exchange for establishing some trust."

Dieter informed that the meeting with the Federal Council in Bern was scheduled for Tuesday and to expect another round of debate with a question and answer session. The meeting would include officials from the cantons (provinces) where the weapon manufacturing factories were located. They were keen to know whether the decisions proposed would impact employment. The Weapon Manufacturers Association would also be represented.

"It appears that our presentation made an impact on the policy makers in Bern," Dieter said, rubbing his hands.

Dieter said that he would schedule a meeting with the Federal Councilors in charge of the Defense and Finance departments, the following afternoon, to discuss the help the Professor Malinofsky requested about the banks in Switzerland.

Twelve

Schaefer called to update Peter that the FBI had not been able to locate the murderers of the analyst agents. His personal feeling was that it was a domestic terrorist cell.

He cautioned Peter to be very careful when discussing anything with the intelligence officer in the U.S. Embassy in Bern.

Peter informed Schaefer about the attempts on his life in New Brunswick and 201 Park Drive. Schaefer said that he knew about the attempts.

There was a silence and Schaefer said, "Peter, I will understand if at any stage of your work, you decide to quit. The job is tougher and more dangerous than I imagined. You know Peter, I tried many times to get the department to issue a special life insurance and pension for our agents, in recognition for the risks they take, but ran into a quagmire of bureaucracy. This is why the Secretary does not allow elite agents with family dependents on the payroll." Peter was touched by Schaefer's forthright explanation.

Peter's phone in the hotel room rang and it was the U.S. Embassy intelligence officer requesting an update on what Peter had been doing. Peter, as advised by Schaefer, gave a vague summary and almost divulged the meeting on the following day with the Council members.

Dieter and Peter drove, in the afternoon, to Bern for the meeting with the Defense and Finance Council members.

Dr Hilfiger introduced the Federal Councilor for Finance, Dr Hutter, who sounded a bit peeved about Peter's encounters with Professor Malinofsky. Dr Hilfiger and Dieter calmed him down. Peter did not respond to some of the wild allegations Dr Hutter made.

The meeting to discuss a strategy on the response to the Professor, turned into a monolog by Dr Hutter who became increasingly agitated and said in finality, "Mr. Miller, please understand that the Swiss banks are aware of the laws concerning transfer of large sums of money. We do not wish to interfere with our banks. I am sorry we cannot help you."

The meeting ended abruptly.

Dr Hilfiger shook Peter's hands and said, "See you tomorrow to discuss your Position Paper on a strategy to stop the sale of arms to hostile groups." There was a pause and Hilfiger smiled, "I know you will do the right thing with the Professor".

Malinofsky called Dieter while the duo was driving back to Zurich. Dieter almost immediately passed the phone to Peter. "How are you my friend? Any feedback from Your clients "

Peter reacted on the spur of the moment, "Yes Hans, most of them informed me that they now also have severe problems in bringing large sums of money into Switzerland. I will keep investigating for a solution; otherwise I will be out of business."

"Any ideas Peter? What do we do now?" Dieter looked worried.

Peter got an idea in a flash, "Dieter, you have a good connection with the Bank? Let us make sure that the bank has accepted the twenty million Swiss francs in cash. They should buy time and inform the Professor that it will take a few days more before a transfer can be made. No, No, damn it!! After all, the weapons were stolen property and the cash belongs to the Swiss Treasury. Tell the Bank that they should inform the Professor, sounding desperate, after a day or so, that the Swiss government has confiscated the funds and the matter is turned over to the Justice department. Dieter, you should tip the professor. That's a winner for the good guys and the bad guy loses out."

Dieter laughed nervously, quite surprised at Peter's spontaneous response to the Professor.

They both decided to have some refreshments at the rest stop on the auto bahn. Peter kept reinforcing his arguments in favor of the plan while Dieter remained in thought and said finally, "OK, I will try, but I cannot promise."

Peter wondered what that meant.

The meeting room with the Federal Councilors was very large and it was full to capacity. An orderly start of discussions soon gave way to loud and noisy exchanges in three main languages of Switzerland viz, Swiss German, French, and Italian. Hilfiger appeared to be the center point of all attacks, but he sure looked cool and even managed to smile at Peter. The ambience was getting hot until someone decided to open some windows. Dieter was intently following the heated debate while Peter slowly felt exhausted. After all, how long can you look alert when you cannot understand a debate?

The Swiss Federal Council filibuster went on until almost ten at night. Peter wondered at the science of politics. He was tempted to stand up and shout, telling them all to shut up and go to hell. But how would he say that in the three languages.

The meeting came to an end and the large number of meeting participants filed out slowly. Some stopped to shake Peter's hand. What about the question and answer session? Peter wondered, but did nothing because the filibuster noise had left him exhausted.

Hilfiger came up to Peter in the hall of the Federal Building. He still looked fresh and had a winning smile.

"Mr. Miller, we are making headway. This is a true democracy at work.

In a democracy, people must be given the opportunity to speak their minds, specially the elected politicians. The proposal will be now discussed at the Canton (state) level with town meetings, demonstrations and all that. Don't forget the press, the media, and all the theater that follows. We have for strategic reasons, mentioned your name as a consultant, although you are the true originator of the proposal. That is to avoid clouding the important issues with any narrow minded issues. What we are debating is a Swiss initiative that comes from within the Swiss government. We will need to continue picking your brains as we make progress.

"You are now a guest of the Swiss government as a consultant, therefore all your living costs in Switzerland will be to our account. Thank you, until we meet again which I expect will be soon."

Dieter had barely parked the car in Zurich, when the Federal Councilor Hilfiger was on the telephone. Dieter's facial expressions were serious. He put the phone off and looked at Peter. "The Federal Council will meet again tomorrow morning on other matters, and Hilfiger wants to introduce you as a consultant on matters of Security."

"Yes, but, Hilfiger just told us that I should maintain a low key," responded Peter, sounding somewhat confused. "What caused this change of heart?"

Dieter sounded tired, "I don't know. We will find out tomorrow. I will pick you up at 6:00am at the hotel."

The Council meeting room was smaller than the one day before. The room had wonderful paintings of Swiss artists and quotes from Gottfried Keller, Pestalozzi, Henri Dunant, J.J. Rousseau, and other great minds. The colors were cleverly blended to give a calming affect. How appropriate, Peter thought.

There were eight Councilors present. Hilfiger introduced Peter to the council members. Dieter appeared well known. "Perhaps Mr. Peter Miller would like to say a few words."

"Honorable members, I am indeed honored to be here. I come from a family heritage of Swiss and Italians that blended in the United States, in an environment that allows free speech and thought. I feel privileged to be in the land of my fathers, for a noble cause to contribute in seeking a peaceful solution on the sale of weapons sold to hostile groups who have caused a plague of terrorism. The solution, in my humble opinion, requires our understanding the message of some of the great peacemaker personalities, philosophers and thinkers. The human being has created Conflicts since creation and human beings who understood what it is to be a human being, have resolved the conflicts peacefully. We live in a time that conflicts are a way of life and we owe it to our fellow human beings to reduce the damage that conflicts inflict on human life specially the innocent masses. I am dedicated and highly motivated to the concept of the peaceful resolution of conflicts."

Some of the council members also expressed their desire for peace.

Councilor Schiller made an important observation, "It is because of a world of conflicts, that Switzerland's founding fathers, decided that we become a Neutral nation, while actively participating in peaceful actions, the Red Cross being such an example. Our founding fathers understood human nature well. If you take sides in any conflict, you become a part of the conflict. Every action, well intended or not, provokes a reaction. We have found that well intended actions do not ensure a positive reaction. Switzerland therefore decided, hundreds of years ago, that our people can live a life of peace if we stayed away from taking sides in any political conflicts and simply 'mind our own business.' This policy of Neutrality has served our country well.

"We are proud that we are a pure democracy. The Swiss people decide by holding referendums on all issues that concerns the well-being of our nation. We must be very cautious if we seek solutions, even if they are peaceful, that go beyond our national borders. The reaction by the conflict instigator can provoke actions that will hurt our peaceful way of life.

"Our people, some years ago, voted in a referendum to accept refugees from other nations in severe conflicts. Some of these refugees have blended into our way of life while some, instead of being thankful for all our help, have become conflict generators. We are coming up with a referendum on whether or not to send them back to their countries. Mr. Miller I would like your thoughts, in writing, next week please, on this subject. So think neutral, see neutral, hear neutral, speak neutral, breath and act neutral."

Peter left the meeting after a warm shake hand with each of the Council members.

Peter was now beginning to understand Swiss Neutrality but could not stop pondering over what Councilor Schiller said. Peter thought that the conflict between Good and Evil was time immemorial. Fighting or standing up for a Good cause was just, valiant, and essential in building the character of a nation and its people. Not taking the side of Good in an international conflict would devastate the moral fiber of a Swiss who must discriminate between Good and Evil in every day life in order to survive. Peter wondered what emotions the Swiss mind must have gone through during the evil expansion of the fascist, Third Reich. Perhaps the desire to survive overwhelmed the cause of Good over Evil.

He was beginning to understand why, the Swiss he knew, were reserved , timid, and shy, noncommittal in the international scene on political world issues. He was committed to the cause of peace by action. He had no passive feelings about peace.

Peter remembered a joke he heard in Switzerland from a taxi driver who said that there were numerous conflicts all over the world and Switzerland was the only country that stayed quiet in three languages.

Thirteen

Peter was busy preparing a position statement for Councilor Schiller when his special cell phone rang. He expected the voice of Schaefer but it was Cathy.

"I am having a great vacation but all good things must end.
Can we meet, off the record?"

"Yes, of course, but what do you mean by off the record? Where do you suggest?" Peter wondered what that was all about. It did not matter, because the thought of seeing her thrilled him.

"How about dinner in Basel at Restaurant Schloss Binningen, at seven tonight?"Cathy said, in her confident voice.

"OK, Cathy. See ya." He tried not to sound excited.

Peter noticed that he had to hurry to catch the train to Basel and felt that he was being followed. The man did not look Swiss or for that matter a European. Peter took a taxi to the restaurant and looked around to see if the man was still on his tail. He went in and ordered a table for two. It was a quaint castle that belonged to an Earl from the region. It looked well maintained. The dining room was impressive and Peter felt that it was telling its history if anyone took the time to listen. Peter asked for a table in a very private area. The restaurant was not full and people appeared to be speaking softly. He ordered a bottle of Dole, a Swiss red wine. The waiter ceremoniously poured a small quantity for the ritual of taste approval. Peter gave a sign of approval as he gulped it down and then remembered that the etiquette calls for sipping the wine after looking at the color, swirling the glass and checking the wine's aroma. Peter looked around, and felt comfortable that he could not see the man tailing him from Zurich.

Cathy walked in, looking very special as people turned around to look at her. Peter was sure the men folk felt envious of him, as she sat next to him.

"Don't forget, three kisses," she said, as she came near him.

Peter felt that his cool was slipping as he gazed at her and realized she felt uncomfortable. Peter suddenly remembered a line from Sinatra in a Hollywood movie.

"Don't you know that you can get arrested for looking so good?"

Cathy burst into laughter.

"Stop it, stop it, " she said, with a blush that seemed to radiate about her.

The conversation gradually drifted into all about Cathy. She came from Basel and immigrated with her sibling to New York. She was a Journalist and history major and a graduate of the New York University. She had worked for the New York Times as a staff reporter after graduation. She was in love with New York, like Peter. She traveled extensively in Europe as an assistant to a star reporter. Later, after a short tenure in the United States Department of State, she ended up in the Intelligence Agency.

Peter was deeply engrossed in the conversation when his eye fell on the guy who was tailing him, sitting at a table close to them. Cathy immediately lowered her voice and enquired. Peter explained what had happened to Cathy and without waiting, stood up and approached the guy. The man stood up and smiled.

"I am sorry, but I must talk to you. I was not sure if you were Mr. Miller and that is why I have tailed you here. You look remarkably like your grandfather. My name is Emil Mueller. I am your cousin. I am sorry, but I only recently learnt that your grandfather had changed his surname from Mueller to Miller. Please extend my apologies to your wife. I will call you in your hotel so that we can talk," He the man said, in the long introduction. He appeared to be about sixty.

"Oh! Nice to meet you cousin. You could have stopped me in Zurich. I am sorry you came all this way." Peter was now perplexed about Cousin Emil. He did not look *simpatico* as Peter's mom would have said.

Cathy was visibly annoyed at the interruption.

She spoke with deliberation. "Peter we had agreed on no shop talk, but there is something I must share with you because it is about personal security. The elite analyst aZarracks, made statements to the affect that the US army in Lebanon was a threat to the weapon trade industry in Lebanon. Peace as far as the various factions were concerned was very bad for the weapon traders. I could go on and on. Peter you talk so much about peace. It could get you killed."

Cathy was nervous and looked very concerned. She looked at Peter "Have you heard anything I said? *Capish*?"

Peter nodded and said, "Yes, threat of war, conflicts, uprisings, wars for independence and now terror are indeed great for the bottom line of the weapon and arms industry." He resisted telling her about the attempts on his life. Why is she so concerned? He wondered. Was it that she loved him or just a passing concern for his life?

Peter now had inklings that his ideal solution may be in trouble. The words of the Swiss Councilor Schiller resounded in his ears. His escapes from the attempts on his life and then Schaefer sounding him also, in his strange way, to call it quits and now, Cathy.

Cathy was worried. "Peter your life is in danger, please stop dreaming. You are not taking me serious, I can see. Be serious for Pete's sake." That brought smiles on their faces.

Cathy and Peter parted and agreed to meet before Cathy returned to Washington.

The train ride back to Zurich was a time of reflection. Peter's thoughts were doing a salsa of music of love with overtones of serious emotions about the meaningless life. Peter was saddened by the thought that it was strange how a few controlled the lives of so many. The innocent were trapped, knowingly or unknowingly, as hostages.

He drifted into remembering the accounts of the American Embassy personal held hostages by the Iranians. What a sense of terror, frustration, and above all, hopelessness they felt especially after the failure of the Delta forces to save them. The treatment in the hands of their captors had gone from bad to worse. The masses in Iran had held the hostages as a reaction to the support of the Shah's regime by the U.S. The U.S. had misread the desperate will of the people from the oppressive regime of the Shah.

Nixon as a V.P. in the Eisenhower administration had a taken a tour of South America, having pumped money for years in foreign aid. He was welcomed instead by rotten eggs and tomatoes. Had the U.S. Intelligence failed or was the support of dictatorial regimes, deliberate? A lot of the foreign aid to South American countries was in weapons. Guess who made tons of money?

He had read how the public in the U.S. was shocked at the reception Nixon received. The papers had carried the headlines 'No more foreign aid.'

Peter woke up from the salsa of drifting emotions where the romance of life had given way to the ugly realities of life. The train had arrived in Zurich.

His thoughts did a rapid instant replay on the business of surviving as he walked to the tram and the brisk fresh air refreshed him. Quitting now, he thought, after he had come so far was a copout. No way, as they said back home in New Jersey.

Peter picked up six messages from Dieter, "Call Malinofsky. URGENT!"

"Hello Hans, I just got back, sorry I missed your calls," he said, trying to be casual.

"Peter, Peter, I must see you immediately. Now!" Malinsofky responded, sounding very desperate.

"Yes, Hans I will meet you at the lake right away," Peter said in a confident tone of voice.

"My Swiss Bank has accepted the twenty millions of Swiss franc deposit," Malinofsky said almost out of breath and jumping to the point.

"That is great news Hans! I will tell my clients the good news so they can bring money into Switzerland."

"No, the Bank said that it will take several weeks to clear before a transfer can be made. A few days later we had second thoughts and we decided to withdraw the entire sum, the bank responded that the Swiss authorities were tracing the deposit and any request for withdrawal will result in the confiscation of the funds deposited in the account," Malinofsky was desperate.

Peter waited before responding, as if in thought of a solution.

"Oh my God, Hans, did you not say that the containers with weapons were stolen?
My God, that could make it all very messy. After all, the Swiss are probably still looking for the lost weapons in the container."

"Don't be silly, the container of weapons was insured, and they have already paid the manufacturer by now. The Swiss don't make a move without first insuring it."

"I see. Can Dieter help with the Swiss Bank in Zurich?" Peter sounded naïve.

"No-No-No! Dieter is just a low level *beamter (*official), " Malinofsky said, in utter frustration.

"Hans, this is really bad news for you and me. I do not understand the money transfer business."

Malinofsky felt that it was hopeless to talk to Peter. He made a vague attempt at a hand shake, turned around, and walked away looking disgusted.

Peter called Dieter the next morning to report the development.

Dieter responded with excitement in his voice

"Don't worry Peter; Malinofsky has just been arrested with five others from his gang. I talked, in fact, with the Professor yesterday and he told me that they had monitored your drive in the Container truck into Germany and watched you come out from an expensive car at your hotel. He was anxious to do more business with you. He was impressed at the speed you were able to make an exact cash payment for the container of weapons. He was perturbed by the delays in his Bank and wanted to talk to you. Be careful if someone from his gang now tries to make a contact with you. I am not worried because you already are a pro at the game."

A day later the Herald Tribune carried a small column, that the Swiss authorities had confiscated twenty million Swiss francs in cash in a money-laundering attempt. No more information was divulged since the investigation had not been concluded. Several arrests had been made and more arrests were expected shortly.

Peter was walking to the Parade Platz from his hotel and his eyes met a well dressed girl who was staring at him. Peter hesitated and before he could think of his next move, she came along side and motioned him to walk with her. Peter racked his brains to try to recall who she was but was drawing a blank. She directed him to the restaurant around the corner. She stared at him and then spoke with a hesitant smile

"You really don't remember me, do you?"

"I am afraid I can't place you, my apologies," Peter said, as he tried to recall.

"I am Tanya. I saw you when we took possession of the money in the garage in Zurich. You are a handsome man. Are you married? Malinofsky took a liking to you. He has asked me to take care of you. We take care of each other. That is our culture. We are not superficial, like people in the west." She talked in a sexy voice.

There was a variety of information in what she said. Peter smiled politely and said, "I am married, and thank you for the compliment. Taking care of each other is a good culture. I am sorry but I should move along."

She tried to catch his hand and said, "Malinofsky and some of our associates have been taken into custody but we have great lawyers who will get them released. I have been asked to caution you. The police may come for you. You should not say anything about our business. Our lawyers will get you out in case you are arrested."

She let go of his hand reluctantly as he waved goodbye to her. Peter had barely increased his walking pace when he heard shots. He looked back to see Tanya fall to the ground. He ran back to where she lay and a policeman, who had immediately responded, was at her side, calling an ambulance. She was conscious and Peter kneeled down to her. She looked at him, smiled and said, "I love you, save yourself." She lost consciousness.

The Police were all around and he was asked to go to the police station. He called Dieter and told him about the encounter with Tanya after showing his ID from the Ministry of Defense. The Policeman saluted him and spoke in broken English, offering to take him back to his hotel.

Peter had a stiff drink at the hotel bar. He was shaken by the incident. Dieter arrived and suggested a drive along the lake of Zurich to talk.

The police arrested the man who shot Tanya. It appears that he and Tanya were not arrested to draw other members of the gang that may have been left out. Peter's appearance with her confused the undercover policemen that were following her. Fortunately they saw the gang member who shot her and arrested him.

"Peter, were you having an affair with her?" Dieter had paused before posing the question.

"Nuts!!! Hell no! She spotted me and I just could not recollect ever having met her. She came to me and told me that she was Tanya and she had seen me in the garage when the Malinofsky gang was counting the money. She was probably wearing a facial mask like the rest of the gang." Peter was on the defensive.

"I am sorry, Peter, but she died in the hospital and her last words were, 'Take care of my friend Peter, I love him very much," said Dieter, in a very somber tone.

Peter was stunned, "Gee, I am real sorry. I am honored by her love. No one ever told me those words before."

"So there is love among culprits and peace lovers also. If only she knew who you really are." Dieter suddenly realized at his wrong choice of words, "I am sorry Peter, forgive me."

Peter could not take it any more so he suggested lunch. He had a hard time keeping his composure but the wine helped him relax.

"Lets review the response I owe to Councilor Schiller on the refugee issue in Switzerland."

Fourteen

Peter reviewed the position paper on refugees in Switzerland he had prepared for Mr. Schiller, the Swiss councilor and mailed it to Bern. The gist was:

The refugees should be issued a stern warning that any attempts by any of them to break Swiss laws will result in an immediate deportation with no recourse of a hearing in the courts. The refugees should report any grievances to special offices located in all major cities in Switzerland. All grievances reported and the actions taken by the Swiss authorities shall be made public to assure fairness.

Peter received a thank you note promptly from Mr. Schiller.

Peter called his dad and mom to say hello.

"Dad I met an Emil Mueller, who claims to be my cousin, in Basel. I will meet him soon. Do you know Emil?"

"How did he know about you, Peter? Yes, I know him. He is trouble. He is a suspect accomplice on my list, responsible for the murder of granddad."

The conversation was kept short, because the exchange made his mom very concerned and she kept repeating, "What are you talking about." Peter could hear his dad consoling his mom that he will explain later. Peter knew that his dad will brush the whole conversation aside with his mom. Poor mom. Peter thought that he would call his mom later and console her that there was no problem.

Sure enough, Emil called and asked Peter to meet in the Raeblus Bar in the Niederdorf. Peter wondered why Emil had not invited him to his home; after all he was a long lost cousin.

Peter felt bad vibes. He received no response when he enquired how Emil had learnt about his whereabouts. In frustration he decided to confront Emil about Grandfather's murder. Emil aggressively responded that it was this type of behavior that gets one killed. Two muscle types closed in and Peter screamed "Hilfe," catching the bartender's attention and he promptly threw Emil and his musclemen out of the bar. The incident caught everyone's attention. Peter decided to leave but the bartender asked him to wait, while he made a call. An undercover policeman approached him at the bar and offered to walk him back to the hotel. The bartender nodded confirming the credentials of the policeman.

This confirms Dad's suspicion about Emil, Peter thought; He now had to find a way to dig in deep to get the facts out.

Peter called Breder from the weapon factory in Schaffhausen. Breder invited Peter for a tour of the factory and lunch.

"I am Joseph," Breder said, as he extended a warm welcome to Peter and get on first names basis.

Joseph got to the point immediately as they entered the conference room which was luxurious in every sense of the word.

"Our management and the Manufacturer's Association are interested in licensing U.S. products in the defense industry for manufacture in Switzerland. We request that you arrange meetings between the Swiss and U.S. defense product manufacturers so that we can work out suitable agreements. In return the Swiss manufacturers would agree to share with the U.S. manufacturers and the U.S. government their complete reference list of clients, in good faith. The open communications would reduce the chances of selling products to suspect hostile clientele worldwide. Defense products sold by each group to their respective Defense Departments would be considered confidential information and hence not shared between Switzerland and the U.S. The European Union had also proposed such a bilateral agreement with Switzerland, which was under consideration.

The meeting had gone well, and Peter could see that Joseph was a professional. The lunch at the Golden Stube in the city was a mercurial delight. The wine, a Maienfelder Reserve, was poetry. Both had relaxed and the conversation covered various world politics. Peter felt confident talking about his grandfather. His death was suspicious and how it still pained Peter's dad and the family. Joseph listened attentively and offered to help Peter investigate. The manufacturers' Association had a vast data bank and Joseph could easily check any historical data of people and events.

"We work with the Police and other Swiss government departments, but we keep our own records and data. I must confess that I checked you through our and the police data and found that there was also data on Heinrich and Karl Mueller. Karl Mueller (Peter's grandpa) had worked as a consultant for the Manufacturers' Association. There is more data but I have not paid any attention. I suggest that you come on the Saturday to the office so that we can look at the data in peace." Joseph suggested cordially.

Peter was thrilled at the progress. He called his dad to give him the good news.

"Joseph Breder! Yes that name rings a bell, but I must look into my information," said Peter's dad.

Saturday, 2:00 am, Peter got a call. The connection was bad but certainly an oversea call. Finally after several hellos, Peter was connected with his dad.

"I think Joseph Breder is the son of Francis Breder who also met a suspicious death. I am very sure that he was also murdered. Be careful Peter," Peter heard his dad say and the line went dead.

Peter drove in the taxi from the train station in Schaffhausen to the weapons factory and Joseph's office on the saturday. The security guard pointed Peter in the direction of Joseph's office, after sticking the security visitor's paper badge on his lapel.

The office door was ajar. Peter knocked and heard a moan. Joseph was leaning over the desk. He had been shot in the arm. The window in his office had a telltale bullet hole.

Joseph looked up, "Lock the door, Peter, it's only a flesh wound." Peter quickly performed first aid and suggested calling an ambulance and the police.

"No, No," Joseph said. "I am eager to get to the bottom of all this. The computer screen was open on the page tittled 'Karl Mueller'."

Karl Mueller, Peter's Granddad, had worked on the' Meridian Project' which started as the joint effort of Britain, France, Germany and Switzerland to develop a high powered multi turret RPGs unit mounted on a model sized pilotless plane built out of stealth material to avoid detection by radar. The airplanes were to be electronically operated from a mobile ground station. The project was abandoned by Britain, France and Germany before contracts between the four countries had been signed, because of budget constrains.

Switzerland had continued with the development and manufactured three-test model sized airplanes at a total project cost close to one billion Swiss francs. The Swiss factory completed the prototype test airplanes which also had operating capabilities with lasers and other break through new technologies with energies never deployed before. The write-up was not specific. The news of the success by the Swiss somehow leaked and caused a major stir in the French, Britain and the German quarters. The Swiss, finally, decided not to share the know-how after lengthy secretive negotiations failed to reach an agreement. Upon pressure and political threats by several European intelligence agencies, Switzerland decided to hide the three test airplanes and all the documents finally at a secret location. Switzerland had expressed interest in negotiating agreements but not under threat.

Karl Mueller and Francis Breder were entrusted in the safe keeping of the secret location of the airplanes. One European Intelligence Agency had managed to infiltrate agents into Switzerland and both Karl and Francis were abducted within a week. Subsequently their bodies were discovered at two different locations in Switzerland. The autopsies showed that they had died from poison injected in their bodies. In order to avoid causing an alarm in Switzerland, the Swiss government decided to report their deaths, as heart failure. The Swiss had no doubts that the two stalwarts had refused to cooperate and therefore their murder was the only way for the culprits to save their face. The last data on the subject stated that the secret was safe and Karl and Francis were true national heroes.

Joseph's face was drenched in tears and Peter also succumbed to grief.

Joseph called his boss, who appeared with two plant security guards. An intruder had shot the guard at the north gate of the plant with a silencer.

The security system in Switzerland worked swiftly. Peter was transported in an unmarked police car to the hotel. Dieter was waiting in the hotel lobby and suggested the evening dinner on the lake cruiser. Dieter was up to speed and expressed regret at the outcome.

"Peter, the authorities are somewhat nervous that you have been privy to highly sensitive information. Hilfiger and Schiller have requested we meet the following day."

My, my, Peter thought, no respect for Sunday! Peter's grandma had once told him in New Brunswick when Peter was servicing the lawn mover on a Sunday, that he would be fined, in the good old days, if he worked in Switzerland on a Sunday.

The two Councilors appeared in jeans. Peter and Dieter appeared in light suites and felt out of place with the hip. They both expressed their condolences to Peter but felt that although the air of mystery had cleared, and Peter and his father could find a closure to their grief, the incident had opened a Pandora's Box. They requested that Peter and his father maintain strict silence in the interest of national security.

Schiller had changed the subject and appreciated Peter's input on the refugee problem. "Your suggestion will be incorporated in the forth coming referendum in Switzerland."

Peter's thoughts reflected on the matters of security of the state on a weapon placed in hiding in a secret location versus the lack of compassion for the grieving families of the national heroes. Again the human element played second to a weapon that could kill masses of human beings.

Fifteen

Peter was worried about Joseph so he called him on Monday at the office.

"Thank you, Peter. If it had not been for you I would have never found out the truth about my grandfather either. Just imagine the confidential information has been in front of my nose all these years. I had no idea. My office is in full operation as if nothing happened on Saturday. The windowpane has been replaced within hours. The death of the security guard has become a matter for the police. Robbery may have been the possible motive but I know that someone did not want us to know about what we now know. My bandaged arm was caused in a domestic accident, is in the press release. How is that for instant secrecy, or shall I say re-cover-up? "

While on his first chance to get a cup of coffee, the special phone rang. Schaefer 's calm voice came on.

"Hi Peter, I got the good news about the Swiss manufacturers willing to make concessions in the interest of more business and security, in that order. I have cleared it with the Pentagon and the Director of Intelligence and Security. The Secretary of Defense has discussed with the U.S. Ambassador to set up a conference with the Swiss Association of manufacturers in Switzerland and U.S manufacturers that are interested in the program. See if you can coordinate the conference between the Ambassador, the commercial Attaché and the Swiss groups involved. Good work, Peter. The Secretary of Defense and the HS Director would like you to stop by in their offices next time you are in DC so that they can thank you personally. By the way, they are tickled by the fact that the Swiss government has made you a consultant and is picking up your living costs in Switzerland. You can be sure that some agency in the U.S. government will object to you serving two countries.

By the way, Cathy is in Switzerland. Have you been in contact? She has not reported back for work and has not called. Not like Cathy at all. Call her home and investigate. I am getting worried that she might be sick. She is with her parents in Bruderholz. She has a Swiss cell phone 709 71 7011. Her dad's name is Franz Schaefer.

Peter responded that they were by chance on the same flight to Zurich and had met in Basel recently for dinner. "Now I am also worried because she was going to call me before flying back to DC. I will check and call you."

Peter called repeatedly and got no response. He decided to take a train to Basel and call her again from the train station.

Peter finally got through. "*Guten Tag,* may I speak to Cathy please? My name is Peter and I am her friend."

There was a brief silence and the response came, " Please come 19 Bruderholz Alle *so bald wie* (as soon as) possible." Peter had the feeling that man had exhausted his vocabulary in English.

An elderly gentleman opened the door, without a smile, of course and motioned him to take a seat in the *stube* (living room). The room was dark, with a Victorian décor. Somehow lively Cathy did not fit in the environment.

Moments later Cathy called "Peter I am in the room next to the living room".

Peter stumbled in the dark following the direction of her voice. He kissed her three times of the cheeks and she smiled. Cathy lay in bed, looking weak, which alarmed Peter.

"Schaefer is worried that you did not show up for work in Washington nor called. What happened?"

"I was confronted by two dark skinned men when I went to have a coffee in town who warned me to stay away from trying to make peace 'a la Americana', in the lands America is trying to forcibly control. I told them to take a hike and one of them attacked me, hitting me unconscious. The police took me to the hospital and I receive a call on my Swiss cell phone that I will be killed if I refuse to listen. The men had an east European country accent. My back is badly hurt and I am drugged with pain killers."

Peter immediately called Schaefer, who talked to Cathy and instructed Peter that Cathy should throw away the chips in her cell phones. He asked Peter to transport her to a secure convalescent Nursing clinic. Schaefer would make all the arrangements and call Peter back. "Don't leave Cathy alone and I will request the Swiss police, protection for her."

Schaefer called again, saying that the Swiss police insist on taking care of it all and Peter could stay with her.

The clinic was near Luzern, on the lake. No telephones, cell phones were permitted on the premises. Peter had a room next to Cathy. She had been sedated for the transport from Basel. A security guard stood outside Cathy's room. Peter was glad that he had a break from his hectic schedule and be near Cathy.

Dieter visited them both and updated Peter.

"The shooting at the weapon factory in Schaffhausen was an informer for the Swiss Department in-charge of the Meridian project, working in the weapon administration of the factory. He erroneously understood that Joseph was about to leak information on the Meridian to an American and took matters into his hands. He has been reprimanded."

Peter sat by Cathy's bed reading the newspaper. Nurses came in periodically to check on her. Peter had almost dozed off when he saw a doctor feeling her pulse and preparing to give her an injection. Peter jumped to his feet, "What medication are you injecting?"

The man mumbled and Peter saw that he wore dirty sneakers, which alarmed him. Peter called for the nurse and the man dropped the injection knocking Peter to the ground and ran out. The security guard struggled with the intruder and used the taser gun to disable him. The man was trying to inject saline water into her arm. She would have gone into shock.

The security had been compromised

Schaefer was of the opinion that it may be the same group that murdered the agents in the U.S. and scared agents Gina and Tina into quitting. Peter was puzzled by why they would earmark Cathy. The FBI and the CIA had been on the case in the U.S. and had no leads or Schaefer was not telling Peter. Were Cathy and Schaefer, both with the same surnames somehow related? Lots of questions, but no answers. The police promptly transferred Cathy and Peter to a maximum-security clinic in Zurich.

Peter requested that he be allowed to talk to the intruder. The intruder went by the name of Janez Popovic, with a police record and was on the police list for deportation. Popovic spoke some German but was quite fluent in English. Peter decided to deploy his plan to gain the confidence of Janez. He visited him every day and brought him American cigarettes.

Cathy was improving and felt comfortable with Peter close by. They talked about light subjects such as, opera, Broadway shows, food etc. Peter had decided not to talk about any thing serious unless Cathy broached the subject.

A policeman woke Peter in the morning in the clinic, "Janez wants to talk to you."

Janez looked like he had enough of the daily police harassment. Janez spoke in a low tone that he felt Peter could be trusted. Peter assured that he would let no harm come if Janez would cooperate fully. His family in Switzerland would also be protected from any harm.

Janez began, "I have been in a terrible state the last ten years. I was born and brought up in Belgrade. My father was a Serb, a medical doctor by profession and, Buddhist by religion. He peacefully opposed the Tito regime and frequently spent time in the jails, as a result. Mother was an angel from Ljubljana, the Switzerland of Yugoslavia. Chaos became the rule of law when Milosevic took over. The ethnic killing became rampant. My father decided to take the family to Ljubljana to protect us all from the increasing tyranny. We had walked along dirt roads, harassed by people we met on the way. It was not even safe to buy some food. We walked for about ten days and finally came to the border at Ljubljana. My mother was allowed to enter alone. My father and my two brothers protested, begged on their knees saying that we were a family, to let us enter. The guards laughed and kicked us telling us to walk back. My father after many failed attempts decided to take my two-brothers and me back. The border guards into what was now under Croatian control refused to let us return. We were in no mans land. My father insisted and was shot at point blank and so were my two brothers. I failed to understand why they spared my life.

"I was finally allowed to go into Ljubljana and put in a juvenile jail before being released in the custody of my mother who was in trauma. I attended school and looked after my mother who never recuperated and died after four years. I was allowed to finish school with morsels of food, and then told to leave Ljubljana. I walked for days alone and crossed into Austria in the dark with only a school certificate and a Serb identification card for collecting rations. I was caught and spent time in refugee camps but treated like a human being by the Austrian authorities. I was then allowed to work as a farm hand for a miniscule salary and transferred from farm to farm. After what appeared an eternity I became eligible to enter Switzerland. The refugee program required that I look for employment. My only experience was working as a farm hand. I became like a gypsy going from farm to farm and getting work for a very limited time. I had saved some money and decided to try my luck in Zurich. I managed to get a job as a cook's helper in a small restaurant in the Niederdorf. One day, after the restaurant closed, usually at midnight, I decided to walk back to my room. The police arrested me on suspicion of a break-in of a shop close to the restaurant I worked. It was alleged that Yugoslavs caused robbery and break-ins. I was, therefore, each time there was a crime, immediately arrested and became a criminal suspect. Finally I found myself shuttling in and out of jails when my only crime was that I was a Yugoslav. Thanks to the legal system in Switzerland, I was always released after no evidence could be found of guilt.

"A man stopped me as I came out of the jail. He had a friendly face and told me that he was in the transport of mail and packages and could hire me for minimum wages. I worked out of a warehouse where cars and trucks brought mail and packages for delivery. I was given a bicycle and I went around town delivering packages. I later met an American who told me a story how his wife was dying in a clinic but not allowed to die. He had tried to give her poison but was caught each time and not allowed to visit her at all. The American offered me a thousand Swiss francs to do the job and when I refused, increased the offer to 10,000 Swiss francs. He threatened to report me to the police that I was trying to sell him explosives, if I refused to cooperate. The American gave me

10,000 Swiss francs and the injection vial. You know the rest. I will help you find the man who caused all this."

Peter took a breather and drank coffee in the commissar's office. The interrogation officer looked at Peter.

"Do you believe the story?"

Peter thought for a moment and said, "Yes."

The officer did not contest the response. "We have it all on tape, if you need it later."

Peter called Dieter who showed up with a Colonel. Peter explained that Janez could be helpful in cracking a case in the United States that has bewildered the FBI and the CIA. After several calls and meeting sessions among the brass, the Police Commissar agreed to transfer Janez to a special prison, making him available for Peter's investigation.

Peter felt encouraged and dialed Schaefer's phone to tell him about the development, but put the phone off as a last minute; second thought.

Cathy was wide-awake. Peter introduced her to Dieter as the man who makes it all happen. The doctor informed Peter that Cathy's injuries were healing well but she was not fit for travel back to the U.S. The doctor highly recommended absolute rest to avoid complications later. Cathy had a spinal injury. Cathy did not take the news well. She was anxious to start working again and resigned to 'doctor knows best'.

"Do you wish to go back to Basel before going back to DC?" Peter said, trying to get a dialogue started.

"No, no," came a vehement reply from Cathy.

Peter thought it wise not to initiate talking about the incident and wait for Cathy instead. Was he just getting impatient or was it the increasing desire to crack her shell of secrecy or was this a hard to get woman's game.

Peter had certainly lived through a life full of the secrecy back home. The mere thought sent a shot of pain in the neck. Anyway there was hope after all his Dad had come out of his shell of secrecy. The thought of dad reminded him, that he had not called Dad to tell him about the encounter in Schaffhausen and all that they had discovered.

"Dad, how are you doing?" he asked, sounding his normal self.

"Damn it, Peter! I have been sick to death, worrying about what happened."

"Dad, how about I get you and mom tickets to make a visit to Switzerland"?

Peter expected the usual "No" for an answer.

"Ok Peter we will come, after all, it is just as cold there as here."

"Swell, Dad, I am so happy. I will call and set up prepaid tickets for you and mom for pickup at the Newark airport. Swiss has a direct flight to Zurich. Next week OK?" A very definite "Yes" was the reply.

Peter was sure now that the healing process with his dad was well on its way.

Sixteen

Peter called Schaefer in DC to update him about Cathy and his programs with the Swiss authorities.

"I would like to take a week of vacation to be with my parents who are coming to Switzerland," requested Peter.

Schaefer agreed saying, "Peter, you could travel back to the U.S. with your folks and spend a few days with me in DC to work out your next assignment."

"I need to stay some more time to work out a way to infiltrate the gang responsible for the attack on Cathy. They could be linked to the murder of the agents in the U.S.," Peter quickly responded.

There was a rare, long silence and Schaefer agreed.

Janez was ready for the meeting with Peter.

"Are you comfortable?" Peter asked.

"Yes, thank you. I am in a four star prison".

"We have decided to keep you protected from the American, so we have two unmarked police cars with powerful video cameras. The cars will drive in the warehouse, restaurant and in the general area where you met him. The police each have a copy of the generated image you gave of the culprit. You can watch the monitor and you tell us if you spot him."

The procedure was repeated for a few days to no avail. The police then suggested that Janez be allowed to walk around the city, wired and with a RFID, to monitor his location all the time, as live bait. Janez agreed and proceeded with walking around the city. Two days had passed when the culprit suddenly spotted Janez. The American appeared to be carrying a weapon in his pocket, which he had thrust against Janez. A plain clothed policeman approached Janez and the American, and without making a scene, arrested the American, quickly transporting him out of the public area. It was over in seconds.

It filled Peter with a sense of admiration at the efficiency displayed by the police. We would have seen a drama back home with police cars and lots of policemen with the media coverage. It was clear that Peter never liked the drama and the fanfare with the police and considered it wasteful.

The American did not cooperate. In the meantime his personal data was transmitted to the CIA and FBI. The American was a fugitive from justice by the name of Richard Tuft. The police Commissar liked Peter's style so he said *Bitte schoen* (please) get the show on the road.

Schaefer was on the phone and told Peter that he will start the proceedings to get Richard Tuft extradited back to the U.S.

"And what?" asked Peter. "So that he can get a great lawyer and start a drama for a few years?"

"Vow Peter, what a reaction! But I know you are right. You can start your magic but the rules require that I start the extradition process which takes a few months and a ton of paperwork," Schaefer responded.

Peter felt a bit of camaraderie in Schaefer's voice, and felt surprised when he heard him say, "Stop being so Swiss; call me John, but don't you dare call me Johann."

Peter told Cathy that his parents were coming to visit him in Switzerland, the following week.

"How nice to have caring parents," Cathy said, with some emotion in her voice.

"Yes, but your father in Basel!" Peter was surprised by her response.

"Yes he is my biological father, but he never showed me any affection because he wanted a boy. He was bad to my mom, as if it was her fault. I did see one tear in his eye at my mom's funeral." There was clearly, pain and anger in Cathy voice.

Peter comforted her and was so pleased that Cathy was talking again. He thought of keeping the flow going. "You have no brother or sister?"

Oops, Peter had asked the wrong question. Tears were rolling down her cheeks.

"I am so sorry," he said, as he embraced her, trying to console. His heart said 'Bingo'.

Peter walked up to Richard Tuft in the interrogation room and sat down.

"Hi Dick! I am Peter, Can we talk?"

"What are you FBI, CIA? Nice to hear an American voice though."

"None of those guys. I am an analyst agent and I work for the Intelligence Department."

"The extended arms of the U.S. , you mean," came an irritated response.

Peter had a good laugh. "That's a good one, and you are right. I never thought of it that way." The humor brought a smile on Richard's face. "I am from New Brunswick, New Jersey, and how about you?" said Peter, sounding friendly.

"No shit! I am from Chicago but I was born in Hoboken, New Jersey. We beat your pants off in basketball, when we played New Brunswick High."

"I played baseball! In playoffs around the state but never heard about a team from Hoboken."

"You kidding? Why our Jersey league won four state championships in a row."

"No Shit! Yousa guys must have been real good."

"So what is this all about?" Richard interrupted the sports lingo.

"Attempted murder." Peter responded.

"Gee whiz, what next?" Richard Tuft seemed to resign.

"Please Dick, let's cut out the crap. I need your help. You are a pawn in a rotten and dirty game that is creating chaos back home. Your pigs make the rats look good in comparison."

"What's in it for me?" Richard reacted as he saw an opportunity

"A chance to lead a decent life. You know what that means?" said Peter, like a priest

"Ya, it's been a while, I was a cop once. Let me think about this. Do I get to make a call?" Richard said, with nostalgia.

"Let's make a deal first and you can make all the calls you want." Peter sounded as one in the driver's seat.

Seventeen

Cathy was all dressed up and ready to go as Peter walked into the clinic.

"I must get out of these walls or I will go nuts" she said with some desperation. They strolled along the lake of Luzern, outside the clinic. It was a cool evening.

"You know Peter, I am sorry that I have not thanked you for all you have done for me. So many thoughts go through my mind, worries, and questions. I am sure I should talk to someone. Some times I think I should consult an analyst," she said.

"Well, that is easy to fix. I am an analyst," Peter replied promptly They both burst into laughter.

"You know what I mean, Peter," Cathy said

"It happens to me also," Peter said, reassuringly. "We are all lonely human beings, some more than others. I can be a good listener," Peter continued when Cathy remained silent.

Peter decided to continue and change the subject. "I will pick up my parents tomorrow at the Zurich airport. I would like you to meet them. We can all spend some time together, if you like."

Cathy's face lit up, "Yes, I would love that."

The Commissar called Peter very early in the morning. "Mr. Peter, Mr. Richard would like to talk to you."

"OK I will be there in an hour," Peter said, as he sensed a possible breakthrough.

Dick gave Peter a warm handshake and spoke

"Thank you, Pete, for giving me a chance. I am willing to spill my guts. I went to the University of Chicago on a scholarship after three years in the army. I flunked out after the second year and joined the Police service and made it to Detective. It was a very rough life all around. We put our lives out everyday and the job demanded more and more. The job, you know, paid lousy wages. I tried to reenlist in the army like two of my buddies and was told that with our army training, we will be shipped to Iraq. My buddies reenlisted and I had second thoughts. Both my buddies were killed within a week of arriving in Iraq. I continued being a Police detective and one day temptation got the better of me with drugs. I was suspended without pay.

"The department chief called me in and asked me to do a job for the Department. I was told that there was a woman terrorist in a clinic in Switzerland and she should be eliminated in the interest of national security. I will be reinstated as an undercover agent in Chicago with a fat increase in salary, if I succeeded. I would get a dishonorable discharge if I failed and I would never is able to get a job with such a record. I was given twenty thousand dollars for expenses. I did not want to do the job myself and I soon realized that the yugos were the criminals, so I got me one. I know that if I return to Chicago, having failed the mission, I will be discharged and since I am privy to very sensitive information, be eliminated. I know guys who failed on such missions and were found dead. Chicago is the murder capital of the Midwest."

"OK, Dick. Let me put a plan together. I will be back in a couple of days," Peter answered.

Dick continued, "The chief is waiting for my call. My last call to him was a few days ago when I told him that the mission was in progress. I suspect that the chief must know about my failure and is probably ready to get a contract on my life."

So the department chief in Chicago gave the assignment. Who initiated the assassination? Who is the ultimate culprit behind this assignment? Cathy was still in danger. Perhaps Peter was also in danger. Anyway, it was a good start, Peter thought.

Peter picked up his parents and checked them in the Hotel Luzerne, a block away from the lake in the city. His mom and dad were thrilled to be in Switzerland. It was his mom's first visit to Switzerland. Peter's grandmother had declined to take a trip to Switzerland. His dad said that she gave no reasons, something that Peter had grown accustomed to with regret. They decided to take a quick snack and get some rest not having slept on the overnight flight from Newark.

Cathy was not in her room in the clinic. The security guard looked lost. Peter missed a heartbeat and before reaching a panic state, saw her sitting on a bench by the lake.

"Hey Cathy, your life is still in danger, you should..."

Cathy smiled and embraced Peter. "Come; let's go somewhere far away from this mad job, and world."

"Cathy do you feel strong enough to talk about madness?" Peter asked.

"Hey, Peter, you forgot to give me the three customary kisses on my cheek."

"OK, OK. So what is happening these days?" Cathy said, with a tired look. "Have you hung the man who tried to kill me? Oh! I am sorry Peter; I forgot your Strategy is non-violence. Mahatma Gandhi will be so proud of you," she said.

The nurse came out and reminded Cathy that must take rest and took her back.

Peter arranged a dinner with Joseph Breder in Schaffausen so that his dad could hear and bring a closure to the loss of granddad. It was an emotional evening for all. Joseph recalled the confidential information in the computers at the weapon manufacturers Association. Joseph, in addition was able to read the confidential information in the Swiss government intelligence as well as in the Swiss defense department's files. The intelligence information tallied with each other with notes commending the heroic feats of Karl Mueller (Miller) and Francis Breder.

"The timing of your dad's visit is perfect in Switzerland. The Federal Council has decided to award our grandfathers, posthumously, the Helvetica Medal of Honor for exceptional service. The award ceremony, I have been asked to tell you, will be held without the media on this Friday in Bern. The proclamation will not make any references Or give any details, because of national security. My dad is unfortunately bed ridden and suffers from Alzheimer." Joseph said, with some pride.

Joseph also informed Peter that the U.S. and Swiss meeting have been scheduled for December. The expectations are high. The Swiss and the U.S will sign the cooperation agreement at the Whitehouse on November 21 on the sale of weapons to private and NGOs, with a number of conditions acceptable to both the governments.

Peter and his parents took train trips to Interlaken, Zermatt, Davos, Basel, Geneva and a day trip to Lugano. Peter's mom was thrilled beyond words and Peter was very satisfied that they were all able to enjoy, an extensive sight seeing trip, together. He had carried a burden all these years about their family bond and granddad. He now felt that the closure and the healing process were progressing well.

Cathy had made a reservation for dinner at the *Luzerner Stube,* very famous for its superlative Swiss cuisine in Luzern. Peter's parents were delighted to meet Cathy. Peter had tried to persuade Cathy to include her father, but there was no changing her mind when they discussed the dinner arrangements. Cathy had a last minute change of mind and had invited her father, which turned out to be beneficial, in healing their father and daughter relationship. The evening was a complete success.

Cathy's father made an emotional appeal to Cathy, confessing his inexcusable, bad, insensitive behavior towards her. It was an emotional moment to see father and daughter embrace for a long time in tears.

So a very sumptuous dinner in a private room which only Cathy could arrange, resulted in healing all around. The happy and content looks around was a testimony to better days ahead.

Dieter called Peter, to inform that Janez had started a fast food restaurant with funds from the Swiss refugee program. Janez had hired some Yugos so that they could lead meaningful lives.

"Another feather in your cap Peter," Dieter said.

Peter felt some contentment, but worried about the other Janez's in the world, who also needed help desperately and became more resolute in his thoughts to help his suffering World family.

Dieter was intensely involved with the Swiss-U.S. government cooperation program. He had received an invitation, for the Friday ceremony in Bern, honoring the two fallen heroes and showed his pride.

"By the way, I am also invited at the signing ceremony of the Swiss-U.S. cooperation program on the sale of weapons, in the Whitehouse. I did not see your name, the chief architect of the program, in the list of invitees," Dieter said.

Peter was unaware of the signing ceremony scheduled at the Whitehouse and felt some disappointment that Schaefer had not informed him about it. He thought for a moment as he pictured the fanfare of the ego loaded participants all trying to be photographed for posterity. The document on the joint cooperation would undoubtedly make no mention of his efforts anyway. There would be roster of big shots, attending the ceremony, all claiming their importance and contribution. The fanfare he pictured started to turn pathetic and he was glad that he did not have to participate. All the same an invitation from the Whitehouse would have been a nice gesture.

Peter had racked his brains but had not come up with a game plan for Richard Tuft. He felt the subject was too sensitive to discuss with Schaefer. The phone rang and it was Schaefer.

"What is Richard Tuft's fate now? I suggest you get as much information you can get from him specially the telephone number and name of his chief in Chicago. I will do some preliminary investigations and we can discuss the action plan when you are here. Give my greetings to Cathy. Let's not try to rush her back. Let her recuperate. I have a new temporary assistant for now, but she is not Cathy."

Richard prepared all the names and contacts in code and Peter transmitted them to Schaefer, when he met Tuft. Peter explained to Tuft that the U.S. law required that he be extradited to the States to be tried but it was a Performa process since, it would mean exposing Tuft to a sure attempt on his life by the culprits in Chicago. "Pete, I don't care ever to return to the U.S., although it is my home. My experience back home was a nightmare and I would rather forget it all and start a new life here. I know that my ancestors came from the United Kingdom and I will drift back there if the authorities permit me. Please help me. You are the only hope I have. I trust you," Richard pleaded.

The Police Commisar in Zurich had kind words for Tuft, that he was an invaluable help for the department. After a thoughtful pause, the Commisar said that Tuft did not show any traces of criminal element in his demeanor and could be fully integrated into the police department.

"Tuft uncomplicated matters for us. He is very reliable and professional. I hear only praises for his work with all the English speaking police agencies we work."

The honor award ceremony in Bern was scheduled for the afternoon on Friday, so Peter decided to see Cathy before picking up his parents. The nurse that attended to Cathy came to Peter in the lobby of the clinic.

"Mr. Miller, I must talk to you before you see the doctor. We are very concerned about Cathy. She is suffering from Depression. She has talked about her past but we have not been able to find the cause. The doctor is considering giving her strong medication but I am concerned about the after affects."

Peter was puzzled by the news. He had not detected any symptoms. But then, what did he know?

"Cathy, how are you today?" he asked, not forgetting to give her three kisses on the cheeks.

"I had a wonderful time at the dinner. You have fine parents. I am glad I invited Dad also. You know Dad insists on taking care of me as soon as I get out of this prison," she responded.

"Well, say something, Peter. Why are you looking so glum?" Cathy startled Peter with the question.

"Well...Your doctor is worried that you are depressed," Peter stammered.

"You bet I am. This place can send anyone to the nut house. The doctor wants to make me into a guinea pig so that he can test all kinds of medications. Look at all the pills they wanted me to take, as she opened an envelope in her purse. My security guard does not let me out of his sight except when I go to the loo. I am getting out from here on Monday," she responded, with disgust.

"Okay, Cathy," Peter said, as he gave her a comforting embrace.

Sitting in the car with his parents on the way to Bern for the Honor Ceremony, Peter felt the hesitant urge to consult his mom on depression and its possible causes, and before he could formulate his sentence, his mom beat him to it.

"We had a great dinner with Cathy and her Dad the other day. How is Cathy doing?"

"Quite well, mom. The doctor thinks that she is depressed and may put her on medication." Peter surprised himself.

"Depression! My foot! You are a true father's son. You are a zero when it comes to females," his mom shot back.

"But, but, mom..." protested Peter.

"I know what the problem is, you thickhead! We women know what is going on when it comes to the affairs of the heart. Cathy is in love with you and you are, when it comes to romance, just plain stupid like your dad! Boy! You need to spend sometime in Italy, to learn. Wake up the Italian blood in you! Mama mia que stupido!"

Peter was dazed at the sudden bashing he received from his mother and was at a loss of words, so he just smiled. His dad seemed to approve his reaction.

The Honor ceremony in Bern, for the two fallen heroes, was held in a room reserved for such occasions. Councilor Hilfiger awarded the Medal of Honor posthumously, and pinned the medals on Peter's dad and Joseph Breder. Peter and his mom did not understand the Swiss German so a running translation in English was made for them.

They all moved to another room where refreshments and snacks were served.

They drove back to the hotel. Peter saw, his mom and dad in tears from the corner of his eyes and could not contain himself either.

Peter drove his parents to the airport the following day and received another barrage of motherly lecture. Peter's dad was in a very good mood and laughed as Peter felt being shredded apart. He felt pained as he thought about his mother's lecture, which was downright demeaning and terribly insensitive. She insulted him, downright. He had spent a good size of his savings for the trip for the parents hoping that it would make them happy. A positive parting and some motherly love could have softened the hurt and pain Peter felt.

He always wondered why his mother always belittled his father and him just because he did not act or behave like a boisterous member of her family. Why in Gods name did she marry him in the first place? He found his father often living in quiet desperation. His parents were obviously misfits in their relation as man and wife.

It was early in the day but he decided in favor of a stiff drink to deaden the pain. He wondered that perhaps encounters such he had just lived through, is what drove men to the bottle. He thought of his zillion uncles and cousins of Italian decent, most all of who had married Italian Americans. Were they reasonably happy or were they miserable?

He recalled when one of the Italian uncles told a joke about the man who was celebrating his sixtieth wedding anniversary and sat looking very sad. His old lawyer friend queried him about the reason for his sad face. He responded that he was reminded of the time he wanted to kill his wife and his lawyer friend had told him that he would get twenty-five years in the slammer. If I had done it, I would have been a free man today. All the men were in stitches after hearing that joke. Peter wondered whether the intensity of their laughter was directly proportional to their extent of marital misery.

A smile came on his face and the pain subsided.

Eighteen

Peter was now coming back to his usual self when Schaefer called.

"The data you sent me in code from Richard Tuft was beginning to unravel the mystery murders. Let's meet in my new office on the P Street in Washington next week".

"Okay," said Peter, sounding hopeful

The Commissar in Zurich was worried about keeping Richard Tuft in the four star prison.

"Well it is my budget that is feeling the strain," he said.

"Can we put him on somebody's payroll?" asked Peter. "You know, he is a police detective by profession."

"Yes, like I told you the other day when we met that Tuft does all our coordination work which is almost all in English with the European Union Police Commission etc. I just don't know how to get the funding for Mr. Tuft without going through the complicated clearance and approvals from the Federal Police Department in Bern. Could Mr. Dieter help us."

"I will get on it right away," Peter answered, reassuringly.

Dieter was very responsive and said that he will get it approved including the salary he should be paid. "I think that Richard Tuft could pay for his keep in the secure hotel, I mean prison, to protect him from some cowboy taking a shot at him."

Peter checked on the arrangement with Richard Tuft.

"Gee, Pete. Thanks a lot. I can go back to being human again. I have started taking lessons in Swiss German with a fine police language teacher. Thanks a bunch, man. Let me know if I can be any help in the investigation, stateside. I will give my left arm to see the bastard Chief in the slammer for good, for all the murders he is responsible. Pete, watch out he ain't alone for sure," said Richard Tuft.

Peter stopped by at the Clinic to see Cathy. Somehow the romance in his heart had lost its umph from the severe bashing from his mother. He informed Cathy that he was heading back to the States.

"When will you be back?" she enquired

"I don't know," he said.

It was a cool goodbye and he headed back to make calls to Dieter, Janez, and Joseph that he was returning to the U.S. Peter did not see a trace of so-called love in Cathy for him, as they took leave of each other. Peter was not ready to go down on his knees to Cathy. What if she really felt no love for him! He would make a complete idiot of himself and would seriously crumble his self respect. Maybe his mother was all wrong. His heart ached for Cathy but he did not have the courage to make a confession to her. His confusion increased as he drove further from her. He wondered why the affair of the heart was so damn complicated.

Peter went to Bern to take his leave from Councilors Hilfiger and Schiller.

"Thank you, Mr. Miller, for your invaluable contributions. Please don't say goodbye because we would like to see you back working with us. We don't think that you should stay in the U.S. too long. Remember the terror within your Agency has not been resolved. We will be very sorry to lose you just because some bad cowboys want to kill all the good cowboys. It is strange that sometimes what happens in the United States comes to haunt us after some time. Globalization ! You can call us at any time if you have an emergency or contact us through Mr. Dieter

Hopf. You can also contact our Ambassador in Washington Dr Meyer for any message you may want to communicate to us. Remember that you are now a dual citizen. We suggest that you check with your State Department for any implications if you agree to work directly on our payroll. So, we will not say goodbye; we'll say, *see you soon,*" were the emotional parting words from Hilfiger.

Peter sat at his seat in the airplane. He was dead tired and fell asleep before the plane took off for the Washington Dulles airport.

The stewardess nudged him that the plane was about to land in Washington. He opened his eyes from deep sleep to see the smiling face of Cathy.

"What are you doing here? You should be in the Clinic! For Gods sake!" Peter said, trying to contain his feelings for her.

"Hi Peter! You sure slept like a baby! Surprise, surprise! What, no three kisses?" she said, appearing her usual self.

"Cathy, but you have not recuperated well. Why did the Clinic release you?" Peter protested.

"I am fine. I am fine, Peter. Stop fussing over me, please. I will rest for the weekend and restart the grind on Monday," Cathy said, sounding very confident.

"Does John Schaefer know that you are returning to work?" Peter inquired

"I will call him now," she said, collecting her things with a deep sigh.

They both walked out the plane and went through the Immigration and Customs as strangers. Peter wanted to talk but he thought it best to stay quiet. Cathy remained a mystery and he felt a bit pained at the chance that he could lose her.

There was a tap on his shoulder as he was picking up his bag.

"Mr. Miller," a custom official who had been watching him said, "May I have a word with you, sir? May I ask you in what line of business you are in?"

"I work for the Intelligence Department," he said, pulling out his badge. The custom official looked at the badge as if he had never seen one.

"What does an analyst agent do?" he asked.

"Analyze information, data," Peter said, with some puzzlement in his voice.

"My boss would like to meet you, if you could spare a moment, sir," the custom agent said.

"Of course," Peter responded, wondering what this was all about.

"I am Bill Jameson, Mr. Miller," said the section supervisor, shaking Peter's hand.

"The Secretary mentioned your name, as someone who is making strides in the war against terrorists, during a recent seminar."

"Thank you. It is really quite a team work, isn't it?" He sounded humble.

"Oh! But, sir, the Secretary lauded you as an example of one who came up with a plan and, had a great talent and ability to implement it." He sounded pert.

Peter stood up and shook hands. "Duty calls."

"Oh! Sir, the chief gave me this envelope to hand over to you, when you returned from your assignment overseas," Jameson said.

"Thank you. The chief? What's his name?"

"Winston Tomas," came the quizzing reply.

Peter did not open the envelope and decided to open it in front of Schaefer.

Peter saw Cathy waiting at the curb and before Peter could go up to her, he saw a man standing next to her with his arm around her shoulder. Peter felt a jab of jealousy and walked up to them.

"Ah there you are, Peter, I thought I had lost you. This is Jack Schaefer," she said, as a matter of course. She waved and sat in a cab and drove off, before Peter could barely say, "Nice to meet you, Jack." But there was no response from either of the two. Feeling a bit offended, Peter waved at them and took a cab.

"Hotel Madison. Please."

Nineteen

The taxi was almost in Georgetown when the taxi driver said, "I am sorry, but the blue car behind has been tailing us. I will drop you at the Hotel Madison, just walk out from the side entrance and I will pick you up."

Peter followed the driver's instructions.The taxi driver drove, making rapid turns and shook off the car tailing them.

A couple of minutes later they were heading back into Georgetown, when Peter thanked the driver and asked him to stop at the Hotel Four Seasons instead" Peter smiled and gave the driver an extra tip.

Peter wondered who the cab driver was. He was an American judging by his accent. He felt uneasy and remembered Hilfiger that he was not out of danger. Peter walked in the hotel lobby and waited a while and decided to eat in the Restaurant while looking around for any suspicious characters.

The glass of red wine and the club sandwich hit the spot. Peter walked out of the side door and took the shuttle bus to the National airport. He took a Hotel courtesy van to the hotel Mariott and checked in instead of Hotel Madison, hoping to at least confuse any one who might still be stalking him.

Peter called Schaefer in the office, next morning.

"Welcome back, Peter. You have an appointment to meet the Secretary of the Department of Security for lunch tomorrow. Why don't you stop at my new office and we can meet before the luncheon with the Secretary."

"Cathy traveled back with me from Zurich yesterday," said Peter.

There was no response from Schaefer.

So Peter continued, "I have a letter from a Winston Tomas handed to me by the Immigration Customs officer Bill Jameson. Do you know any of these guys?"

"What does the letter say?" Schaefer asked.

"I have not opened the letter and thought that I open it at our meeting," Peter responded.

"I have a better idea, we open it when we meet with the Secretary," Schaefer promptly answered.

Schaefer embraced Peter as he walked into his office, which surprised him.

"The Secretary is deeply disturbed with the murders of the agents and the attempts on your life. I have also updated him about the attempt on Cathy and her injuries. He also has all the information you sent me from detective Tuft. He had believed that one of the terrorist cells had infiltrated the department but now is convinced that it is the establishment."

The Secretary was very pleased to meet Peter and thanked him for the remarkable work he had carried out with the Swiss weapon manufacturers. He informed Peter and John Schaefer that several of the U.S. defense contractors will participate at the coming seminar. He sounded very casual as he wandered around different political topics. It was a fast lunch and Peter was pleased that it was over, when the Secretary requested for the check.

The Secretary lowered his voice as they were leaving the restaurant, and said that Peter and John Schaefer should follow him about half an hour later to his office for the meeting.

No sooner had the Secretary left the restaurant, when his office called John to inform him that the location for the meeting had been changed. They were directed to proceed to the Restaurant Chang, on J Street and that a taxi would pick them up and drive them to the place for the meeting. The taxi driver's name was Jason. Schaefer looked concerned as he shook his head very worried. The taxi driver drove them to the Blair House and left.

The Secretary apologized, "We are now so sophisticated in this country that we have become our worst enemies. Make sure that Richard Tuft is well protected. The word is out that he is a whistle blower. The 'establishment' is behind this chaos. They have had sweetheart deals with the defense contractors for decades and the lobbyists have practically run this country's defense policies. It was a system that worked great for the export of weapons and what have you. The Congress really had no objections and played along. The administrations changed but each president felt that a highly weaponized United States would be the best defense in the world. Then came Reagan, who sharply increased the defense budget adding projects like the Strategic Defense Initiative as a defense against the communist ICBMs. The defense contractors and their R and D machines went into high gear. You will be surprised at the cost of the high-tech weapons that have been developed. Remember the Drone model plane, which was being developed, and the costs were running in hundreds of millions of dollars? The Israeli offered to sell their drone planes well tested in the war against the Palestinians for 200,000 dollars a plane. Reagan then formed the famous Grace Commission to audit the national expenditures to reduce the waste by the government. The Grace report of hundreds of pages made some fine recommendations and most of which fell to the way side and business returned to the usual.

"Well, so much for the history lesson. Our defense industry is very powerful, as ever, so that the word PEACE is a direct threat to the moneymaking industry. How many nuclear weapons do we need? Our arsenal is adequate to wipe out the entire world sixty times!

"Don't get me wrong, we need to remain militarily strong, but not at a cost that starts killing any sane notion of peace. We are a Democracy and not a tyrant nation. Sorry for the preamble but I want to be sure that you understand the course that the President has taken. The policy is simple and one that recognizes that in order to reduce terrorism in the world, there must be Democratic Free societies all over the world, that are responsive to any dissension in its people, creating an environment of freedom and opportunity for its citizens to live in peace.

"We are reorganizing the intelligence community in the government so that we can act on our intelligence effectively in order to protect our nation. We simply must treat all nations with respect and dignity. Nations should build the world into a community where all individual human rights are respected and grievances are rectified. We can eliminate all the various types of terrors that plague the innocent. The President recently said that our nation must join all peace-loving nations to take the initiative to help the needy all over the world. We are taking steps with other countries to disarm the enemy of the people." The Secretary took a deep breath after the long speech to Peter and John.

The Secretary then looked at Peter and said, "I am very proud of you for taking the nonviolence approach to dissolve tension, but I must caution you that you have an uphill struggle because there are people in our capitalist society that unequivocally believe that violence makes a hell of a lot more money than nonviolence."

The Secretary stopped a minute and continued, "The buck stops at my desk, so I am requesting all in our administration to feel free in emailing me directly any comments, recommendations, gripes any one may have that would help us all become better and responsible human beings."

The Secretary paused again and continued, "We have almost completed our investigations identifying the culprits, and the murderers, responsible for the horrific murders of our agents and who threaten those amongst us who work for peace. These murderers will be charged with the due process of law."

Peter and John were about to leave the Secretary after the meeting when Peter suddenly remembered the letter he had not opened and that Schaefer had suggested they open it in front of the Secretary. Peter explained to the Secretary that he was handed a letter from the Customs Chief at the Dulles Airport addressed to Peter when he arrived from Zurich and handed him the letter.

The Secretary took the letter, opened it, and read aloud.

"Dear Mr. Miller

You are indeed a remarkable young man and I congratulate you.

I understand that you are involved in a program to reorganize the Intelligence Department, as a member of an elite team of analysts. Those of us who have years of experience and have followed our history of defending the core interests of our nation have been left out of the reorganization process.

We have protested and made many attempts with the new administration that they hear us out before they disregard years of valuable experience, but have had no success. The departments responsible for the security of our nation are being reorganized with no regard to the system of the vast Intelligence know-how that has been collected over several years by agents that have laid their lives for the country. We are not against changes as long as they are done in a manner that improves the security and not in the manner it is being done which will weaken the security and make our nation more vulnerable to increased terrorist attacks.

We agree that young blood is vital but not at the expense of experience that has been the backbone of security of our country. Our experienced human resources are being shredded mercilessly by thoughtless reorganization, relocating them into wrong positions and some given meaningless tasks. It is a national suicide and those of us who care are desperate.

Peace is the objective of all, but it is not the language terrorists understand. We are not consulted nor asked to participate in the new policies and strategies that are being planned. This will have dire consequences.

Will you also turn us down or will you join us to save the nation from insanity? We hope you will decide for the latter option.

Thank you

Sincerely
Signed
Winston Tomas
Director."

The Secretary looked up at John and Peter and said, "Tomas is a good man. It is sad that he has joined a group of revolutionists that threaten our security and stop at nothing. Tomas is mistaken when he says in the letter to you that the Administration disregards them and their opinions in the reorganization effort. The truth is that they, known as 'The establishment', have held many administrations and the Congress, hostage to their will. 'The establishment' believes that they are the Government.

We found lots of weak spots in the nation's ability to collect intelligence and use it in a well coordinated response to terror before it strikes Americans. 9/11 is a sad example but it was a wake up call and our Administration took it very serious only to see 'the establishment' block most of the reorganizations considered mandatory and they offered no alternate solutions either. We know that for every security issue there are as many opinions as people involved in searching for a solution, but this is ridiculous."

The Secretary was visibly very disturbed.

Peter spoke, "Can we not talk to the establishment?"

There was a long, thoughtful moment and the Secretary responded.

"Yes , I suppose we should but they are so numerous. We have identified some of the criminals and they face murder charges."

"I could meet with Winston Tomas, for a start and get to meet some of 'The establishment' before dissension runs totally out of control," Peter suggested and John agreed.

The Secretary pondered over the suggestion and responded, "Winston Tomas has exposed himself by what we have found in our investigation and now this letter to you. He may negotiate with you but the rest of the establishment will not show their faces for obvious reasons. OK make an appointment to meet Tomas. Needless to say be very careful. You may be sticking your head in the lion's mouth. Keep me informed."

Twenty

Peter walked out of the Blair house with John Schaefer, who murmured that the Secretary would make a very good President if he decided to run one day. Peter agreed wholeheartedly.

It was a crisp cool evening, and Peter thought that a stroll from the Blair House to Georgetown would do him some good after having sat through intriguing lectures, first with John and then with the Secretary. Peter saw some students walking towards him on the bridge. He overheard a student say, "This country is going to the dogs, and even the Secretary of the Security is not safe."

Peter increased his walking pace when his cell phone rang. It was Schaefer.

"Have you heard that the Secretary was the victim of an assassination attempt as he left the Blair house?"

"My God. What the hell is happening?" Peter reacted.

Schaefer instructed, " Peter! Check out of the hotel you are in now. I will have an agent pick you up in the lobby. We are both targets next." There was urgency in his voice.

Peter did a quick turn around on the bridge and jogged back to the hotel. He quickly packed and came down to the lobby to check out. A TV reporter rushed up to him.

"Are you Agent Miller?"

Taken a back by the camera and glaring lights, he paid the bill and made a dash for the door where a man stood waving. Seconds later they were speeding over the bridge to Georgetown and through the University campus, heading to Maryland.

The man driving the car turned to Peter, "Whew! Boy that was close. I am special agent Draper, Director Schaefer is waiting for you at his residence." The car made a few quick turns and drove into the driveway of the house. Agent Draper waved and took off.

Schaefer opened the door and beckoned Peter in while looking to see if they had been followed. The TV was on and breaking news flashed that the Secretary of Security was rushed to the hospital following an attempt on his life.

"Peter, the Secretary was shot as his car left the Blair House. He received a flesh wound in his left arm. The ambulance, that was rushing him to the hospital, suddenly disappeared and was later found on the Turnpike south at the Crystal city exit, minus the Secretary. Let's check the tickers," he said, as he walked to his situation room.

One of the many tickers was printing out coded message so John switched on the decoder and the message was electronically displayed on a special screen.

'Ambulance driver shot now out of danger and moved to an undisclosed location for security. No sign of the Secretary yet, all roads and exits out of DC on high alert. President now in Whitehouse situation room. Standby for message from President.'

Schaefer poured a drink for Peter and himself while keeping an eye on the special screen.

The TV channel, flashed 'Breaking News Update.'

The reporter said, "We have just learnt that the Secretary was in a strategy meeting in the Blair House instead of his office. The police are searching for the two men in meeting with the Secretary, just before he was shot. We are awaiting news about his condition as soon as we can find out the hospital where the Secretary was rushed. This just in, the ambulance carrying the Secretary was found near Crystal City. The ambulance driver had been shot and is in critical condition."

Peter was in deep thought at the sudden change of events, when he saw Cathy walking into the room in her dressing gown.

"Well, well, well, first it was me and now it is the Secretary, boy am I in some company! Peter, the hunter of peace, is now being hunted by the devil," she said, with sarcasm.

"Please, Cathy, this is not a joke." John sounded very irritated.

Peter was at a loss of words. Cathy wore that mischievous smile on her face. What was she doing there? Was she married to John Schaefer or was he an ex or her fiancée? Who was Jack Schaefer he met at the DC airport? The hour of the destruction of his dreams was upon him. He just did not want to find out what she was doing there. He felt very tense and wondered if he could handle the suspense and the hour of truth.

The special ticker started again: President wants to see you in the Whitehouse. Special transport on its way to pick you.

John jumped up and ran to his bedroom only to return in a flash. All dressed up, wearing his badge.

"No comments, in case reporters call. I will be back soon. I am hungry, please make pancakes." A moment later, John Schaefer was being sped to the Whitehouse to meet the president in the White House situation room.

Cathy plopped on the sofa, and waving her hands said, "Peter. Peter, I told you, let's go far away from this crazy world."

"Yes, you did. But what will your husband..." Peter blurted sounding fearsome.

"What husband? I am not...Oh, you thought that John and I...... what a wild imagination you have Peter!" Cathy rolled over laughing.

"John is my brother and Jack, the tall one you met with me at the airport when we returned from Zurich, is my cousin and he works at the Pentagon. No wonder you had your famous quizzical look! Say something. Will ya?"

Peter collected his composure, and said, "Sorry, I am just trying to digest the situation."

"Take your time Pietro otherwise you may suffer from indigestion and we don't have Alka Selzer for sure, knowing John." She laughed.

"You are laughing at me, ridiculing me. Why, Cathy. Why?" Peter was reeling.

"Wait a minute, dear Peter; are you worried and jealous? How wonderful!"

Cathy clapped her hands.

Peter could not hold it any more and started laughing, "You are soooo smart! Me, confused? Yes. But jealous? No way, Jose."

"Peter, Peter, pumpkin eater. Peter is a liar, liar!" Cathy jumped with joy looking like a teenager.

"I am not the smart one liner type who can match all the belittling I get subjected to by the very few females that I came in contact including my mom. I don't understand what pleasure people get by belittling others." Peter was hurting.

Cathy suddenly embraced Peter, "I am so sorry, I was just teasing you. The truth is that I subject the very few special people in my life to a kind of teasing. You may call it distorted love. The truth is, I am dying for their love and can't find a way to tell them how much I love them for fear of rejection. It is a very warped way of doing it. I am so ashamed. Peter you are very special and...I love you!" Cathy was in tears.

This was an unexpected response and Peter was overwhelmed. He held Cathy in his arms.

"Darling lets just stay like this forever. I love you too."

The two were lost in each other's arms as two lost souls who had found each other.

Time had lost its significance. A Greek philosopher, considered an authority in the affairs of cupid, had written that a soul comprises of a female and a male part which somehow separate in cosmos, and wander in the universe in pain looking for each other. When the two parts of the soul find each other, there is a heavenly sparkle as they unite in oneness.

Twenty-one

The unison was shook when a car pulled up in the driveway. The door, which had seen better times once, creaked open in protest. Two massive masked men stood pointing their weapons of mass destruction at the united souls. The scene was simply pathetic. Aggression had no respect for romance.

Cathy screamed as Peter was marched out into the waiting car, which sped into the night burning tire on the driveway.

Cathy was in shock when John returned from the meeting in the White House. John immediately issued an all points bulletin.

The morning papers had headlines about the assassination attempt and then kidnapping of the Secretary of Security. The papers alleged that for some very strange reason the Secretary met with two individuals in the Blair House after having lunch with them in the city. The office of the Secretary would not confirm nor deny that one of the two visitors was of Middle Eastern decent. One of the TV stations had an exclusive that the Secretary was about to make a major policy announcement, when the incident happened. The talk shows speculated that the administration was taking a long awaited get-tough policy on the Middle East. The nation's alarm system had gone to deep red alert.

Peter felt a sharp pain in his neck as he came to. It was a well-lit room in an office and Peter could see the capital dome. His hands and legs were taped to the chair he sat on, and ached. An elegantly dressed man, wearing a mask came in.

"I take it you are well rested, Mr. Miller," came a muffled voice.

"What is this all about? Who are you? What do you want from me?" Peter demanded.

The masked man shook his head and said, "As they say in the movies, you are in no condition to ask questions."

"Oh yea? Which movie was that?" Peter responded.

There was silence and the kidnapper and the victim started to laugh.

Peter made the move. "Please, sir, could you cut me free? I am a very civilized man. You obviously have a problem and I am a troubleshooter. I will help. It's my job and I love it."

"I suppose you will ask me for a coffee next, perhaps some breakfast," said the masked kidnapper.

"Yes, sir. You read my mind. You must be a gentleman with a few strange habits such as kidnapping people you wish information from instead of merely requesting in a civilized manner." Peter was fully in control of his wits.

Much to Peter's surprise the man walked up to him and said, "You are an interesting man indeed. I will take my chance and trust you."

The kidnapper pulled out a Swiss knife from his pocket and cut the tapes. He picked up the phone.

"Two coffees and some Danish, please." There was a knock at the door and the man quickly removed his mask and lit up a cigarette. "We allow smoking since all our employees are smokers and we rarely have visitors," he said.

Peter stood up, under the watchful eyes of the man, and sat in a comfortable chair in front of the man. The man was probably in his fifties, professional looking.

"Thank you for the breakfast, sir. I owe you one. How may I be of help to you?" Peter said, feeling better and amused at the situation he was in.

"What was your meeting with the Secretary yesterday about?" the kidnapper queried.

Peter responded, "The Secretary thanked me for my work in Switzerland and reinforced the administration's policy to combat terrorism with peaceful means. I am part of a so-called elite team of agents specially formed to seek a peaceful way to eradicate terrorism that plagues our nation and the world. Two of our agents were found murdered some months ago and two were scared out of their wits, which resulted in their quitting the jobs.

"The Secretary thinks that the dreadful murders are the work of the Washington DC establishment, which believes that acts of aggressions, wars, conflicts etc. are good for the bottom line and peace is a sign of weakness and drives people and nations to the poor house. The weapons industry accounts for a significant part of the trade around the world and makes tons of money with no value for life."

"Kind of naïve approach for a nation, when we have all those rogues trying to kill our way of life, wouldn't you say" The kidnapper snapped back.

"Yes, sir, you are right. History, on the other hand, teaches us that might when considered right brings destruction ultimately to the aggressor. I do not see an alternate to peace and just want to be a good decent human being. Aggression only provokes aggression. How much of our foreign aid went for years to support dictators, tyrants. The aid programs destined to help a nation barely helped the needy because of rampant corruption. Was our nation oblivious to all this or are we so self centered that we turned a blind eye to the truth." Peter was now tired as his voice trailed.

There was a pause and reflection and Peter continued, "Why don't you tell me what your problem is. It would also help me knowing who you are. I will get started and find a solution, unless your business is to kill people as rebels without a cause. I promise no harm will come to you. I will report this incident as a case of 'comedy of errors' and give no details whatsoever."

"OK, Mr. Miller, you are free to leave and we have a deal, subject to the approval my associates. My driver will drop you back in a hotel, sorry not at Mr. Schaefer's home in case the police is watching. We meet in the lobby of the Hyatt Hotel at the Capital for lunch tomorrow and no games please."

Peter walked out after a handshake, and a driver in uniform guided him through the offices down in the garage, where he was gently blindfolded.

"Sorry, this is for our security," he said.

The car moved out into the street and the driver after a few moments, asked Peter to remove the blindfold. Peter noticed that they were passing the White House. Peter asked the driver to drop him at the Four Seasons Hotel. He freshened up in the men's room and walked out still feeling the pain in his neck from the blow one of the gooks gave.

Twenty-two

Peter called Schaefer, who calmly informed him that the intelligence had determined his location and they were waiting for a signal from him to rescue him.

The police were monitoring the location where the Secretary had been taken, who likewise had not pushed the panic button for rescue.

"The President is aware of the situation but is hopping mad that the Secretary has not been rescued as of this hour. By the way Cathy is terribly worried about you, so you better go back to my place at 300 Jefferson Glade in Bethesda, Maryland."

Cathy looked as if she had been crying a long time and was glad to have him back in her arms. She reminded him to call his parents in New Jersey.

She watched him, intently, as he talked to his mom. Peter decided to pour the unripe news on.

"Hi, mom. Yes, it's me, Peter, and yes, I am in love with Cathy and we hope to get married soon. No you are the first one to know. I have not even asked Cathy if she will marry me. This is all fresh off the press and the ink is still wet. Give my love to Dad. I am glad he speaks to you in Italian. Why don't you answer him back in Swiss German? No! No! No! Mom, please don't tell the family anything until Cathy agrees to marry me. OK mama, Bella mamma, Ciao!"

Peter put the phone down and turned around to look at Cathy. Her eyes were closed with tears flowing down her cheeks.

"Darling, Cathy, will you marry me?" Peter proposed. He was surprised how naturally the words came out without an ounce of hesitation.

Cathy gave him a very hard squeeze. "Yes, I will my love. Darling, don't forget that as an elite analyst agent, you cannot marry for another two years and some months."

"How can you get so technical at a moment like this?" Peter asked. They both laughed.

Peter gave a briefing to Schaefer, at the office, about his encounter with his kidnapper and that he was going to meet him at the Hyatt.

The newspapers reported that the Secretary had been rescued and the culprits were in custody. Schaefer however informed Peter that the Secretary had walked into his home early in the morning. He later drove to his office and issued a statement that there was no cause for alarm and that he was well. The ambulance driver was in good condition and would be released in a day or so. The press was intrigued at what had happened and chased the Secretary around the city for answers.

"I will brief the Secretary about your incident in the next hour, Schaefer said to Peter. What's this about Cathy and you? Well, we will talk about it later." John waved and left their meeting, without even a smile.

Twenty-three

Peter was nervous as he walked in the hotel lobby of the Hyatt Capital.

The kidnapper waved at him and they walked to the restaurant in the hotel. They were seated in the corner table where the usual noise level was somewhat subdued.

"I am clean of any devices. How about you?" the kidnapper said.

"Yes, I am clean," Peter said, confidently.

"I am retired Brig. General James Strong. I work as a lobbyist for the MacLean Industries, for the past five years. MacLean, as you know, is one of the largest defense contractors in the country, employing some three hundred thousand professionals around the country. Almost all the previous administrations have had a strong policy to maintain our armed services with capabilities second to no other country in the world. This has been the corner stone of the Congress and the Administrations.

"The 9/11 disasters gave a further boost to revamp the nations defense capabilities. There are several troubling issues, as you know concerning the consolidation of the multiple intelligence agencies.

"The El Qaida-type of groups have changed the ball game. In fact it has once again shown that the U.S. armed services can fight a war like the Gulf war effectively but not a guerrilla type of a war such as in Vietnam, Afghanistan, and Iraq. The armed services are undergoing changes in the training of our soldiers but it falls short and hence the slaughter of our boys. We have had several highly experienced Generals, Admirals whose recommendations to create a separate guerilla trained army have been overruled by the civilian Secretaries of Defense and State. Needless to say that the rift in strategies amongst the civilian brass and the army chiefs in each administration has been widening over the years. Very important decisions concerning the security of our nation have been compromised for political and what have you reasons.

"Now let me come to the point. The newly created Department of Security, which is basically a good idea, disregards the years of experience that has been accumulated, in its attempt to reorganize and streamline operations. New blood is good but not at the expense of knowledge and incredible experience. In fact there is a war between the old guard and the new blood, which has resulted in compromises that is having terrible consequences.

"The differences in opinions led to loud sessions, then some fist sessions and now some outright killings. It is becoming a free fight with no referees. Who is responsible for this mess? No one stands up to take charge so as not to get exposed and be held responsible while things go wrong everyday.

"The industry has been watching this internal war but any attempts to intervene were brushed aside by the elected and appointed brass in the government, as special commercial interests.

"Mr. Miller, the MacLean Industry made a bold move to get all parties to meet and come to senses but one group or another in the government vetoed the attempt. The U.S. Congressmen, who constantly bashes out at each other across the aisle, did not respond, so that they can take put shots at the administration. There is a lot of lip service and no meaningful action. A bloody mess, while our boys are out there fighting an enemy, that now consists of multiple guerilla cells, which they know very little about and are elusive. We have observed the formation of several special interest cells each carrying its own agenda in the government, while we are told how great the nation is doing.

"The Secretary of the Security Agency turned down many attempts to meet with our group. I took the bold move with some of the concerned group of Lobbyists, as patriots and pulled the kidnapping of the Secretary and later you. It was not our intention to hurt anyone and I deeply regret the injuries.

"Let me tell you this...the Secretary listened and realizes the terrible problem he is in charge of resolving and will soon become a scapegoat for the administration. The meeting was a wake up call for him. He has extended his full cooperation so that we can all pool our resources and find solutions in the best interest of the country.

"I agree with peaceful means to resolve problems, but you must negotiate from a position of strength and not weakness with groups or countries that do not understand any other language. The insurgents in Iraq for instance, are heavily financed by nations and private capital that considers Democracy a threat to their way of life, which to most people of the free world is abhorrent. We must realize that there are insurgents that are fighting tyranny in their countries and they need our support or they will perish, Sudan is a great example. We must bring about some semblance of sanity starting at least in our nation.

"The Secretary has agreed to work in coordination with all concerned groups and I really hope you will too."

Peter was confounded at what the General had to say.

"General, I am shocked at what has happened because voices of dissension were not heard by those responsible in the government. What ever happened to dedicated public servants, I deeply regret the horrific outcome. General, could the cause of lack of cooperation by the Administration, stem from years of power, almost unflinching at times, that the army used over the past Administrations on policy and strategy decisions? Kind of, a backlash, to show who is the boss?" Peter shared his thoughts.

The General was pensive and offered an explanation. He spoke with slow punctuated deliberation

"A sound Government, in my opinion, is one that respects the balance of power, understands the burden of responsibility, and acts in the true interest of the nation without clouding decisions with political agendas. We are far from this idealism and we have strayed to extremes at times. Power has a habit of corrupting those in power. It is a human frailty perhaps.

"I am also pained by the extreme reaction leading to murders by some who lost control of their senses in the heat of the moment. Our law will hold them accountable.

I have made a full written confession of my part in the revolution or mutiny to the public, following the shooting, kidnapping and the meeting with the Secretary.

The revolution caused by the dissension is not controlled by a central group. It is more like a guerrilla warfare with cells following their own agendas and gripes, so be careful."

"I have been invited to join the cause of the establishment in a letter I received from a Winston Tomas. What do you suggest I do, General?" Peter tried to solicit some advice, Showing him the letter.

The General reflected for a while and then said, "Peter, I know him and watch it because he may be indicted in the murder of intelligence agents. I would have suggested that you write a polite letter to him but now that I know you, please meet him after clearing it with the Justice Department or your department lawyers."

The General gave a warm handshake as he took leave of Peter. "I am sure we will meet again, unless the government decides to throw me in the slammer. Nice to meet a man of peace."

Twenty-four

Schaefer, upon being briefed by Peter, suddenly reacted.

"What? I remember meeting the Brig General and frankly he made a whole lot of sense to me. My boss did not show any interest whatsoever when I reported to him about my meeting with the General. You know, Peter, the General committed a crime in kidnapping but the Secretary has issued a no contest plea against the General so perhaps no charges will be brought against the General and his merry men."

"Hey Peter, you cannot marry Cathy for another two years. The field job you have exposes you to near death situations and that is why the Secretary strongly felt that unmarried individuals would be better suited. I am also single although I would like to marry and settle down with a family. This job is too damn exciting. It's an intoxication that might kill me someday." Schaefer spoke with a hint of emotion.

"Yes, I know, John."

Peter could not resist his desire to call Winston Tomas, so he called the general counsel of the department, Ralph Munch giving the background and soliciting his advise.

Ralph read Peter the riot act and umpteen reasons for doing nothing. He finally agreed that Peter should at least call Tomas for the sake of courtesy.

Peter called Tomas, who picked up his call and recalled having sent the letter to Peter.

"What have you decided?" he asked, abruptly.

"I will be glad to do all I can to assist, but I am not a mutineer and I love peace." Peter replied.

"What the hell does that mean? You can either join our cause or stay out of our way." Tomas was very irritated.

"Sir, what I am suggesting is that negotiations are better than aggressive confrontation with the Administration, who we are sworn to serve. We must find a just resolution of the dissension. Nothing like an open dialogue with those you disagree with." Peter tried to calm Tomas.

"How many people did you show my letter?" Tomas sounded more aggravated.

"My boss and the Secretary. Oh! also General Strong. They all agree that your grievances should be discussed with you so that they can be resolved. Sir, I can arrange for a meeting with the Secretary and others in the Intelligence Department so we can address your serious concerns and recommendations. What dates are suitable for the meeting? I am available at your convenience to prepare an agenda and an outline of your concerns and recommendations, for the meeting. Shall I proceed?"

Tomas was surprised at Peter's refusal to be non-confrontational and find a solution, peacefully, instead.

"Well, okay. let me check my schedule and others and I will get back to you," Tomas said, somewhat pacified.

Cathy and Peter decided to dine at the Palm restaurant. It was a very cold evening and there were some snow flurries to add romance to it all. The lobsters were just impeccable. The soft-shell crab cakes although not in season went well as starters. They both enjoyed the Robert Mondavi red wine, which they had a preference for, in the dinners earlier. The tension in the pre courtship days had given way to love and a sense of security that only blissful marital relationship brings. There was some anxiety in Cathy's voice as she talked about marriage.

"Pete, waiting two years would drive me absolute bunkers!"

Peter realized that this was his first of many dousings to follow, of female logic. How does one respond? Stay meek or strike back? So he stayed calm and said, "Are you going to leave me? No patience, my love?"

Cathy did not expect this blunt response. She waited, dropped her head and attacked with tears in her eyes.

Peter, seeing the tears, melted, fumbled, and lost the moment to be tough.

He tried the consoling strategy, and said, "What's the difference, love? We can get engaged in New Brunswick and invite your folks from Switzerland. We can move in together and we are, for all practical purposes, married. We can then have a church wedding in Switzerland, when the two years are over. How does that grab you?"

Cathy continued to look pensive and said, "How can you be so cruel? All I am saying is that I love you very much."

It was clear as mud, so Peter decided to kiss her instead. He now realized that he was entering the world of the famous love's twilight zone.

After a reflective silence, Cathy said"Well, come to think of it, what troubles me is that you will continue to work in a highly life threatening job environment during the so called two year waiting period arbitrarily set by a man who is married and has three wonderful kids and got kidnapped."

"Well, well, well! Why, its Peter having a night out!" It was the Secretary of Security taking a seat at the table next to theirs with his family.

"Mr. Secretary, this is indeed a great pleasure. May I introduce my fiancée, Cathy?" Peter stood up to make the introduction.

"So when is the big day? Soon, I hope. You must both be so excited" said the Secretary.

Cathy jumped right in. "Pete has signed an agreement with the Department, which will not permit him to get married for three years."

"Oh, yes, I believe that is right...Peter has, however, turned his job from a high security risk to a normal risk. You know he has this admirable talent of diffusing his enemies. Tell you what, I will send a memorandum on Monday canceling the non-marital stipulation from his employment agreement. After all we cannot have you two love birds held apart," said the Secretary, who was in a great mood.

No sooner had Cathy and Peter sat at their table, when Peter saw General James Strong Enter the restaurant with an entourage. The General walked straight up to Peter and shook his hands as an old friend.

"So good to see you, Peter. You are looking great and radiant. Oh! I see why," he said, as he turned to face Cathy.

"My fiancée, Cathy. Darling, may I introduce Brig. General James Strong," Peter said, as he introduced Cathy.

"So, I am going to ask you the same question everyone does. When is the big day?"

Cathy was fast and responded with a very radiant smile. "Peter has just been cleared for marriage, by the Secretary, so we will get married soon."

"Why that calls for a celebration! Debra, my wife, and I would love to have you both join us this Sunday at our home in Virginia for dinner at seven so that we can celebrate in a more festive setting. Sorry but I will not take a no for an answer. Please, please!"

Cathy and Peter finally sat down, in total disbelieve, trying to absorb the rapid blessings that had showered them in the past few moments. They held hands and gazed at each other enjoying the precious moment.

"Pete, my love, I am beyond words. I have never been so happy."

Peter remained speechless as he gazed at the deep blue eyes, black haired, angel face, and his wife to be, in a rapture of indescribable love.

A feeling of victory came upon him as he remembered the first time he set his eyes on Cathy, along with two other potential suitors. The pride he felt slowly faded into sadness as he remembered that the two Analysts agents who would have been potential suitors had been murdered.

Peter stood up after quickly paying the bill and stretched his hand out to Cathy.

"Honey bun, lets leave, this place has no respect for privacy."

Twenty-five

The General had a sprawling ranch for a home, about a half hour drive from DC. Large trees dotted the landscape, with manicured lawns and attractively spread areas full of flowers. The setting was pictorial. The General and his wife Debra were very charming hosts. Dom Perignon flowed all evening as they went through a dinner of wild game. The chocolate and cream mouse was out of this world. The conversation had been light and lively. It was very clear that the General and his wife hosted many parties. There were photos of the General with present and past Presidents and other dignitaries tastefully displayed and made for some very lively conversation.

The General proposed a cigar and cognac in the study with Peter while Debra put her arms around Cathy and suggested she show her around the ranch. Yes, it was now time for some business.

"Peter, the MacLean and other groups, I represent, have expressed a desire to meet with you, after the forthcoming Swiss—U.S. defense Contractors' seminar. Now I know that you will not attend but it is very clear to all of us that you have been the man that has made it all happen. Peter you have a business background, so you will understand when I say that you have managed to convert a confrontational situation between Switzerland and our country into a business opportunity for both the countries. The news has not gone unnoticed in the European Union headquarters either. By the way, Peter, the Secretary is also very pleased with your performance, and said that he was very glad to have you on his team."

Cathy decided to drive back to DC because she said that Peter had had a bit too much of the good stuff.

Peter started to brief her, starting from the time she was attacked in Switzerland. She took it all in with only an occasional emotion. She had received some updates from John and prompted Peter to go on fast forward from time to time.

It was now wee hours of the morning and both were exhausted.

"Cathy. do you know why you were attacked in Switzerland?"

After a moment of introspection Cathy said, " Working as an assistant to brother dear gave me access to a lot of sensitive information. Perhaps that became a threat to some. I met the police chief from Chicago; he had come for a meeting with John. There were some allegations in the meeting that he may be involved with the disappearances of some of the detectives in Chicago. I had a file on him in the office and I caught him glancing through it. He looked surprise when I caught him in the act and begged me not to squeal on him. He had stopped by my office later and made a statement that the department had very little intelligence on him. I don't know why, but I said that there was a lot of intelligence information we carried in our heads, that was not committed to paper, just in case the file is compromised. The police chief had looked nervous and left abruptly without the usual goodbyes. So…so, he hired Richard Tuft to do the dirty job for him."

John was up and early, having coffee when Cathy and Peter came looking dreary. Peter talked about their dinner in the Palm restaurant and the chance encounters with the Secretary and the General. Cathy interrupted the dialogue.

"The Secretary has agreed that Peter and I can get married and he will waive the stipulation in Peter's employment agreement." John shook his head in acknowledgement and left.

Cathy came up to Peter. "Don't mind John, he is all about work. He is just Swiss."

Peter had been trying to get John Schaefer to talk about the next assignment.

John finally came out as they sat in his office.

"We have work to be done in Bruxelles with NATO, but it could be very nasty. Look here Peter; you have made my work concerning assignments very complicated. How can I send my future brother-in-law take on work, which the department knows is high risk? I will be criticized if I gave you easy ones. I am damned if I do and damned if I don't."

Just then John's secretary popped her head in to announce that Amin Hasan had arrived.

Amin looked very surprised and happy to see Peter. "So, from nine elite analysts to just two. I am glad to see you alive," Amin said.

"Amin is a member of the task force that is working with the CIA and FBI to streamline them with the other intelligence units," John quickly interjected to change the topic.

"How are you coming along with identifying the Muslim terror cells in the country?"

"The only thing I have been able to achieve is the hiring of more Muslims in the intelligence units, but they are not trusted by their peers," Amin said, with sadness. Schaefer was observing Amin as he expressed frustration about his assignment.

"Peter, you are between assignments. Why don't you give Amin a hand?"

Peter suggested that they take a drive to Mount Vernon. "It's generally quiet at this time of the year and we can brainstorm perhaps."

Amin had issues. He talked at length on how he had struggled in his career. He was a Palestinian by birth and his parents left Jerusalem in 1948 for the U.S. His parents were in the shoe manufacturing business in Jerusalem and had continued successfully in Queens, N.Y. Amin had a college degree and decided to join the New York police department.

"I wanted to help the immigrants coming to the Promised Land. You know Peter; I managed to convince the department to hire cops that were multilingual. After a few years a new Police Commissioner, changed the hiring program because he preferred cops coming from the academy that spoke only English. I objected on several occasions since the multi-lingual cops amounted to only twenty percent of the entire police force of the city, which is a melting pot of people from all parts of the world. I was transferred to DC and I met similar resistance from the brass. I was fortunate to be selected for this job, but I am stuck."

Peter noted that Amin had deep rooted anti-American feelings so he prodded the subject till Amin came out with quite some emotion.

"Peter, my people were literally thrown out of their homes to make room for the Israeli people. The Israeli primarily focused on getting rid of the British. Today they would be ranked as terrorists. After 1948 when Israel was founded, any resistance from the Palestinians was dealt very severely by the Israeli. The country became known as Israel and did not even recognize that it was Palestine, the land of the Palestinians. The U.S. and the British came out always defending the Israelis. The level of frustration in my people increased over time and millions fled as refugees to any nation that would accept them. Out of the fight for our country that was brutally taken over, rose the militant group of Yasser Arafat who became determined to oust the Israelis from Palestine.

"The wars that followed made it even worse for the Palestinian people. The Palestinian freedom fighters are called terrorists. This injustice has made a terrible mark in the minds of the Muslim world that has lost its faith in the so-called free world. The Palestinian people are very bitter and have lost all hope. It has deteriorated to the extent that young people blow themselves up, while the world watches in horror, blaming the true victims of injustice. Reaching out to the Palestinians has become a lip service. The media has made the true victim into a hated terrorist. The western society cannot even relate to the Palestinians but relates well with the Israelis. Palestinians, who have been fighting to get back their land since Israel was born in 1948, are now not even considered human beings. The western world has driven the Muslim world to sheer hopelessness, desperation and wonders why terrorism is expanding. The west supports the leaders in the Muslim world who are tyrants and dictators. The war in Iraq was to stop a tyrant from becoming a nuclear tyrant.

"Return human dignity to the Palestinians including those who are not allowed to return to their mother land and you will see the start of peace. Want to give it a try?"

Peter was reminded how the news coverage had only recently started to show some respect for the Palestinian cause. Amin had thrown him a challenge that he could not refuse.

"Hi honey, you look like...that look of sadness, worry, and determination," Cathy said, as she saw Peter walk in the house.

"Hi, my love! I just had a long session with Amin. He spoke to me about his experience of human tragedy, while the world gasps in disbelieve." Peter was reeling in sadness.

"I love the compassion you feel and the strong desire to do something about the immense suffering. I will work side by side with you with all my love and dedication," Cathy thoughtfully responded.

"Sorry if I stray away a bit from our thoughts. My dad is very excited about us. He suggested that we fly over to Basel with your mom and dad and we can have a very cozy wedding with just our immediate family. We can go to Zermatt for our honeymoon. John wants to also come to our wedding," Cathy said, with an excitement that comes when a life long desire comes to fruition.

Peter was absorbed in his thoughts about Amin and all the pain he suffered back in his home. Peter tried to imagine his own home in New Brunswick, in turmoil, because some people, who had no home moved in, calling it their home, not sharing but displacing him and his kinfolk. Just the thought of it all brought pain and a massive confusion in his mind. It can't be true, it could never happen, in his wildest imagination! So the net equation seemed to be that one homeless displaced another. What kind of a human being came up such a solution? What made human beings do something so terrible? Just thinking about it was painful for him not to mention Amin and his family, for whom it was a terrible reality.

How many times did this happen in the past history? What about the pain of becoming homeless?

Peter recalled a simple analogy, to this tragedy when he popped in a pill for his headache the other day which cured his headache but gave him a stomachache.

He was not getting anywhere with his thoughts because of the pain he felt for Amin. So he forced his depressed thoughts out of the hole, to think of the challenge Amin gave him.

He was grateful to God, to be born in the land of the free. He suddenly felt the urge to jump and shout with joy when he realized that Cathy was shouting at him.

"Hey, Pete! Have you heard even a word of what I said?"

"I heard every word you said, my love. Sorry I am in the process of switching from Amin's pain to our joy and happiness. I did not realize that it was a time delay switch."

Cathy was smiling at Peter in a loving gaze. Who is this guy, I love so much?

"Okay, Cathy, let's go for it! Let me call my folks...." Peter tried to snap out of the moment.

"I already did and they are busy planning for the wedding," she said, with a smile of accomplishment.

Twenty-six

Peter's phone rang.

"Hello, Mr. Peter. I am a friend of Amin Hasan. I saw him the other day and he was so excited at the prospect of you joining our operational board. Sorry I forgot to introduce myself in my excitement. My name is Ben Sargans and I work for the United Nations Children's Emergency Fund with my childhood friend Ram Barua, who is a program Director. Amin, Ram, and I would like to brainstorm some ideas with you. Can you come to New York tomorrow?"

"Yes. Yes, of course." As Peter realized what the call was about, he tried to contain his enthusiasm.

Peter talked to John, who also liked the idea and suggested that Peter should take Cathy along.

It was snowing in New York as the plane landed in La Guardia. Cathy had booked a room for them in the Grand Hyatt because of its proximity to the United Nations complex.

The meeting room faced the Dag Hammarskjold Plaza with a view of the city. The air in the meeting room was charged with enthusiasm and expectation. They all greeted each other with warmth.

Ben started the meeting.

"Amin, Ram, and I know each other for ages and have felt the urge that we must be able to make a difference to reduce the human suffering in the world. We agree with Amin that a good place to start is Palestine/ Israel. Amin gave us a wonderful introduction about you, Peter, and we decided on the spur of the moment to all meet. We hope Cathy, with her incredible experience, will also be an invaluable member of our team.

"We have met with the Secretary General of the U.N. who wants that we prepare a new program/proposal to resolve the Palestine and Israel conflict. Our concept is therefore to build a team in the United Nations of dedicated people from all walks of life to rebuild Palestine with funding provided by the UN and some Middle Eastern countries that have expressed their support. The program will entail literally thousands of people who will descend into Palestine and work night and day rebuilding a nation. Jobs will be created, homes built, establish the infrastructure of roads, communications, travel, export, schools, colleges, a university, industries etc etc. A blue print of the program is being prepared as we speak that will have target schedules for completion and naturally the total cost. The Program will be presented to first the Palestinian people, and the Israelis for a vote. Next, the Secretary General of the UN will submit the Program to the General Assembly for vote. This will be anything but easy, but we must make it happen.

"The lead team, in charge of the Program shall be us five with Amin Hasan, an American, Palestinian as deputy to the Chairperson, Madam Waheeda Mujim, Home Minister in the current Palestinian Government."

Ram passed around a two-page outline of the Program. We have a meeting with the Secretary General at 10:00am tomorrow in the UN Secretariat building, meant as a kick off session for the Program and to get his blessings.

"Let's meet later today to review the blue print of the Program."

The meeting with the Secretary General (SG) was very business like. He listened very attentively. There was a slight commotion when the schedule came up in the presentation. The Program of reconstruction of Palestine was slated to start in eight months.

One of the UN executive objected that it was totally unreasonable.

Peter defended the schedule. "Several of the events to be completed in the Program had started some months ago. In fact most all the events will run in parallel. We must implement the Program on a fast track basis with periodic reports and updates on the progress of the Program made public." The Secretary General smiled and agreed.

The SG gave some encouraging closing remarks. "It is a novel, brave and very commendable approach to a very old problem growing as a cancer in the society. Your success shall give the world hope. I wish to be updated at least once a week on your progress. I will encourage all nations to cooperate in the Program. We will all work together. Wish you all Good Luck and God speed."

The news of the UN Program initiative in the Editorial section of the New York Times and in the DC newspapers, generally praised the Program with cautious optimism. There was no shortage of critics either.

John had started the approval process with the Secretary for Cathy, Peter and Amin and received an overwhelming support.

The UN team worked fast and a delegation with Amin and Peter met with the Palestinian government in Gaza. The Prime Minister was pleased to see that the Palestinians will be very actively involved in the Program. The Home Minister Mujim was fully prepared with the municipal drawings and supporting data on the construction of the areas in their territories. She had proposed that the areas in the Gaza strip occupied by the Jewish families illegally should be negotiated with the occupants giving them the opportunity to continue living under the Palestinian flag. The Minister had argued that there were Arab citizens in Israel so it should work also in reverse.

Amin and Peter held town meetings to explain about the UN Program. It was accepted with skepticism as expected by Amin because a number of programs and initiatives in the past had been planned but not implemented. They also attended schools and met with various groups who were amazed that such a Program was in progress. Peter prepared a log of all the inputs expressing support or deep concerns as part of the database for the Program.

The meetings with the militant groups were most interesting. They had completely lost trust in the world. They were not reconciled to Palestine and Israel, two nations living side by side. They were deeply divided on the differences in the economic conditions in Palestine and Israel. Amin however felt that for a first series of meetings they did well.

Ben and Cathy were touring Israel giving out information and collecting the thoughts of the people. The Israeli government also warmed up to the Program and there were strong expressions of interest in making contributions to the rebuilding of Palestine.

The first tour by the teams showed encouraging feedback. The touring of Palestine and Israel became an on going process for the purposes of education and to have a continues feedback. The Palestinians and the Israeli public saw encouraging outcomes and had started building confidence on a people to people basis.

Peter was reviewing progress of the UN Program with John in DC, but he was thinking about Cathy. He interjected, "Say, John, do you know when Cathy is returning from her trip to Syria?"

"Do you mind, Peter? Please pay attention to what we are discussing and don't mix family business with our work!" John snapped at Peter.

"Sorry, John."

Peter tried to reach her on the special cell phone but she did not respond. He was told that as a rule the special phones should only be used as an emergency when calling someone in a sensitive area of the world.

The UN Program administrative staff did not know her whereabouts except that Cathy was with Ben and some other members of the UN in Syria. An hour later he was informed that the delegation was due to arrive in New York, the next day and were booked in the Hotel Grand Hyatt.

Peter's thought drifted and he suddenly realized that he had not given a thought about the wedding rings. Cathy and Peter had not talked about the wedding schedule since their induction into the UN Program. Peter decided to give Cathy a surprise in New York.

A snowfall had preceded the airplane landing at JFK. Peter could feel his emotions racing. He finally caught a glimpse of her as she came out of the VIP exit. She was holding hands with Ben as they walked to the Taxi area. Peter suddenly felt abandoned and shocked with a bit of jealousy. The Taxi took off before Peter could reach them. The ride to Grand Hyatt was filled with concern in Peter's mind, but his trusting nature felt that there was a simple explanation to what he saw.

Peter knew one of the supervisors at the check in desk. He enquired if Cathy and Ben had checked in and with some coaxing learnt that they had cancelled their hotel reservation for a double room. In the ensuing confusion Peter recognized one of the UN employees who was a delegate on the trip with Cathy. The delegate was not aware of Cathy's program but said that the entire five-person delegation would meet for breakfast, in the hotel, the next morning.

Peter had a terrible night as he tossed and turned, trying to console his heart.

The following morning, Peter saw Cathy in the arms of Ben, near the lobby. He froze and stared in disbelief. The delegation team had just started breakfast when Peter walked to them, waving in welcome. Ben looked up in surprise, a look that turned to guilt. Cathy's reaction was as if she expected to see Peter. She gave Peter a cold kiss on the cheek and continued talking.

He grabbed Cathy as the delegation members left.

"Not here please, we are in public," she said

"You sure changed Peter for Ben fast!" Peter said, with a hurtful smile.

Cathy stood silent as Peter poured out his heart, and received neither explanation nor the benefit of even a response. Peter's hurt and frustration overwhelmed him and he left the breakfast room.

The romance in his world was slowly falling apart from cloud nine to a free fall. It felt unreal and the pain in his heart was crumbling the dream of a loving life with Cathy. How cold and cruel she turned out to be and how very wrong. He was madly in love only to be shocked back to an ugly reality. He felt pangs of anger at Ben and Cathy, but life had thought him to just walk away from people who caused hurt and pain.

He went to the UN Secretariat building to drop off some paperwork he had prepared on the UN Program. He saw Ben from the corner of his eye watching him but Peter avoided even an eye contact. He saw Cathy walking into a conference room and she stopped looking at him as if to say something. There was a brief eye contact, but Peter was too hurt to stop and attempt a dialogue. He went straight out of the Secretariat building, checked out of the hotel and took a cab to La Guardia airport and then had second thoughts and went to New Brunswick instead.

His dad embraced him while his mom immediately started the pasta routine. His dad observed that Peter was not his usual self.

"What is happening son? Where is Cathy?" his dad inquired.

A moment of silence ensued and as if his dad could sense it he said, "It is Cathy, is it not? Somehow, I had some reservations in my mind about her, if you don't mind my saying so. Please don't feel hurt about someone who is not worth your pain. You are my angel and you deserve an angel and an angel you will find. There is no doubt in my mind."

He had tears in his eyes as he embraced his son. Peter could not hold back the tears either. The sad moment of having lost someone you deeply loved was now embalmed by the wisdom and the unconditional love of his father. His mom had only enquired about Cathy in passing and was too occupied about uncle so and so, trying to update Peter about the family happenings.

His mom was, as always, perceptive and said, "I am shocked. How could I be so wrong?
Don't let her go if you love her."

Peter responded, "Cathy has failed the first time her love for me was put to test. I should be grateful that this happened now instead of after marriage. How does love deal with betrayal? If she is unfaithful once then what is going to stop her the next time she is tempted. I would rather wait for true love, if such a love exists, then spend a lifetime of suspicion."

Peter decided to stay another day at home and spent sometime with his old buddies and walked around the town in an effort to heal him from the unbelievable experience. He simply had to stop and say hello to Joe and broke down in telling him about it all. Joe as usual, in his infinite wisdom told him that love was indeed blind, and although love was a beautiful world to be in, love was deceptive as proven time after time. History had shown that there were only very rare cases when true love bound two souls together. God, he said, had not given many the gift of deciphering deception from true love, until after the crash.

He tried to cheer Peter and said, 'Who was it who said that it was better to have loved and lost than not to have loved at all?"

"I can't remember, Joe," Peter replied.

A moment later, Joe said, 'I can't remember, either."

Peter called John Schaefer upon landing in DC.

"Hi, John! I would like to discuss about a new assignment if possible. The UN Program is well underway and there is some element of routine creeping in," Peter blurted and wondered whether John knew what had happened with Cathy.

"Great timing, Peter, the General wants to meet with you soon. What are your plans for Christmas? I was thinking of Zermat but there is better snow in Steam Boat." John did not sound as if he knew.

Peter wondered how Schaefer had mixed a few topics in a single thought.

"Are you going home? I mean my home," asked John.

"Yes, I wanted to pick up my things and move to a hotel, before seeing the General Strong," he answered, expecting an enquiry in response. No such thing, no whys or buts.

"Okay, stop by at the office about six and we can go for a drink," was the cool response from John.

The two men met for a drink but neither mentioned the name Cathy.

Twenty-seven

General Strong was very cordial on the phone. They agreed to meet in his office the next day.

"Hi Peter. I have taken the liberty of reserving a table for lunch, a Christmas lunch since Debra and I are heading for Colorado for the Christmas holidays tomorrow. General Watts of the European Defence Alliance (EDA) will join us for lunch." The General sounded business like.

General Watts was very direct. "Peter, have you heard about the Swiss Meridian project in your discussions with the Swiss authorities?"

Peter took his time to respond. "Yes, I am vaguely familiar."

"Our EDA intelligence tells us that the Swiss who were not willing to share the technology with neither the U.S., nor us in the EDA, developed the technology that remains the state of the Art in drone planes and their capability to accurately hit desired targets with multiple weapons. We attempted to infiltrate into the Swiss camp but failed and in fact there were some casualties. Of course this is all strictly confidential but our intelligence has learnt that the Swiss are developing or testing bio-intelligence weaponry which allows targeting people or groups that are planning terrorist acts. This amazing technology as you can imagine is of a vital interest to us. The joint Swiss—U.S. technology transfer program is coming along very well for the Swiss and U.S. manufacturers of arms and a few deals have been worked out that will be implemented starting next year. We laud your efforts in formulating the joint program. All our efforts to work out a joint effort on the Meridian technology with the Swiss have failed. We believe that you might be able to help us. "

General Watts watched Peter with interrogating eyes as he talked.

Peter pondered for a while, remembering that the Meridian project had ended the tragic loss of his grandfather. The killers of his grandfather now sat in front of him requesting his assistance. What an irony of fate, he thought. The EDA must have done their background check on Peter and he wondered if they had not concluded that they had in fact killed Peter's grandfather in an attempt to infiltrate or steal the Meridian technology from the Swiss. It then dawned on him that the EDA and the U.S. intelligence had most likely, overlooked the fact that some of the 'Mueller's' who immigrated to the U.S. had changed their surnames to 'Miller', so that they could better blend themselves in the Anglo-Saxon world.

"Well, Peter, what do you say? The DOD and the EDA will give you a monetary Incentive / reward package if you succeed." General Watts continued throwing a glance at General Strong for approval.

"I need to think about it and discuss it with my Director, John Schaefer." Peter was trying to buy some time and felt nauseated at what had landed on him, like a ton of bricks.

"John Schaefer is aware and has already received the approval for you to work on this project from the Secretary of the Security," said General Strong, as if to corner Peter.

"That's good of John. Let me review my notes and I will get back to you, now that I know what you are interested in," Peter said, with a straight face.

John Schaefer talked about how well the agents of Arab descents had been instrumental in reducing the terrorist threat in the nation.

"Amin is a very good man and he thinks highly of you. By the way, did the two mighty Generals manage to convince you about your new assignment?"

"Yes, if you want me to do it," Peter said, with a tone of caution. He could not imagine where John stood in all this mess. Why was suspicion creeping in? Was it because of the Cathy affair ?

"Thank you, John, for obtaining the clearance from the Secretary so that I can discuss with Generals Strong and Watts about some project in Switzerland that I know little about. What is happening?" Peter sounded nonchalant.

"I am sorry, Peter, but the truth is that both the U.S. and our European allies are keenly interested in the Meridian technology and we assumed that you most likely have good information, specially since you are also a consultant to the Swiss Department of Defense," John said, sounding casual about the subject.

"Oh! So you set a trap, for me, your friend, your subordinate in the department, your confidant. Nice going!" Peter responded.

John reflected and said, "You are right, Peter. How could I do that to you? Please forgive me. I am so ashamed of myself. I don't want to lose you nor damage our friendship."

John and Peter casually walked out of the office into a bar. They chatted about the world affairs. John, just before an exchange of Christmas greetings, looked a bit sad and said that he had observed that the relationship between Cathy and Peter had cooled down, but he did not want to know the reason. John then in a round about way tried to find from Peter the amount and terms of the monetary success package, he was offered by the Generals.

Peter calmly responded. "No specifics of a monetory offer were made. I would never take any money anyway. It is a serious conflict of interest and I am surprised at the extent they want to go for the information on the Meridian technology."

A few days later Amin called.

"Peter how are you? I cannot help feeling that something has suddenly gone wrong between you and Cathy. You can't quit the UN Program abruptly!! What shall I tell the team? Cathy does not say a word about you. Lovers quarrel? Damn it man I miss you. Ram Barua had a bad disagreement with Ben last week and the two barely talk and now you quit on us. Listen, I am in DC now so let's meet for dinner. I will hear no excuses."

"Okay, let's meet in Restaurant Diana at 6:30," Peter responded.

The city was in a very festive mood. Amin gave Peter a big hug and they settled at a table where the noise level was subdued. Amin winked at Peter.

"It pays to have a good contact. I have lived many years in this country but my nature is still Middle Eastern when it comes to good friends. Do you know what I mean, dummy?" Amin had tears and became very emotional. Peter worried whether Amin would start howling when he finds out what really had happened between Cathy and him.

"Amin, I have been given a new assignment which in fact I was about to take when the UN Program came around. Yes, I requested reassignment after my disastrous relationship with Cathy. I saw her holding hands with Ben and amorously kissing him. She was silent when I confronted her, as if she owed me no explanation. Damit! She was making arrangements for our wedding and I was introducing her to every Tom, Dick, and Harry as my fiancé." He was going to tell Amin all the sordid details.

"May I take a seat?" Cathy stood at the table, much to Peter's astonishment, but the expression on Amin revealed a naughty conspiracy.

Peter made a strong effort in keeping his cool and not showing the hurt he felt. He stood up and pulled a chair for her and made sure he gave her no kiss in spite of her look, expecting one. Peter said nothing, waiting for one of the two to speak.

"Peter, you really surprised me. I did not expect to see you in New York," Cathy said.

Amin jumped in. "What? You mean it is Peter's fault to catch you in the act of deceit? Cathy, you got caught cheating, infidelity, and you blame Peter!"

"Please, Amin , let me explain, " Cathy protested.

"My recent trip with Ben and the delegation to Israel, Jordan, and Syria was a shocker for all the members of the delegation. On one occasion both Ben and I broke down and were under the pressure to maintain our composure as professionals. We cried in each other's arms in the hotel and for reasons that I cannot explain we started kissing and ended up in bed. The next few days our feelings for each other grew and we spent many an hour in our rest periods together. I realized when I saw Peter in the breakfast room at the Grand Hyatt in New York that I had made a terrible mistake and done all the wrong things for the wrong reasons. Saying sorry to Peter would in no way make my acts of infidelity reconcilable. I could feel the terrible pain in your voice when you spoke to me. I am guilty on all counts and I am in psychotherapy to understand my actions. Ben and I have decided that we keep our relationship on professional level. I am ashamed and I don't know what to do anymore." Her voice was breaking and she sat still.

Peter was at a loss of words. His head was pounding and he felt that there was more than meets the eye. His warm heart wanted to forgive, but he was unable to convert his feelings into some form of a communicable language.

He muscled up some courage and spoke. "Thank you for being candid, Cathy. Thank you, Amin, for your thoughtfulness. I have no idea where this is all going. I think we should remain as friends and let time take its course," Peter said, as he gave Amin a warm parting embrace and barely looked at Cathy.

"Peter, the UN department responsible for the program has received word from Schaefer that you have been reassigned, but that you will be available on intermittent basis," Amin Said, with a grin.

Peter took the shuttle to Newark for the Christmas holidays.

Peter's mom was busy making dinner for a small segment of the New Brunswick family. Peter went to the Woodbridge Mall and the quaint shops in Princeton to pick the Christmas gifts. He was on the main street at the Landau store looking at the sweaters that were a work of art. He remembered Cathy in Switzerland, how she liked sweaters. He had bought one in Zurich and how she reminded him many times that it was her favorite. He was not an impulsive buyer, nor did his income allow enjoying such luxuries, but he could not resist buying one that he knew would blow her mind. Why was he doing this after all they were not together anymore? Somehow buying the expensive sweater, thinking of Cathy calmed his battered nerves. In spite of what had happened, his heart ached for Cathy, but he just did not have the guts to pick up the phone and call.

His fear was, having to go through a repeat of the heartache if she had another fling, after a makeup. His emotions got the better of him as he went through various, "what if" scenarios.

The Christmas dinner preparations were in full swing at home. The table was set for twelve. Peter counted three and wondered who the others were. His mom cracked at him when he enquired about who the guests were.

"What, you don't like the family?"

She was being her rude self and insensitive to his pain. His grandma remained aloof. She had not said anything about granddad either. Maybe it was her way to protect against emotions and pain.

"Where is Dad?" Peter asked.

"He has gone to the airport to pick up a relative." She snapped back at Peter.

"Hey, mom! Which of my questions deserve the display of rude behavior?" he asked.

His mom decided to ignore him and he debated about leaving and never returning.

Peter became busy with the chores his mom kept dishing out at him.

The guests were taking their seats at the table. He heard his dad pull the car into the garage. Peter looked up and saw Cathy entering the house.

"I am sorry mom for the delay," she said, as she handed Peter's mom a huge bouquet of flowers. "Merry Christmas everybody!"

Peter's dad followed her in the house and complained about the traffic on the roads and that more snow was in the forecast for Christmas day.

This is a set up, Peter thought as he lightly kissed Cathy, once, on her cheek. He became self-conscious when he saw that the eyes of most of the guests were on him.

"Don't forget we kiss three times in Switzerland, Peter!"

Peter disregarded her comments, which his mother noticed.

"We get married in Italy and not fool around like the Swiss," said his mom, clearly resenting Peter's cold response.

Peter again disregarded his mom's comments, as he poured Cathy a drink. "Its a *Dole* , your favorite."

"Mine too," said his dad, as he winked at Cathy.

With all that was going on, Peter had no time to clear his head. He could feel the eyes of Cathy on him. She finally cornered Peter and said, "John went skiing and I could not think of being alone at Christmas. You have the right to throw me out but I am not leaving voluntarily."

She was gazing at him and her dark blue eyes pierced through him.

Peter felt strangely comfortable and calm inside. He did not respond.

Cathy came closer and took his hands in hers, which were cold. She held them tightly and rested her head on his chest.

"You are much too dear to me, and I love you with all my heart. Please, please, darling, forgive me. Forgive me, I beg of you. I know how much you are hurting." she was sobbing.

Peter embraced and kissed her, feeling compassion for her pain. He realized now that he was a pushover when it came to the affairs of the heart.

The guests started to open and exchange presents and Peter remembered that the Europeans open the presents on Christmas Eve unlike the general custom of opening the presents on Christmas morning.

Cathy opened her present from Peter and gave him a bear hug.

"You love me, how wonderful! Thank God!" She cried.

She gave him a Gold Cross pen with a card that had a poem:

God Almighty! I pray Mercy take
I for one have made a grave mistake

What must I do to be forgiven
But love between two hearts is made in heaven

It is God who joins hearts
It's not a mere game of darts

But oh! God! I have sinned against my only love, and he
Suffers intolerably because of me

Banish me for a life of pain
No more happiness, just shame

But I pray, Oh Lord, heal my love and bring him everlasting joy
Protect him forever from another such ploy

O Lord! All Mighty, who creates and destroys with a mere glance
I pray with all my heart for a second chance

Peter the pushover, loved it.

"So 007, where is your next assignment?" came the question from uncle Flavio.

"Well, I am heading back to Switzerland for a while "

Cathy gave a look of surprise, "Oh, Peter, I did not know that you are a secret agent?"

The whole group laughed as Peter's mom explained. "Well it has become a joke in the family, ever since Peter started to work for the Security…whatever it is called in New Brunswick. It is a way the family rags him to talk about what he does. Peter is the quiet type and never does talk about his job. There is no trace of Italian blood in him. Just look at him now, smiling."

"What about you, Cathy?" came an inquisitive question from Peter's aunt, Silvia.

"I am working on the UN Program in New York, to try and bring peace between Israel and the Palestinians. I have requested a transfer to work out of the UN office in Geneva. I am never going to let Peter alone," came the prompt reply from Cathy.

Peter was taken by surprise, but he knew that Cathy worked fast and was efficient. Did she plan all this? No, he thought, no one could plan the reunion he just had with Cathy.

"This is all great about James Fond or whatever this character is called. What I want to know is when are yous guys hooking up? Cathy, is you Italian? You sure look Italian." Came from the single-track mind of Aunt Silvia.

"No hurry at all," came the unexpected response from Peter's dad. "I like the idea that they get married in Switzerland...as Cathy had informed us and...and then we have the wedding reception here in New Brunswick."

"Sure, sure, you Swiss only think of yourselves...what about us? We are family too you know.... And we want to have the wedding right here. We can't afford to fly to Swiss unless big shot here wants to buy us all tickets to fly out there". No sooner had aunt Silvia said this, the old noisy quacking session started about yous Swiss and wees Italian...better than thou game."

The laughing, drinking, talking noise level was building up with almost all participating at the same time, except uncle Flavio who had a smirk on his face of enjoyment. He was a master at starting such brawls, especially at family gatherings. The cause of the noisy session faded away and all returned to the normal noise level of yous and wees.

Peter saw his dad get up to get some more wine from the basement and Peter followed him. His Dad had a remarkable wine collection, most of it was Californian. His mom did not mind as long the label of the wine sounded Italian. Peter had noticed that his dad, over the years had taken a lot of interest in wines. He had heard his dad in Switzerland talk very knowledgeably about European and American wines.

His Dad selected a few bottles with Peter and then came close to whisper

"Be careful son; don't let anyone rush you into marriage with Cathy. There is something strange about all this. I cannot put my finger on it yet but it will come. What are you going to do in Switzerland?" His dad felt very close to Peter especially after the murder of granddad had been resolved. Peter also felt comfortable and secure talking to his dad.

"Dad I have the assignment from the assassins of granddad to get the Swiss government to cooperate on the Meridian Project!" Peter whispered.

"Oh! No, no, my God…Peter, the bastards are going to make you the sacrificial lamb." His Dad protested.

Just then they heard footsteps and decided to talk later. It was uncle Giorgio and Cathy, swinging arm in arm.

"We thought you may need help with the wine." Uncle Giorgio was the playboy of the family, having a track record of three divorces and an unending chain of affairs. He lived a life, convinced that the Italian men were God's gift to womanhood.

The next couple of days were festive. Cathy spent most of the day with Peter's mom and the chatty women in his mom's group. Peter was giving his dad a hand at clearing snow from the driveway when he saw two vans parked a distance from the house. His dad had also noticed one since his return from the Newark airport on Christmas Eve. Peter had learnt in his training how to track, listen in, and all the innumerable devices the secret service used or abused in the intrusion of privacy. Peter decided to find out. He made up an excuse to go shopping with his dad and they drove out. One of the vans was indeed following them. They went into the Woodbridge mall and Peter observed that the van had parked close to where they had parked. A man stepped out and lit a cigarette.

Peter and his dad quickly returned to the car and saw the man drop the cigarette and get inside the van. They drove around the mall and parked again. The van again parked near their car. The mall was noisy enough to increase the scramble capability of the special cell phone. Peter called Schaefer.

"Hi John, I am being tailed since Cathy arrived."

"Call you back and alert Cathy also...you know the routine. Stay at this scramble level till I call back."

Peter and his dad decided to buy jeans that were on sale.

"Peter, I think you should give up this job. I don't want to lose you too. Why take this terrible risk?"

"Justice. Granddad's soul must rest in peace. I hate what they did to us and they must repent," he said with absolute conviction.

It had been almost an hour and Peter and his dad were getting tired of walking around the mall. Peter's phone rang, it was Schaefer.

"None of the U.S. intelligence agencies involved. We are working on it. EAD is a possible suspect. General Strong suspects General Watts but does not want to alarm them that we are now wise. EAD listens on frequency bands 250—300 kilo cycles, range Gct779 in the U.S. so stay away from these frequencies. Take Cathy and leave tomorrow for Zurich and follow the routine. Dieter is updated. No fast moves, stay cool. You are officially assisting the U.S.—Swiss joint weapons manufacturing program team as and when required by them. Stay out of their way. The team is all ego the size of a football field. The joint program is getting plenty of publicity here and in Europe. EAD is miffed by not being included directly in the JV program. You know why. The EAD will try to contact you in Switzerland about you know what. Don't sign any document MOU with them. Keep Cathy on a need to know basis. Get married for goodness sake; that will keep her occupied."

Cathy looked very relaxed. Peter's mom had taken a great liking to her. His dad played along. His mom repeatedly reminded that they should set the wedding date. There was talk about a spring wedding. Strangely enough neither of the two talked about any wedding plans since Cathy had suddenly appeared in New Brunswick on Christmas Eve.

Twenty-eight

Dieter received Cathy and Peter at the airport in Zurich. It was very good to meet an old friend. Cathy took the train to Basel to be with her dad and Peter checked into Hotel Central in Zurich.

Dieter spoke, having waited for a quiet moment with Peter. "Peter you sure have a knack of taking on complicated projects, but you are good at it. Some of our brass in the intelligence community is worried about how to proceed with you on the Meridian Project. Hilfiger has arranged for a meeting tomorrow afternoon in a special place you will like, to discuss a strategy."

"Dieter, I must tell you on what all has happened since my meeting with EAD, General Watts and General Strong. I feel I must also tell you also about Cathy. I have some reservations since it might have a bearing on our work." Peter still wondered about Cathy.

"OK, Peter, just relax, you can tell me all about it tomorrow in the train. We will be meeting two of the elite military brass in the intelligence Agency and Hilfiger. These guys are really the tops."

Peter and Dieter took a train to Interlaken. It was picturesque. They were picked up by an unmarked police car and driven up towards Sislech. It was a quaint hotel restaurant, reserved for the meeting.

All were in casual clothes as if on vacation. The atmosphere was very calm and very relaxed but very alert. A police helicopter with all kinds of detection devices flew over the area at a height so as not to catch attention. Plain clothed security men and women strolled near the hotel and around the hills surrounding the hotel in mountain gear.

Hilfiger greeted Peter and Dieter and introduced the two-intelligence brass but no names were exchanged for security reasons.

"Peter, you are between a rock and a hard place. Can you maintain your allegiance to the two countries? We are all familiar with your background and we feel that you will protect the interests of the U.S. and Switzerland, sort of what they say in the U.S. a win-win situation." Hilfiger spoke.

"I must confess that I am very disturbed by what some rouges in the EDA did to my grandfather. I do not wish to discolor the memory of my granddad and his heroic deed. I would like to propose a strategy which will continue to protect the rights of Switzerland and ensure that no government, including the U.S., grab the Swiss technology and know how which will aid humanity and not just the selfish interests of a greedy few," Peter explained.

One of the brass from the Swiss intelligence started his presentation

"We think that you already have an understanding of the basic Meridian drone airplanes. The drones are capable of carrying multiple grenades in their turrets. In fact they are also cable of carrying smaller or more powerful bombs that can be very accurately fired at specific targets with almost no collateral damage. It is a powerful weapon in guerrilla warfare and of course against terrorists. We have last year been able to make a drone with stealth material, making them invisible with our own stealth technology.

"The multi infrared cameras, however, required a fast human evaluation of enemy positions and individuals and then a human decision to fire the weapons. Intelligence from the satellites and other sources can be reliable only a relatively small percentage of the time. Highly sensitive tactical attack and defense data compiled from the Korean War, Vietnam, Kuwait Afghanistan, and now Iraq show that the current technology is frail and does extensive collateral damage and often misses the intended targets. In fact success of a mission primarily depends on the accuracy of the information and the intelligence and then a system that implements the command to destroy the enemy.

"We are actively testing three non destructive technologies to enhance the capabilities of the drones.

"The first of these technologies is one that recognizes a weapon in fact any weapon that requires a firing pin or a fuse, causing a controlled explosion. This would disable all known weapons except plasma, high-energy rays such as lasers, masers, etc.

"The second technology recognizes weapons such as large knives, lances, swords, etc and disables the person or persons carrying the weapon.

"The third technology recognizes and disables any energy laser type weapon and any nuclear weapon including dirty (nuclear) bombs disabling their firing/triggering system.

"These three technologies are in the final test phases. No mass production is intended to avoid abuse. Remember that these technologies diffuse mal intent. We believe that these three technologies are adequate to discourage most types of aggression by people with bad intentions such as insurgents, terrorists, etc.

"We have another technology in development and now undergoing tests that reads the human brain waves and makes a preventive counter attack by diffusing the aggressive decision segment of the human brain. This technology has also several medical applications."

"The strategy," Peter interjected. "Should be that these defensive weapons are never known to any one other than a neutral country like Switzerland.

What ever happened to the Strategic Defense Initiative (SDI), hotly pursued during the Reagan administration?"

Hilfiger responded, "The high cost of shooting missiles from a set of satellites became prohibitive, but the tests showed that the technology works within a reasonable accuracy. We believe that the U.S. has the technology well developed for counter attacking weapons like the missiles. Our technology will be at a fraction of the cost of SDI

diffusing the missiles before they are fired and destroyed by an SDI. Think of the collateral damage an explosion of a nuclear missile will have when it explodes at the source. Our weapons diffuse the missiles at the source therefore there is no destruction to human life."

The select group concluded the evening with some cocktails and a great meal. All the participants turned in for the evening. The hotel was quite full, Peter realized, so as not to catch any attention.

The group met the following day again. Hilfiger spoke again.

"The development of these technologies we discussed yesterday has been under heavy guard. There are only four scientists who are in charge of the entire program. Only two Federal Council members follow the activities and are sworn to secrecy. All the other scientists work on only specific segments, for security reasons. There has been no leaks so far whatsoever. The cost to the federal government is high. There are a few politicians who oppose the government spending more on this program. We want you to think it through and propose course of action as you see it".

Hilfiger took Peter to the side. "We communicate well with John Schaefer, also on a personal level. Schaefer because of safeguarding his security does not know any thing about the Meridian Project. His sister Cathy has also done good work for us in coordinating with some U.S. manufacturers. The U.S. authorities are watchful of both John and Cathy. To tell you the truth, most immigrants and new American citizens are held under watchful eyes, especially if they are working on sensitive areas that concern national security. We trust the brother and the sister team implicitly. The psychiatrists who treated her in Luzern have advised us, because she performs work treatments on top secret matters, that Cathy has suffered because of her rather hard nosed father. She is very efficient but the attack on her life last year has been a severe blow and shaken her confidence level. She needs a type of stability that perhaps marriage brings. I know that she can continue to not only help you but also us. Her strange behavior at times is merely a defensive mechanism.

"We consider you an important member of our world community, one who has a high respect for human life and dignity. I am sorry if I spoke too frankly but I know that Americans appreciate frankness. I must also inform you that you are also under constant surveillance when you are in the United States. You can be sure that EAD and the U.S. are trying to increase their surveillance of you because of the new assignment you have from the U.S. You have our trust."

Peter had a quiet ride back to the hotel in Zurich. He was very tired and decided to turn in for the day.

Twenty-nine

Peter woke up in the morning to a call.

"Hi honey! Remember me?'

Peter burst out in laughter. "Why would I forget you, darling?"

"I miss you very much. Can you come to Basel now? We must talk," Cathy said.

It was snowing heavily as Peter made his way to the train station. The trains were so comfortable that Peter always enjoyed the trip. He could reflect on just about anything as his mind wandered about the work at hand. The background to his thoughts was the indescribable Swiss landscape changing rapidly as he headed to his destination. How strange, he thought, the past few months had been when he went from absolutely madly in love to sudden pain and then doubt and more doubt. Compassionate Amin, saw only love between his two friends, in spite of the infidelity, and wanted them to reunite. John in his strange unemotional way, who did not want to know the rift between Cathy and him, asked him to get married to his sister. Dad had doubts about Cathy while mom had pounded him to tie the knot. Now Hilfiger, a truly great man filled with compassion had opened his heart to advise him marriage to her.

All these inputs but what did his heart say about all this now. He tried to focus on the cause of doubt in his mind. It was fuzzy at best but he could single out one emotion that caused pain. It was seeing Cathy in the arms of another man. He felt a burning sensation as he thought about Ben and Cathy. So how does one heal such a pain? Time! Could heal or would it only reduce the pain. A band aid solution at best. Cathy could cure the pain with tons of love; after all she is the one who caused it in the first place.

Yes. Yes, that's the solution! Peter was slowly coming to terms in his thoughts when the PA system squawked, "Basel, end station, everybody out", sounded better in Swiss German.

Cathy's dad was very cordial.

"I am so glad to see you, son. My other son I rarely see.
What a tragedy of life."

Cathy's dad was very talkative, kind of unusual for him. They talked about the local politics of which Peter knew little, so the dialogue became a monolog until Cathy came to the rescue.

"Hey Dad I want to talk to him too!"

"Okay, okay! You love birds go and get me some fresh bread and cold cuts for lunch."

The sky was overcast but the sun was peeking in places. Arm in arm, the two looked like a cozy romantic pair as they walked to the town. They both had much to say to each other but somehow their thoughts were communicating and the occasional gaze at each other confirmed the lovers' dialogue in process.

Cathy's dad had set the table with plenty of garnishes. He served a rich goulash soup

And he talked about his last trip to the United States. He liked DC, specially the area where John lived. Peter could feel that Cathy and her dad had come to terms with their past. They were happy, laughing, talking, joking and it all felt genuine.

The snow had turned to sleet so walking outside was not a good option. The three settled down on the comfortable antique sofas. Cathy's dad opened a new bottle of red wine from southern Germany, a good setting for starting a dialogue.

Cathy started talking about what had happened between Peter and her. She went on to express her desire to settle down and have a family. Her dad complemented Peter for his willingness to consider forgiveness, and started to confess.

"We are very often our own enemies. We cause pain and hurt when that was not the intent. He blamed ego as the main culprit in human behavior. His own upbringing taught him stubbornness and the strong desire to insist on having it his way. The result was that as I went about blinded by my own ego, I became oblivious to the terrible damage it caused for the family. The element and desire to control overlooked that my family was human too with their own desires and aspirations. The struggle, in retrospect was wasteful and meaningless."

His tearful sessions with Cathy finally opened his eyes and he was determined to make amends and bring his family together. John, he recalled, was a very sensitive young boy and could not handle the father's controlling and overbearing behavior. He had done the right thing by taking his sister and immigrating to the U.S., the land of the free.

"Just imagine he put his sister and himself through schools and the universities, in the United States, when it was my responsibility to pay attention to the importance of good education in life for my children. I am sorry to rattle on my agenda but I want the family I lost, all because of my fault. I would love to pour my love on to my children and my grandchildren."

Cathy frequently gazed at Peter as her father spoke and Peter while listening had flashbacks of what he had heard in his meeting with the Swiss intelligence.

"Why don't we all go to Zermat for a few days to ski and relax? It will give Cathy and me a chance to also talk."

He glanced at Cathy, who said, "How about we start the process to get married in Basel, please. Please, or are you never going to forgive me for kissing Ben and holding hands?"

That was a bombshell. Peter started to laugh and Cathy's dad started to laugh. Cathy looked serious and stood up as if she was going to leave.

Peter embraced her and said, "Honey, I love you! Will you marry me?"

"Wait, wait! Let me get a provisional ring to complete the ceremony."

Cathy cried, "I would love to marry you, my love!"

Cathy's dad made a ring out of a fern leaf in a hurry. It was an act of comedy as Cathy and Peter were laughing, and Peter put the organic ring on Cathy's finger.

Cathy and Peter took the tram to Marktplatz in the center of the town to buy a ring. Peter bought Cathy an engagement ring and they picked the wedding rings. It was off to the Spiegelhof to register for the marriage Certificate and start the paper work, which they were told would take three weeks. The civil wedding ceremony was set for the last day of January. They went to the very romantic Restaurant Schloss Binningen for the wedding dinner, where their romance started.

Peter watched in amazement as Cathy moved, organized, and called out for printing invitations to friends and relatives. She called Peter's parents in New Brunswick and organized their tickets for Switzerland. Peter talked to his dad who had rethought his reservations about Cathy and blessed him. His mom was overjoyed.

Cathy's dad insisted that Peter and Cathy live with him in Basel. The house was very big and Cathy decided to give it a face-lift.

The wedding ceremony had the parents and the best man and best girl. Peter had asked John to be his best man. The wedding reception had about one hundred invitees including Ram, Ben and Amin. Cathy's dad footed the bill for the entire wedding affair.

"But that is a much lot of money!" Peter had remarked.

"Don't you worry, darling, Dad has pots of money. He is swimming in money."

The newly weds, Mr. and Mrs. Peter Miller went to Zermatt for their honeymoon.

Peter was preoccupied with what lay ahead and Cathy, who had observed it, said, "Pete, we are now married and I am your partner for life. We must pledge to each other that we keep no secrets from each other. We must tell each other everything and I mean everything. We must seek the spiritual truth together and attain enlightenment together. There are many aspects of life that are a puzzle, which pains my soul. I know in my heart that we can find the light together. Our devoted love for each other will pull us through."

Peter marveled at what Cathy said, "Exactly my sentiments, my dear. I agree whole-heartedly."

Peter gave an outline of the meetings and the events he had in the recent months. Cathy was a good listener and her mind started working on the proposal with Peter. They summarized it on the back of a menu while enjoying a great meal in a restaurant in Zermatt:

- The Meridian project must be completed and made operational in the interest of world peace.
- Outsourcing segments to a country like India could reduce the cost.
- Switzerland must maintain its Ownership, Operation and Control.
- The **first option** would be, Switzerland operating it in troubled areas of the world without the knowledge of the sovereign government.

The **second option** was that a world body such as the UN orders its use in top secrecy and pays for the service.
Since it is a weapon for peace, Switzerland will be the constant target for Individuals, Groups and countries that will try to steal it such as the attempts by the EDA.

The **third option** was that any government could request the Swiss Government for its use and the Swiss government would evaluate if the request was an abuse or justified. The implementation would be for a service charge.

The **fourth option** was that Switzerland works with a select body of world personalities well known for their Peace efforts, to decide on a request from a government or United Nations if the use of the peace weapon is justified.

The **fifth option** was that Switzerland as the leader work with Neutral Nations of the world, including countries like India to implement the use of the Meridian technologies.

The option of EDA ordering its use should be ruled out because it does not represent the world body.

The world population being about 6.4 Billions, our data shows that there are about 10 Million that are listed as criminals. Freedom fighters are not included, which are estimated at 20 Millions. The people classified as pure terrorists who are considered 'rebels without a cause' number some 1 Million of which about 500,000 are extremely dangerous cross border types.

There are about 20 active conflicts around the world.

The attack strategy on the culprits should be under cover, causing turmoil within the ranks of the insurgents.

Dieter met with Peter and Cathy to review the proposals and submitted it to Hilfiger.

Thirty

The Swiss intelligence committee met to review the departmental proposals on a strategy for the Meridian weapon for peace and the proposal from Peter, Cathy, and Dieter. The deliberations continued for three days. The only decision was that the Swiss manufacturer explores reducing the cost of the various systems with India. India had been selected because of several recent reports by Swiss manufacturers who have been very successful in outsourcing electronics and highly specialized software to Indian companies. The highly skilled labor costs in India were a fraction of the costs in Switzerland. The intent therefore was to sublet all of the highly labor intensive components.

Hilfiger requested Dieter, Peter, and Cathy to explore the possibilities with the Swiss Ambassador in India.

The Swiss Ambassador was very current with the business and political climate in India. He suggested that the possible dialogue with the Indian Government be deferred until the initial evaluation of the cost savings had been ascertained.

The Swiss manufacturers association who had been working in the various areas of outsourcing with Indian companies requested for firm price proposals on the highly labor intensive components. The results were astounding and the total cost of all the Meridian groups of weapons amounted to a number that could finance at least a dozen of each type of weapon. Peter suggested that once the program gets underway, the income from the legitimate uses could finance additional Meridian units/systems.

Joseph Breder had just returned to his office when he got a call from a company in Malaysia about their interest in doing software projects for Swiss companies. A day later he got a call from a company in The Peoples Republic of China making the same request. He called Peter.

"We may have a leak, somewhere."

Peter called Dr Vishwanath in Bangalore using code words, as they had agreed.

He responded, "No, Peter. No leak possible from our side. I can assure you but I think I know how it may have happened. We have to inform our government each time we receive new orders and the source country. This information is then reported in the government statistical report, which is public domain. Our competitors all over the world have access to this information. The Malaysian, Hong Kong, in fact all countries do the same, except the Republic of China. I see our Swiss activity surged about two years ago and the calls you have received is the reaction. Don't worry about it. Some of my colleagues had thought that we get a waiver on the special sensitive work but the government advised against it because any attempts to cover information like this catches more attention."

Peter was reviewing the update on the Meridian project when he got a call from General Watts on the special cell phone, surprising Peter.

"How are you coming along with Meridian Joint Venture with EDA?"

"General I have feelers out since I cannot as you know do any thing directly. I am trying to get the Swiss to agree on working with U.S manufacturers as part of the Joint weapon program." Peter responded.

"What? God damn it! How would the involvement of U.S. manufacturers help EDA?"General Watts screamed.

"Well, I thought that the U.S. is important and works with the EDA, so if the Swiss do not want to work out a JV with EDA then the way around would be through the U.S.," Peter replied.

"What the hell are you trying to do, screw us all up with your own strategy?" The General slammed the phone down.

Peter updated Schaefer on the talk with General Watts.

"You said the right thing, Pete. I was talking to the Secretary of Defense the other day and he hinted that their was a group in the EDA who are at the behest of some European members trying to take a lead on access to new weapons, one of which is being developed by CERN under cover. This is a laser of very high intensity, adjustable to the job requirement, mounted on a new cobra type helicopter. We have a similar weapon operational but there are many safety aspects not resolved. The SDI is a 'go' also, but we hope we never need it. EDA had opposed the SDI but now that we have it, they want it in Europe. The President says that too many cooks spoil the broth. The U.S. has not made any overtures with the Swiss on the Meridian, on which by the way is not much known here in the U.S. The Israeli folks have also a couple of drones but they function as spy satellites in local areas. They are low cost and have proven effective.

"The Secretary of Defense was thinking about starting talks with the Swiss about Meridian but was terribly upset when he learnt about the murderous attempt by EDA some time back, giving EDA a real black eye. The crazy mavericks in the EDA are still up to old tricks, so play it safe. The politics of bringing some unity is getting complex since the rift between the U.S. and Europe on several matters is increasing.

How did the General contact you?"

"On the special cell phone. How come EDA has access to our secure line?" said Peter

"No way! Mmmmm...I will call back," Schaefer responded

Cathy, was having her morning coffee with her dad when Peter joined in.

"Pete, I am going to Geneva for a day on the UN Program meeting, why don't you come?"

"Good idea! Me too! I will take you to a restaurant where they serve Fondue au Truffle," said her dad.

"Alright, let's all go, but in the train please. Driving conditions are quite bad."

The trains were full on the return trip and it seemed to take forever. It had been a good visit but the trio showed signs of fatigue. The silence in the train compartment was suddenly broken with the special cell phones of Peter and Cathy ringing simultaneously. It was the Assistant Director of Security Ted Bahner, in DC. "An assassination attempt has been made on John. He is all right and is in a secure area until we can find out who the rogues are. I strongly recommend your taking shelter in the U.S. Embassy compound now. I will update you later."

"Where are we now?" both Peter and Cathy seem to say. Almost immediately the PA system came on that the next stop was Fribourg.. Cathy asked her dad to go on back to Basel and they had to get down at the next stop.

They took a taxi to the Embassy in Bern.The night security guard took his time in opening the gate.

"Please check in with the night clerk...please wait there are two vans outside, are they with you?"

"What vans?" asked Peter.

"You wait here. I will send the marine guard to check."

The marine guard opened all the entrance lights to the Embassy compounds. No sooner had he stepped out, there was rapid firing from the two vans and the guard returned the fire. One of the vans sped out while the other looked like it was hit. The guard alarmed the police, who came in a flash and more firing from the van with the Swiss police returning the fire. The marine guard closed the gates and walked back.

"There are three guys in the van, shot dead," the marine guard informed.

There was a commotion in the embassy living quarters, people waking up from the firing. The Intelligence Officer came out to meet Peter and Cathy, in his night attire.

"Gee I expected you folks tomorrow, sorry about that. Come on I will show you to your room. I will see you in the morning with some coffee and brot." He seemed relaxed, as if this was a routine.

Cathy called her dad in Basel. He had made it back safely.

Cathy and Peter were exhausted and fell asleep. There was a knock at the door. Peter looked at his watch; it was 10:20am. It was a young lady.

"The Ambassador will see you in ten minutes. Sorry to rush you."

The Ambassador was very cordial and offered them coffee. He spoke with soft overtones and looked very elegant and polished.

"Thank God that you are both safe. I have received a briefing and the U.S. Government has lodged a strong protest to the EDA. I have been in touch with the EDA Secretary General who has opened an enquiry, but he assures me that EDA has nothing to do with the assassination attempt on Mr. John Schaefer, who I understand is also your family. You are in the business of 'Cloak and dagger', do you know who is behind all this including the two vans that apparently followed you yesterday to the Embassy and opened fire on our marine guard. The Swiss police are investigating and the media is not covering the incident. One van that got away was confronted on the main highway to Fribourg, they fired and the return fire killed the two occupants. So the police have two vans and five bodies riddled with bullets."

No sooner had the Ambassador spoken when news was flashed that there was a gang style riot in Zurich and in Geneva. The Swiss military and police had their hands full. Emergency was declared and the TV and radio was advising all inhabitants in Zurich and Geneva to stay indoors. The whole day the news coverage showed pictures of the two cities with wild gangs firing at the police and the military. Where did these gangs come from?

The situation was going bad to worse with similar riots breaking out in Luzern also. The Swiss felt that they were under siege.

Peter called Dieter.

"What is happening? We are in the U.S. Embassy since last night. You heard about the assassination attempt on John Shaefer in DC. Who are these gangs rioting in the cities"?

"Yes Peter, I am aware. Stay calm and watch; the M weapons are about to fire. It will be safe to move in a couple of hours. Stay in the

Embassy today and listen to the police radio band on 670 kilocycles. I am sure that the U.S. Intelligence Officer has one in his office. Please keep quiet. I will send a police car to pick you up tomorrow morning with the pretext that they want a statement from you both about the shooting last night."

The police radio channel was giving continues reports as the police in the cities of Zurich, Geneva and Luzern were communicating. There was a sudden silence. Then a police called out, my God the gangs are being wiped out. They are falling all over the streets like flies. We are not hearing any weapons being fired. The voices were now screaming as if they were seeing some science fiction movie. The police was rushing to examine the fallen bodies. There were more screams that the damn gang men were all unconscious. The police moved swiftly and transported the gang members to the jails. The police commissioners were requesting that the neighboring towns take the culprits to their jails since their own were being overloaded. The news coverage began to report that the Swiss police had the riot gangs fully under control and the public was now free to move around. At the end of the day the Swiss public was in awe and full of praise for the excellent and effective response by the police in wiping out the intruders. The media had the most fantastic theories on who the culprits were. The police reports started to inform the peace loving Swiss that most of the culprits were from East European countries trying to start unrest in a country that has remained safe from Chicago gang style killings.

An interview on live TV with some of the men under arrest was more revealing, when one of their leaders spoke.

"We are frustrated in our so called freedom and the European Union that has not done any thing for the public. Democracy has allowed the criminals in our countries to take control and exploit the blood of the people. Some of us are criminals and some of us have formed various groups to defend ourselves. A majority of us want jobs to be able to feed our families. Our free government is deceiving the citizens and too occupied with lining their pockets. No one in the world gives a damn about us and nor are welcomed anywhere, as if we are some kind of a contagious disease. We lived under tyrant governments for many years and now we live under the control of thieves."

The interviews had a major impact on the public in Switzerland, who were touched at the plight of the eastern European nations, but were unable to comprehend why they chose Switzerland to voice their frustrations with violence. These insurgents should push for reforms in their own countries.

Cathy protested in Swiss German when the police car came to pick them up. The policeman obliged by first driving to Basel so they could shower and get a change of clothing.

Cathy's dad was very worried about John and decided to fly that morning to DC so he could see his son. John's secretary arranged for John to talk to his dad, Cathy and Peter in Basel. John was in the hospital and was brief on the telephone with his Dad. He was recovering. The injuries were not severe.

The police drove them to Schaffhausen to meet with Joseph who was meeting with Dieter.

Joseph started. "How about those guys! The peace weapon really works and no one so far has picked up on the phenomenon, but the public is puzzled. One newspaper has figured it by announcing that the police had used state of the art taser guns. It was a difficult decision for the government but I am glad they did. The Federal Council voted today to deport the gangs back to their countries. The culprits will spread the word around that Switzerland deals with riots very decisively. Most of the culprits when interviewed off cameras were in a state of shock from what felt like an electric shock. The after affects were temporary headaches and disorientation. The good guys amongst them were given a chance to apply for entry and work permits in Switzerland."

Dieter added, "Peter's Gandhian principles were used in the strategy, as you can see."

The motive of the five men, who had tailed Cathy and Peter and were shot in the gun battle outside the Embassy in Bern, was under investigation. They carried no form of identification. The police was working with Interpol. The Swiss were also concerned about the assassination attempt on John Schaefer and suspected that it was somehow connected to the five dead insurgents.

A few days later Peter received a call from Schaefer.

"Peter, me lad, need you here for a couple of days. The Intelligence officer in the Embassy will arrange for your transport. Yes, yes, yes, I am doing just fine, damn it was a close call. What did you guys do with dad?

He is a totally different person. Ask Cathy to stay in the Embassy till you return, in the meantime she will get a bodyguard if she has to go to Geneva for meetings."

Peter cursed as he boarded the C130 Transport in Geneva for London. It felt like flying in a cargo ship without any comforts. The plane was loaded with UN cargo and some personnel who talked strange languages without pausing to breathe. His head was pounding when they landed in Staffield Air force base in the U.K. He then boarded a F16 and had a hell of a ride to the National airport in DC. A U.S army car picked him up and he was given a bed in the military officer's quarters where he dropped totally exhausted.

He woke up next morning to coffee and doughnuts, still feeling groggy from the transport ordeal. To top it off, he was interrupted, early in the morning, by a smart uniformed officer who saluted him.

"Good morning, Mr. Miller, I trust you had a pleasant trip back, Sir. I would like to escort you to the meeting."

The meeting was in the military barracks. The room was poorly lit. John Schaefer smiled and gave him a brief hug, then introduced him to Mr. Ken Pollard and Mr. James Maynard from the Pentagon Intelligence Agency.

Maynard opened the meeting.

"We have been doing some digging and want to explore a theory with you. We believe the rouges who attempted the assassination on John and then threatened you and your wife, believe that you know more about the Meridian weapon than what you have disclosed to your departments. John here assures us that he knows no more than what we already know. What do you think about the strange phenomenon that suddenly subsided the riots in Switzerland, Mr. Miller?"

Peter reflected and could see the strained face of Schaefer, who was unshaven.

"The trip I just had was a torture and now I am being subjected to an interrogation. Listen, all I know is that the Meridian is some project about model planes. I do not have that sort of hobby so I have not paid any attention. General Watts of EDA and my Department has asked me to dig around in Switzerland. I suggested that we try to include the toy planes in the Swiss-U.S. weapons joint venture program underway, but the General got mad when I suggested that we focus our efforts through the U.S, which is my assignment, and the General responded by hanging up on me, for changing the strategy. Hell, I don't work for the EDA. Don't tell me the great Pentagon cannot make toy airplanes." Peter responded, tired and grumpy.

"Drones are not toys," came a stern response from Pollard.

Peter continued. "The news papers in Switzerland and some photos in the news media showed a couple of the policemen with a taser type gun in their hand. It is a shocking experience I understand."

Pollard interjected, "Peter we are not trying to give you a hard time. We want to find the people who are trying to kill you three, for Christ's sake."

"How about the EDA?" enquired Peter.

"They are clean. We have checked," came a prompt response from Maynard.

"I don't agree. Did you know that EDA tried to infiltrate the Swiss intelligence and killed some Swiss? What makes you so sure that they will not try to kill again?" Peter's temper was now showing.

"Damn! We did not know. Is this new intelligence information that the CIA is withholding from us?" asked Pollard, startled at the news.

John, who was listening with a tired look said, "Your boss, the Secretary of Defense gave me that information."

The meeting suddenly went into a lull, and Shaefer said, "Okay guys, thanks for your help. Let's keep digging. Sorry we have a meeting with the Secretary of the Security in half an hour and I must shave before we go."

John and Peter smiled and shook hands with Pollard and Maynard and left the meeting.

The Secretary of Security and the Secretary of Defense were in a session with some Senators. Their meeting ended, so John and Peter went in.

Both the Secretaries looked very worried.

"We are getting a lot of flack from the Congress concerning kidnapping, and now the attempted assassination on John. The Security and Intelligence Agency is under siege. How can we be expected to keep the country secure? We have serious issues on the consolidation of the several Intelligence agencies under a single Intelligence Czar. The agencies are dragging their feet after having run their own show for years."

"If I may, Mr. Secretary," Peter said. "In my opinion, the multiple Intelligence agencies should be allowed to operate somewhat independently with the proviso that they report to a central Intelligence office, like a project Manager who then consolidates the Intelligence and makes it available to all concerned. Each Intelligence agency has years of experience in sourcing information and contacts. The real problem as I understand is that there is duplication of efforts but most deficient aspect is that there is poor coordination and sharing of intelligence information collected by the various Intelligence Agencies. The newly created central Intelligence, should in fact act as a Project Manager in the industry. Our elite analyst group is really a kind of marketing research group. Our group faded rather quickly because we were looked upon as a threat to the job security of all the intelligence agencies. The various Intelligence Agencies in the country should be asked to form the Central Intelligence office and make it rotational for the sake of training the Intelligence Agents and improving their experience."

The Secretary of Security stood up and said, "All right, Peter thanks for your comments. Let me reflect on the idea. I have to leave for another meeting. I will see you both later tomorrow."

The Secretary of Defense waved his hand at John and Peter to remain seated

"I need to discuss with you about how the Swiss quickly defused the recent riots in three major cities in Switzerland. It may or may not be linked to the Meridian drones that we believe the Swiss have been working on. It must be a sophisticated weapon that does not kill the rioters. The President would like to receive a report and explore a dialogue with the Swiss. I have no doubt in my mind that once we know what the weapon does, someone will come up with a counter weapon. Peter, I have read some your reports where you suggest cutting the roots of the problem by non violence solutions, as the best defense weapon.

It is idealistic in our times. What about might is right? Do you believe communism would have fallen if we had been weak militarily? The only threats we face now are the terrorist cells operating all over the world . You know that General Strong has finally convinced us to create a new segment of soldiers trained as guerrilla fighters in the army, marine, navy, and air force to deal with this threat. Sorry, I got side tracked. So, could you two go on the fact finding trip to Switzerland and report to us asap."

The military police van drove John and Peter back to the military base. The van driver saw that they were being tailed and called in the reinforcement that stopped the car but he kept driving till they were back in the security of the base.

John poured a drink for Peter and himself.

"Interesting, eh! You must know a lot more than you have told me about this damn Meridian project. Any idea how to tackle what the Secretary has asked us to do?"

"Quite elementary, my dear Watson We start the exploration through Dieter. This guy is really well connected," Peter suggested.

"Hell, I can do better with Hilfiger and some assistance from the Ambassador, John answered.

Peter's cell phone rang. "Darling, I am sorry to call you on this line but I am worried and I miss you so much. Come back now."

Peter smiled and winked at John. "Yes, my dear, right away. We will return within a couple of Days."

"Who's we?" Cathy asked.

"John and I," Peter answered.

Thirty-one

A military transport plane flew John and Peter to New York.

"Gentlemen you are cleared to fly to Germany on a military carrier, leaving in two hours but we have been advised by the EDA transport office that they have some brass returning to Bruselles and they would be glad to give you a free ride."

"No Thanks. We have to fly to London." John replied.

Peter understood the quick response and they went over to American Airlines and caught a flight out. John explained that he felt very uncomfortable with the EDA flight option.

"How interesting to have the whole family working together," Hilfiger said as he looked around the table at Cathy, John, Peter and the U.S. Ambassador.

The Swiss government expressed serious concerns that the Meridian weapon could be misused. Hilfiger talked about the peace weapon that disables the culprits temporarily. The U.S. and Swiss cooperation was discussed but the Swiss insisted that the use of the weapon should be as a service provided by only the Swiss. After a lengthy session, which was not going anywhere, Peter suggested that they continue the following day with some fresh ideas to see if an arrangement or an agreement can be reached.

Peter felt a bit uncomfortable, playing a double role in the meetings. He had to stay focused in not allowing politics to compromise the real mission of the Meridian, weapon of peace. Why was the United States acting like a bully when all they needed was to ask the Swiss to help them in the guerilla war conflicts, with the weapon of peace? Damn political ego, he thought, that does as much harm as crime. He wanted to talk to the President in DC, directly instead through all the puffed up middle men who had their own agendas.

The group returned to the Embassy and after dinner sat in closed session to brain storm. The Ambassador saw no inkling on part of the Swiss to have a cooperation of sorts. John and Cathy lectured at trying to reach an understanding without first establishing some trust with the Swiss. Peter suggested that they prepare a draft proposal that represented the U.S. intent. The proposal can be submitted through the Secretary of Security to the U.S. President for discussion. The basic U.S. proposal could then be signed by the President and hand carried to the Swiss government by the U.S Ambassador.

The group mulled over the idea and finally agreed to proceed on Peter's suggestion. Peter felt disgusted with himself for failing to convince the Ambassador and John on a simple, straight forward plan of action. The U.S. Ambassador proposed that he meet with Hilfiger, alone, the next day and make the proposal.

The insurgent attacks in Iraq seemed to be getting worse, was the headline on the Swiss papers, the next day.

John and Cathy did not agree with Peter's simple plan which overlooked diplomacy. Peter racked his brains for another solution. He called Dieter at night

"Hi Dieter, I am afraid our meeting today went no where with Hilfiger."

"What are you suggesting"? Dieter asked.

"It sounds a bit crazy but how about if the Swiss take the initiative and use the peace weapon in Iraq with the blessing of the U.S. and say the UN Secretary General. It will give a wakeup call on the effectiveness of the weapon and give the negotiation a kick start. I have suggested that we prepare a proposal outlining the U.S. intent for submittal to the

Swiss but I feel it will get lost in the U.S. government. You are the only one who I have talked to about the crazy idea," Peter said.

"That's a thought. It is worth waking Hilfiger up," Dieter said.

Peter's cell phone rang. Peter looked at his watch and it was 2:00 am. Cathy was also wide awake.

Dieter in his tired voice said, "Hey Pete, my wife wants to know who this guy is who does not let us sleep, after all what is so important that cannot wait until a civilized time. Hilfiger liked the idea but he feels that Meridian should be used now with perhaps the blessing of the UN and the Iraqi government only. It will give a polite message to the U.S. Any way he needs to discuss with others, before implementing the crazy plans."

The Ambassador, John, Cathy and Peter met for lunch later in the day, and took the opportunity to walk around the beautiful shopping arcades in Bern. John reflected on one of his professors in the university, who came originally from Bern. The Professor had an interesting philosophical solution for solving problems in the world. He said that one should observe and do nothing, because problems have a habit of solving all by themselves.

The meeting between the Swiss and the U.S. Ambassador continued in the afternoon. Finally the Swiss agreed to receive a proposal from the U.S.

Dieter informed him later that some of the Council members considered the crazy plan too crazy, but workable.

John decided to visit his dad with Cathy and Peter. Cathy's dad was in his glory to see the family all together and showed it with tears rolling down his cheek.

John insisted that Peter return to the U.S. for briefing the boss and the Secretary of Defense. Cathy was not willing to stay back in Switzerland. So the trio boarded a flight back to Washington DC.

"What are you so busily writing since we took off?" John remarked.

"The proposal," Peter said.
"Really? Pete, a meeting report would do the job," John suggested.

"Well it's like this; I still have everything fresh in my mind and guess who would have to prepare the proposal draft. By the way how come we are all traveling commercial? What about the security?" Peter replied.

"The bad guys are probably tired and given up on us. We will have to take precautions again if another attempt is made on our lives. You guys stay with me at my home," John suggested.

Peter prepared a short meeting summary and the draft Proposal which the trio went over and over again with several drafts.

John informed Peter, "Our boss will meet us tomorrow morning".

Peter hurried with the Draft which in essence said that the Swiss were willing to consider a joint program. It was agreed that the U.S. will submit an official Proposal outlining the intent. The Proposal was very direct with little flowery language to avoid any misinterpretation. It stated that the U.S. was deeply involved in several peace making efforts around the world, where conflicts had broken out and which threatened the peace and security of the world. The U.S. has always resorted to negotiations but when all efforts breakdown and violence breaks, weapons were used as a last resort. The Swiss peace weapon offers a solution never available before and would serve as a valuable tool to resolve conflicts. The insurgents should learn that conflicts must be resolved with negotiations. It was also clear to the U.S. that the UN should take a more active role in peacemaking so that the parties in conflict receive the attention and aid in resolving their conflicts amicably.

John submitted the report together with Peter to the Secretary, who appeared pleased and was going to review the draft Proposal with the Secretaries of State and Defense.

It was a Sunday morning in DC and John, Cathy and Peter were settling down to a breakfast of bagels. An alarm in John's situation room rang and the three rushed to investigate. The Security status printer reported that several people, believed to be insurgents in some cities in Iraq, had fallen unconscious during a series of attacks by the insurgents. The Iraqi Government was arresting the fallen insurgents and transporting them to jails where a team was interrogating them. The news release by the Iraqi government reported that the weapon used was unique and coordinated with the Swiss government.

John, Cathy and Peter looked at each other in surprise and then burst out in laughter.

"Boy the Swiss are clever indeed," said John, as his phones lit up like a Christmas tree. He could not stop laughing and finally picked up one that was from his boss.

"What do you know about what just happened in Iraq I am blamed by the Secretary of Defense?" the Secretary said

"Really, Sir! It appears to be a great event and we should be rejoicing in the U.S. as the Iraqi's are also rejoicing. Show the critiques our report and the draft Proposal, and give 'em hell for not celebrating. Sir I suggest that we all meet the President so that we can report on our meetings in Switzerland. We are also surprised about the great news in Iraq."

Later John learnt that the Secretary of Security had in fact met with the President, but without John or Peter.

"Peter! Is there something you have not told me?" John asked

"There you go again John! What do you think about the Swiss? You think that they developed a peace weapon, tested its effectiveness and went back to sleep," Peter replied.

Minutes later Peter and John were speeding to an emergency meeting of the cabinet in the Situation room of the White House.

Accusations shot against John and Peter like a machinegun. Both stayed calm and real cool, until the national security advisor looked at Peter.

"Mr. Miller, what do you know about what has happened in Iraq?"

John answered instead. "Sir, I am just appalled. We know nothing about Iraq other than what we read. If you are referring to the meetings we had with the Swiss government at the request of the Secretary of Defense and approval of our boss, then you should know that we went to explore the feasibility of working a joint operation with the Swiss on the weapon of peace. We have submitted a draft proposal to outline intentions as we see it. Now it appears that the weapon used in Iraq was in fact the Swiss peace weapon. We can request the Swiss for details, if you so desire. We certainly don't expect that they would develop a peace weapon, test it and go to sleep. It appears to me that perhaps the Iraqi government has worked out some arrangement with the Swiss to help at least contain the severe insurgency problem. May I ask what our intelligence tells us from Iraq? Let us await the outcome of the weapon deployed before we jump to any conclusions. I protest the line of questioning my colleague and I have been subjected to as if a crime has been committed and we are the culprits." John spoke with such cool eloquence that it surprised Peter.

John and Peter had not noticed that the President had entered the situation room and taken a chair in the rear, unnoticed.

The President clapped and said, "Bravo, that's telling them." The mood in the meeting became conciliatory and the President spoke

"I have received a call from the Prime Minister of Iraq this morning telling me that the Iraq has been cooperating with the Swiss Red Cross and the Swiss government, under heavy secrecy, in a desperate attempt to find a solution to the insurgency problem we have since many months. The Swiss agreed to help. The entire plan has worked out without a hitch. We believe that we now have a large percent of the insurgency Leadership behind bars . Most of these men are from the neighboring countries, paid to fight and well financed as we all have known all along. The mood of the Iraqi nation is that of hope since the insurgents have been taken by complete surprise and know nothing about the invisible weapon. The Swiss have insisted that Iraq interrogate the insurgency humanely and that the individuals arrested be rehabilitated in their own countries. I am eager to see a very positive effect from the use of this weapon, which we very badly need. My plan would be to announce troop reductions with a target date for completing the withdrawal. Gentlemen I want that we respect the Swiss and continue to work out a program of cooperation with them in the other trouble spots we are involved."

The U.S. media was punching away at the administration. The U.S. intelligence had an idea what the Iraqi had worked with the Swiss. The words plastered all over the press was "Invisible Weapon." Some of the media reported that one or more Middle Eastern countries had also developed the unique weapon and would use it against the Israelis. The Middle Eastern press spread the news like wild fire with statements on who could be the next country to use such a invisible weapon.

General Strong called to express his thoughts of support on the use of the weapon. It may be a very tragic loss for the defense industry. All or nothing philosophy resonated. His input from EDA had been that they had all given up direct negotiations with the Swiss. The Secretary General of EDA had issued stern warning to the EDA brass to desist from any undercover operations.

Amin called from the UN, "Hey Peter, can you find out about the invisible weapon used by the Iraqis on the insurgents? We have not been able to get any information within the UN organization. Boy! This is powerful stuff. We have calls from Palestinians and the Israel, wanting information. The demand is like a spreading fire all over the Middle East. Wait, wait! I am receiving info on the tape from the US intelligence Top Secret, that the weapon is owned and operated by the Swiss. Come on guys what info do you have?"

"We have the same info kiddo as you have but we will investigate and I will let you know ASAP." Peter made a calm response.

News flashed that Switzerland had repelled an attack on Switzerland from the French border at Divonne les—Bains. The C130 Hercules Transport plane landed at the French and Swiss border with a load of three tanks and masked armed men in camouflage attacked the Swiss and French border police. The invisible weapon rendered the men unconscious and the tank firing mechanisms were rendered inoperable.

Within hours the world press agencies were all flashing the news. All the Swiss borders remained open and all roads, rail and air transport remained unaffected, which surprised all, reflecting the confidence the Swiss government had in their secret weapon.

John, Cathy and Peter sat across the dining table in John's home, in splendid wonder.

"The Swiss are moving too fast, but I suppose once the cat is out of the bag, all the bad cowboys will challenge the weapon, like the fastest gun alive in the wild west," John pointed out.

There was a loud bang outside John's house and the front door, crashed open. Four men fully armed walked in.

"This is an emergency please come with us to the Pentagon," one of them said. One of the other armed men looked around the room and asked for the special cell phones at gunpoint. The other walked into the situation room and fired at all the secret service communication equipment.

"Who the hell are you? What is the meaning of all this? You are not from the Pentagon. How dare..." John was hit across the face. Cathy and Peter stood, shocked.

Minutes later an army Hummer was transporting the three, kidnapped. The ride took almost an hour while Cathy and Peter attended to John's injuries.The Hummer drove into a warehouse and the three were gagged, bound, and told to sit on the cold floor. It felt like eternity and the three were stone cold, trying to huddle in order to keep warm unsuccessfully. All three wore night attires when they were kidnapped. They were exhausted from the ordeal and tried to sleep when the warehouse they were in started to light up. Suddenly strong lights were aimed at the three hostages. There were people walking up to them but the strong lights at them blinded the trio.

"This can all end in a few minutes if you can give tell us all you know about the Swiss secret weapon. The alternate is you will be left to die in this place. Is it worth your life?" There was a brief silence and a man came up and untied the gags.

Peter responded, "What do you want to know? You are welcome to know all we know. What do we care about the Swiss weapon! It means nothing to us except it appears to be a smart weapon that disables undesirable human beings like you. The news we heard when you so rudely kidnapped us, was that the Swiss weapon also disabled hand guns and military tanks. Hey fellas! I am an analyst agent and if you guys are Americans then I will do my job and find out more for you. We cannot do anything sitting in this rat hole freezing our butts."

"You are lying!" Someone shoved a gunpoint at him.

"You must know a hell of lot of truth, if you say that I am lying. Well do you? " Peter was starting an argument.

"Shut up you fool," came the sharp answer.

"Listen fellows, you are making a terrible mistake. We are all from the Intelligence Agency. You should know that it would take a few minutes and the army will be all over you."

"How so, Mr.?" came a confident response.

"One of your smart guys destroyed the secret service communications in John's house which sends an alarm out to the army and the FBI. Why don't you guys relax and settle down and we can all welcome the U.S. army."

There was a hustle among the men and the lights were shut down. They could hear that the kidnappers were leaving.

"Could you please leave some lights on, please? I hate the dark," shouted Cathy.

Thirty-two

Dieter was trying to reach the trio and finally was informed that the department was searching for them. It appeared that they had been kidnapped. Dieter alarmed the Defense Department. The kidnappers had destroyed the secret service communication equipment in John's house.

The Israeli captain Moshe had just settled down in bed after the long training day for guerrilla warfare with the new U.S. Army group, when his phone rang. He listened attentively and thought for a while. He put his uniform and woke up Hamid, from the Palestinian contingent there giving the US Army training on guerrilla warfare techniques. The two men thought a bit and suddenly one of them initiated the alarm.

"We are going to do a live training to rescue three American Intelligence officers, now" They went to the air force base in Virginia and waited for a FBI van that was pulling up as they arrived. The FBI agent had a special digital spy satellite transmitter and receiver.

"All our agents carry an ID card which emits a weak signal for about a year and the card is automatically renewed each year. We just have to hope that at least one of them has an ID card on him" the FBI agent said. The system was now scanning and trying to locate a signal. An air force plane with scanning capabilities, took off to search a wider range. It was morning and all attempts seemed in vain.

"Check for any cars reported stolen in the last two days in the DC area," ordered Captain Hamid.

A few hours passed. The army unit cell phone crackled, "We have a stolen hummer, found by the DC police. The army transport tells us that the hummer has done about 120 miles since reported stolen."

The army captain issued an order to the transport plane in the air to cover an area of 120 miles from John Shaefer's residence.

The PA system at the air force command center in Virginia, announced; Swiss *Air Force mirage 778 requesting permission to land.*

"You are cleared for landing on runway 231."

The Swiss plane landed and after some brief formalities, unloaded a drone airplane loaded with gear. The drone took off before receiving the permission to take off. The drone plane was scanning an area of about 120 miles. The Swiss pilot sat in the cockpit of his mirage778, controlling the flight of the drone. It was now about 10:00am and the Swiss Ambassador's car pulled up at the air force base to observe. The Ambassador was accompanied by the Deputy Secretary of State and they approached the Swiss plane. The Swiss Ambassador greeted the pilot who was totally absorbed. The pilot suddenly came out of the cockpit of his plane with a smile.

"Latitude 39.2, longitude 8.690." The two-army captains one from Israel and the other from Palestine drove off with a small contingent of U.S. soldiers. A helicopter was also dispatched to the coordinates found.

Half an hour later the radios were alive,

"We have found the three kidnapped and they are being rushed to the Hospital in Bethesda."

The Swiss plane pilot collected his drone and asked for clearance to take off. Four minutes later the Swiss plane took off for Switzerland. It had taken all by an element of total surprise.

The State Department, Deputy Secretary and the Swiss Ambassador sat trying to recap what had all happened so swiftly.

The State Department official said, "Mr. Ambassador! Thank you for the rapid response by Switzerland to help us out. We have a lot of questions about the weapon. Can we..."

"Yes Sir, there is an on going dialogue between our countries as you know to seek cooperation. I saw the drone also the first time like you. Quite impressive, I think," responded the Swiss Ambassador.

"God damn it! I can't believe you gave the Swiss Mirage the clearance to take off." The colonel was raving mad. "The drone was at our door steps and you guys all slept while the Swiss performed and left. You mean no one examined the drone, any pictures, or videos taken by anyone? All this work, down the drain. My boss will shoot me for all the kidnap drama, the attempted search and then the Swiss mirage, drone operation, all happening under our very eyes while we slept!"

"But sir, we were informed about the arrival of the Swiss Mirage plane when it had done its job and was taking off. I don't know who botched up the under cover op."

Captain Hamid sipped his coke while captain Moshe enjoyed his beer as they sat at the officers' mess room.

"Well that was an interesting adventure. I expected that the joint effort would have been successful. It was a good training for the boys, but the drone appearance out of the blue and its fast action just left me spellbound. How about you, Moshe?"

"Spellbound is the perfect description. What puzzles me most is that the U.S. looked like they were also very surprised at what hit them. The other amazing thing I observed was that the Swiss pilot performed the entire operation from the Mirage. The U.S. did not even hold on to the drone to investigate. How strange," said Moshe.

"I suspect that there was a fast agreement between the Swiss and the U.S. before the Swiss plane even landed" Captain Hamid offered a possible explanation.

Captain Hamid was on the telephone in the Palestinian Embassy.

"Yes, I am calling for Brigadier Salim. Sir, I have some very interesting photographs which I am sending to you on the drone with the diplomatic mail bag."

"Sir, it is Captain Moshe, calling from the Israeli Embassy in Washington DC. I am sending some top secret photographs for the intelligence bureau.

Thirty-three

John and Peter went to the Swiss Embassy to thank them for their help in their rescue.

The Ambassador took them to the secure communication room in the Embassy, and informed them

"The Swiss intelligence is of the opinion that your kidnapping was staged. Let me explain. We received an urgent request from the U.S. Pentagon for help before the three of you were kidnapped. In fact this request came about an hour or so before you were actually kidnapped. Mr. Dieter Hopf learnt about your kidnapping quite some time later. We did not want to take any chances so we dispatched the drone with the Mirage. We became concerned and suspicious that the U.S. complex Security could hold the drone long enough to collect enough data that can be analyzed, but fortunately that did not happen. Any way, we are not sure but we thought that you should be alerted. The other intelligence input we have is that the US Intelligence in the Pentagon suspects you three that you know a lot of details about the Meridian project than you have disclosed."

John and Peter just could not believe that their kidnapping which was not without severe pain was a staged drama in order to secure more information on the secret weapon.

Cathy was furious.

"This country is getting out of control. It is definitely some shady and eager beavers who are behind this plot, and Ha! It failed. This information should go to your boss and heads will roll."

"Yes, I agree, Cathy. I am getting sick and tired of people taking put shots at all of us," John agreed.

John wasted no time and reported the whole affair to the Secretary who sat totally appalled. "Some one is trying to sabotage our efforts on our attempt to work out a joint program on the Meridian with the Swiss. I am reporting it to the President in writing."

Within days of the kidnapping, Peter received a call "Hello Peter, this is General James Jamieson in the Pentagon. I just received a copy of your draft on the U.S. proposal for the cooperation with the Swiss on the Drone Project. I understand that you are using diplomatic language in the Proposal, but it sounds like we are begging for their cooperation. We are the U.S., we don't beg for anything."

"General you are free to change the language and I am sure the State Department will in any case use their own language. My task is to make sure we get what we want. Personally, Sir I am still stunned after being kidnapped with John, the Director of Security, and my wife here in DC. All of us suffer from the trauma we recently went. We are investigating who the culprits were and Sir, I can assure you that I will make my findings public. We are grateful to the Pentagon for requesting help from the Swiss. The drone located us and saved our lives." Peter responded.

"I am glad that you are all safe. Let me know if I can assist in seeking out the culprits." The General was cooperating with Peter.

Within minutes of the call from General Jamieson to Peter, John received a call.

"John , this is General Strong. I must meet with you and Peter. I suggest we meet for cocktails tomorrow. I can pick you both from your office. By the way you guys keep changing your office. So where are you now? You know that it is better I pick you guys up at Joe's on L street."

"Thank you, but we can drive and meet you at your home," replied John.

The General Strong looked very disturbed and wasted no time on getting to his concerns "The Swiss drone weapon has caused a hell of a stir in the Defense industry. The Swiss-U.S. joint weapons manufacturing program that Peter initiated has come up with only one billion Dollar of potential revenue for the U.S. I have information that the Swiss weapon manufacturers are also not pleased at the outcome. The defense industry worldwide is feeling the pinch, which is some forty percent of the world trade. We need to brain storm on what can be done to save the back bone of our industry. The automobile industry in the country has been facing losses now for years, and now the defense industry is edging away. Are we going to become a third world country soon?"

John tried to be rational. "We boosted our economy in the industrial revolution and pretty much kept the growth, taking measures to adjust with the changes in the industrial economics. We are and have been since ages leaders in the economic world. I am confident that the American ingenuity will find a solution to the Defense Industry."

"We must not forget that the human beings, the innocent bystanders, have increasingly become over the years, hostages to all kinds of acts of violence and weapons that threatens the annihilation of the world many times over. We have a chance to possibly find peace for the Joe Blokes in the world who have been totally forgotten by the very governments they elect each time. What's wrong with us? We should be celebrating at the chance of world peace, instead of worrying about the bottom line of our defense industry. We have lost human respect and value and sold our souls to a select few who are totally blind in greed." Peter said with a tone of sadness in his voice.

General Strong poured his guests another drink. "To our savior!" I have information that your kidnapping was staged by someone in the Pentagon who is now in deep trouble for having failed the mission."

Thirty—four

Cathy looked very perturbed when she saw Peter and John upon their return home from the meeting with General Strong, looking morose.

"I am very deeply worried at what is happening to us. We have become the target in our own country. What next? You know the way things are happening we will soon have to live like fugitives, all because of a peace weapon that offers the world a chance of some peace? What an irony ! I can't even think of having a family as a fugitive from some terrorizing mafia." Cathy cried.

John looked at Peter as if to say, you handle the situation.

Peter spontaneously suggested, "Yup, it is time to do some serious thinking. Your dad called yesterday all upset with our 'kidnap theater' as he called it. I shared his concern and promised to think. My mom and dad called in desperation, and terribly concerned about our safety when I talked to them the other day. My mom was very direct as usual. She wants me to stop being macho and give her some grandchildren."

"Hey, got an idea! Why don't wees take a brief vacation in......San Juan, Puerto Rico. It will give us some time to relax and think."

"My boss has broken the news to the President and I am sure that a storm is brewing. Why don't you love birds take off and I will join you when the coast is clear," John said with reluctance.

Cathy and Peter checked into the Caribe Hilton in San Juan. It was still high season and expensive but not crowded. The check-in clerk had it figured out, when he said that the tourists are scared to travel and have less money.

Peter called the room service and ordered a planters punch and a pina colada. The drink was delicious and seemed to calm his nerves.

"Hey Mr. Macho, I am ready for some dinner and please no room service, darling." Cathy cuddled with Peter.

The dinner at the Restaurant Don Pepe was a delight.

"Peter is it my feeling or do you feel it too?", Cathy asked in almost a whisper.

"What?" said Peter, in a way that the folks sitting at the next table looked at them with a smile.

"Maybe I am oversensitive but I see people around us giving us the look over," she said "Gee hon! they are looking at a beautiful women. You are simply the most beautiful women in the restaurant. Stand up and take a bow."

Cathy felt flustered and went to the powder room. She returned looking very embarrassed.

"I had forgotten one plastic curler in the back of my hair makeup. A lady in the powder room pointed it out to me. Gosh! How embarrassing! How casual can I get?"

Peter had paid the bill in the meantime, so he stood up, gave Cathy a kiss and walked out of the restaurant arm in arm. They sure looked like a romantic pair.

Cathy and Peter sat the next day. The morning swim in the sea at the hotel was very refreshing and the breakfast with plenty of fresh fruits, made it complete. Cathy sat enjoying the ambience and remarked that they should live in a vacation area.

"Why do we live in DC when there are such wonderful places in this world?"

Peter was somber about his life. "When I take stock of my life so far, I must say that I have had an exciting and challenging life so far. My objective in life remains finding peaceful solutions to any kind of conflict. The recent events have given me a kind of wakeup call, that my country has drifted into greed and is rapidly losing human values. The political process does not encourage the Mahatma Gandhis in our country to lead the nation. Special interests, political and non political, are running the wonderful people in this country. The silent majority is screaming but the terrible environment has muffled their screams. It is now becoming clearer to me that the weapon of peace is our most important hope and we should be actively part of the process, working with people who share our beliefs, for the benefit of world peace."

Cathy suddenly stood up. "Are you saying its time to find a new pasture?"

"Yes, my love. I do not want to fight city hall any longer. Our administration, our politics is giving lip service to the real American cause and is misled into the corrupt hands of greed. I have been thinking of talking to our friends in Bern. Maybe they have a job for me where I can work to keep my American dream alive," Peter said, with resolve.

The next two days they relaxed and reflected on the plan to start a new life in Switzerland.

John sounded depressed when he called. He had been in three meetings with the Secretary and the President. It was all about how we had failed to get our hands on the Meridian drone weapon. This failure, the President felt will cost the leadership that the U.S. has had for years. John now strongly felt that he was made the scapegoat. John finally gave in to the repeated requests by Cathy and Peter to join them for a vacation in the Caribe Hilton.

It did not take long for John to take the next flight to San Juan after the call with Cathy and Peter.

The hours past and John sat gloomy and sad in his hotel room, despite all the attempts to cheer him. Finally, Peter and Cathy decided to tell him about their plans to quit DC and their jobs for a fresh start in Switzerland. John listened and suddenly he became alive.

"I had not thought of this option."

The discussions became alive with hope. John became animated and ready to enjoy his vacation. He loved his job in the department but the job had started to weigh him down when some of the agents were found murdered and some resigned because of the establishment terror group. The excitement and job satisfaction turned into frustration and disgust.

John received a wire message from his secretary that the Secretary wanted to see him in his office on the following Monday morning.

"Why should I leave this island paradise only so that His Majesty can have the satisfaction of telling me that I am fired?" he said to his office secretary.

"No John, the rumor has it that you will get a new job. What will happen to people like me if dedicated people like you quit," said the encouraging voice of Jane, his secretary.

Peter called Dieter to update him on the situation John and he had befallen.

"Cathy and I will look for jobs in Switzerland. I am not sure but I think John will also join us." Peter informed Dieter.

"Excuse me, Peter, but has the Swiss Ambassador not called you about Hilfiger's message. Well Hilfiger feels that it is neither safe nor interesting for you three to stay in the U.S. That is Hilfiger's way of saying that he wants you three to work for your old, and first Heimat (first motherland). Think about it and don't do anything stupid in the meantime like getting kidnapped again," Dieter responded.

"No it's probably safe here. We are vacationing in San Juan de Puerto Rico," said Peter, trying to hold back his excitement.

"So, I tell Hilfiger that you agree. He will not take no for an answer"now Dieter sounded worried.

"Dieter, I have a suggestion that you travel to San Juan to convince us about what Hilfiger has proposed. You can have a vacation and return home victorious. How can you beat that?" Peter suggested.

Peter told Cathy and John about the great news. Dieter is coming to San Juan to convince us. The trio looked cheerful again.

A few days later, John decided to leave for DC . "So I can look at the Secretary and say thanks but no thanks, for the new job, whatever that is," he said.

Dieter joined Peter and Cathy with his wife Maria. They criss-crossed the island and savored the delicacies of the creole food. During one of the dinners Dieter confessed "I informed Hilfiger that you three appeared to accept his offer and your suggestion that I join you on a vacation. This great man laughed and winked when he said that I should take a business trip with Maria to San Juan. So this is an honest business holiday for Maria and me. You see Maria works part time for the Ministry of Defense."

John Shaefer was indeed offered a new position as a "Senior Administrator" in the department of Securities and Intelligence. The Secretary had given John the job description, which read like a genuine "chief of paper pushers." John reflected a moment and then handed the job description back to the Secretary.

"Thank you Sir, the new job you have kindly offered me reflects the confidence you have in me. I will take leave now, Sir, resigning my post of Director with my gratitude to the administration for giving me an opportunity to serve my country."

The Secretary was shaken but not stirred.

The wire services caught on and gave the administration another black eye. The press had almost an accurate coverage of all what Shaeffer had been subjected to in the line of duty by the very government he served for twenty years. John particularly enjoyed reading the editorials on him. He was relaxed about the whole situation, a pleasant surprise for Cathy and Peter.

Peter and Cathy returned to DC all excited at the prospects of a new beginning in Switzerland. They met three Security agents, Peter knew, at the airport, upon arrival. The agents were returning from a seminar where the directives, they said, confirmed that Big Brother was not only watching but had taken over their lives. They were quite concerned about the rights of the American people. They mentioned in passing that one of the SI agents was questioned at length just because he was a Muslim returning from a home leave to Lebanon.

We miss good sound leadership in the department. There is no unity among us and we appear to be under siege not only from the outside world but also from within the department. They felt that the KGB style of operation was creeping into the department. The 'establishment' within the department made the job very difficult. The resignation of John Shaefer they said was a blow to the group. John was able to cut through red tape and drastically reduced hindrances that kept them from doing their jobs. The new guy is a mere puppet of the boss.

Peter resigned from the SI Department in DC. The new Director, John Walsh looked up after reading the letter of resignation

"Does this have anything to do with the resignation of Mr. John Schaefer?"

"No! I have been harassed by the Administration about the Swiss Meridian Drones. I was given the task of exploring a joint operation with the Swiss. I submitted a proposal to the Secretary on proceeding with the joint operation, following the meeting John and I had with the Swiss government. I never heard any response. I can understand that the U.S. was surprised when the Swiss used the weapon in the Middle East upon request by the Iraqi government. My government is trying to pick John and I as the scapegoats, instead of proceeding with the task we were given," Peter replied

"I understand and regret what has happened. I wish you the best of luck in the future," said the disinterested new Director, as he accepted the letter of resignation from Peter.

John decided to sell the house, and being a good area, sold it within a week. Cathy and Peter helped John to pack up so that the movers could ship the household items to Switzerland.

Peter collected all the special gear like the cell phone and left it at the office, when the secretary handed him a message from the Secretary of Defense.

"Peter, I am sorry to learn that you resigned. I could use you in the Pentagon, please contact my office if you are interested."

Peter sent a polite letter in response to the Secretary of Defense. He remembered to structure the letter in a way that did not burn any bridges remembering the words of a friend, who once said, "Ya never know."

Peter was disappointed that the Secretary of Security had not made any attempts to contact either John or him to bid farewell.

Thirty-five

Hilfiger welcomed the trio to Switzerland with a warmth that they missed in Washington DC in their jobs

Hilfiger gave a brief outline of the operation and success they had with the Meridian Project.

"We have decided to open a new department to manage all the operations and applications of the Meridian Drones. We are appointing John Shaefer as the Director and Peter as the Deputy Director. Cathy, we are appointing you as the Director of Administration. We believe that the operation of this department should be conducted by a key group who can efficiently run the affairs, closely coordinating them with the Foreign and Defense Departments. You three have a proven track record".

The UN Program for the Palestinians and Israeli had made good headway. The special team in the UN insisted that Peter and Cathy stay on as team members. The Swiss government found this to be totally acceptable, assuring close cooperation of Meridian applications with the United Nations.

The governments of Israel and Palestine were now more confident that peace agreements between them would have a better chance of success. There were several calls by both the governments for the use of the Drones and an environment of trust started to build between the two parties. Each application was closely coordinated with full agreement of the Governments of Israel and Palestine. The UN had observers on the ground to ensure against abuse of the use of the Drones. The UN started raising its prominence in the world affairs.

Joseph Breder met with the trio and expressed the satisfaction of the Swiss manufacturers with the limited agreements with the U.S. There was a growing pressure from various countries on the Swiss weapon manufacturers and the Swiss government for licensing the Drone technology.

Peter recalled that General Strong in DC had informed him that the Swiss manufacturers were also disappointed about the outcome of the limited Swiss/U.S. trade agreements. Where did Strong get his information? Was it Strong's own agenda?

John and Peter initiated an agreement with the United Nations to serve on the Swiss Meridian Board, as an Observer. The UN Security barely passed the resolution. The word had it that the countries that opposed strongly felt that they were losing an important control element in the power of the UN. The debates were heated but fortunately wisdom prevailed. The biggest problem was from the weapon industries that were seeing a decline in sales in conventional weapons, but Research on New technologies was increasing after the success with the Meridian weapons.

Joseph saw a great deal of interest to apply the Meridian technology with the use of satellites, and felt that a dialogue should be opened with the U.S. contractors. He also felt that it was only a matter of time before the Meridian technology would be duplicated. A close cooperation and coordination with the U.S and perhaps the European Members would be a better policy instead of a confrontational development. The Swiss government agreed to review the concept of cooperation.

The United Nations was anxious to find a way to reduce the threat of nuclear weapons. One of the Meridian technologies had partially tested the system that disabled the fuse of a nuclear weapon. The Swiss research team was interested in implementing the anti nuclear capability but lacked the funds to go at it on their own.

John and Peter were sent to New York to put feelers out with the UN. The number of areas in the world, which had used the Meridian drones to disable the conflicting parties, was increasing. The news made headlines, whenever Drones were used but the novelty was fading slowly. The impact was astounding as more conflicts were being addressed across tables rather than in a battlefield atmosphere. The political impact was also increasing as warring factions found the peaceful resolution, the only option.

The United Nations Secretary General had realized the power of peace in the Meridian Drones and was intensively involved in all the sessions with the Swiss.

The SG started the meeting between the UN brass and the team of John and Peter.

"We thought that we present an update on the status of the impact of the use of the Meridian Drones. A new era of peace had made its long awaited debut. The SG cited fifty violent conflicts that had been defused, forcing the conflicting factions to seek a non-violent resolution. The new peace initiative was in its infancy but the major impact was in the reduction of harm to the innocent citizens which all the peace loving nations wholeheartedly welcomed. The SG continued to encourage the countries to lend their active support to the conflicting factions to ensure resolutions acceptable to the parties. We are hoping that more countries will join the peace movement. The Meridian is a powerful peace weapon."

There was a surge of excitement within the UN participants when they heard from John and Peter about the Swiss technology that could disable nuclear weapons. The discussions favored the development of the Swiss technology with the International Nuclear Authority. Peter voiced the reservation the Swiss government had always expressed in the possible political implications that might negate the effectiveness of the program and its use. The consensus appreciated the concern after a very lengthy debate. John suggested that the Atomic Energy Authority, IAEA prepare a position paper for the UN Security Council and the UN members. Peter left the UN meeting very contented that the progress of peace was finally taking shape.

It was very festive in the city with all the sales after the year-end holidays. Peter was taking it all in with a touch of nostalgia. He felt the immediate future would be best addressed by working out of Switzerland. His America, he felt would not stay on the side lines as peace starts to envelope the troubled spots around the world. What would America do? Would they join the bandwagon as preachers of peace or would the ugly politicians launch another disruptive sets of undertakings to show the world that we are the greatest, mightiest the best and what not. Huh! A good test of the real guts of his beloved America, he thought. He was still lost in thought when he walked in the hotel room and saw the open arms of his Cathy.

"Darling! What, no three kissy-kissy on my cheeks? This lovely custom does not expire when one gets married. It fact the intensity of the three kisses increase."

"Of course, darling." Peter held her in his arms and smothered her with kisses.

"Peter, you are so engrossed in thoughts. I love it. You have a kinda glow, an aura about you. Are you by any chance Saint Peter, back again amongst mortals to spread the word of our Lord? Come on come on lets hear it, my honey bunny."

Peter was amused, "I am not a saint, honey! The meetings in the UN went very well. I was just recapping the recent past and taking stock to where we were as I walked back from the UN Secretariat building.

The Meridian drones operating around, are a set back, for the weapons/arms manufacturing industry. Light weapons such as rifles, rapid-fire arms, RPGs, grenades and the like are affected. These were the weapons of terrorists. General Strong, I recall, had informed me that the so-called small arms were the bread and butter of the industry. The larger grade of weapons were capital intensive and over the years saw a decline in the bottom lines because of increasing competition, and also because the governments, like the U.S. tightened the cost controls. A set of agreements with the UN the IAEA and the Swiss on the defusing of the nuclear threat would further enhance world peace. How often we heard in our travels around the world that a handful of powerful countries held the world masses hostage. These threats had to be minimized if not eliminated all together. Know what I mean?"

"Hang on, for Pete's sake. This is getting heavy. Let me fix two powerful loving drinks so we can sip and cuddle as we watch the snow flurries," said Cathy, as she poured drinks.

"Are you pulling my leg in my moment of revelation?" Peter laughed.

"Of course not, you ding dong! I am savoring every moment. I just wanted to add some liquid into you to keep your thoughts well lubricated. Sorry, sorry.... I just love you to eternity." Cathy smothered him with kisses.

Peter took a sip of Jack Daniels and continued, "You know dear I should feel a sense of achievement, kind of a silent victory on all our humble contributions towards sanity. How fortunate I feel. But, the happiness and bliss I expected is not there. I feel a void after all this as if I have done nothing. Gosh this could turn into a depression instead of euphoria. God, Cathy what's going' on?"

"The problem, my dear, is that you are very sincere in your objective of life. You are suffering because you have humility. It's the ego in us that gives us the euphoria you expected. You have practically no ego. You are very sensitive in a very positive sense! How lucky can you be? I share your sentiments because in spite of it all what I have been doing in my life, I feel like something is missing. Don't get me wrong, you are the best thing that happened to me. Without you I was drifting towards insanity. You have given me a renewal of life and I feel that we must search for the cause of this emptiness. I have yet to meet someone who has understood the riddle of life. Lots of theories and strange beliefs, customs and what have you," Cathy said, in deep thought.

"Hey kid," Cathy said. "We are at the gates of something, I just don't know what." She and Peter slowly faded into the arms of sleep.

Peter and Cathy had slept in late when the phone rang,

"Get up you lazy love bees. We have a flight to catch this evening to Zurich." It was John just checking up on them.

"Yes! Jack Daniels never fails to give us that sound sleep. How was your evening yesterday?" enquired Peter.

"I had a great evening with a friend and we caught a show before dinner," John responded.

"He or a she?" asked Peter.

"Why do you want to know?" questioned John.

"Well boss, it is like this. You are also my family. I worry about you.

Cathy and I hope you find your partner of life, so you also can take the Nestea plunge. Know what I mean?" Came the reply from Peter

"All right wise guy! Let's meet for breakfast in twenty minutes." John sounded amused.

Cathy got dressed hurriedly. "Damn! The flight is in the evening. You guys can talk shop during the flight. John is a confirmed bachelor so there is no juicy story awaiting us."

Cathy and Peter suddenly bumped into John as they entered the coffee shop.

"May I introduce Maria? Maria, my dear, these are my sister Cathy and brother-out-law Peter Miller."

Cathy lost her composure in utter surprise. "Well I'll be darned! Nice to meet you, Maria. Where have you been hiding her?"

Peter smiled, also in surprise, wondering at Cathy's reaction.

They settled down at a table, smiling and at a loss of words. Cathy gave John that enquiring and wondering look with a nervous smile.

Finally John broke the surprise. "Maria and I went to the University together and, and...

"And what?" Cathy started to laugh.

"Well, we met again in this wonderful city and...discovered that we really have deep feelings.... aaaa...love for each other." John was struggling for words.

"Really? No Kidding? Well I'll be darned!" Cathy continued.

Peter broke into the strange expressions of surprise. "Maria, sorry, we are very pleasantly surprised because we only know John as a serious guy. All work and no play most all of the time. We just don't know the romantic side of John. What a wonderful surprise."

Maria composed herself and said," John is a super wonderful man. I lost my heart to him when we were in the University. He was so studious and reserved. I felt that I had not made his heart flip, after many attempts. Anyway I never could overcome my love, so I followed his career and stalked him a few times when I visited DC. I purposely bumped into him, several times, but he seemed to have little recall of our encounters in the University. I could not get him out of my mind so I called him and we met yesterday. I was going to pour my heart out to him as a last resort before going to the insane asylum. I really could not prepare for the worst, if he would have said that he was married or he had no feelings of love for me. We met and he kissed me, to my real surprise."

Suddenly Maria looked serious. "There is something you should know. I had a car accident when I went to visit a friend, a girl friend, in Denver. I had rented a car at the airport. It was snowing and all I remember is being hit head on. I lay in the hospital and when I came to, the nurse smiled and said, 'How do you feel Dr? You have a head injury.' My head was all groggy and when all the questioning started I could not remember my name and where I had come from. The policeman and the hospital staff kept calling me Dr Gina Antonelli. When I asked for my belongings, I was given a bag that had clothes which did not look familiar at all. The hospital staff looked at me as if I was plum loco, which in fact did describe my state. They then showed me an ID that was damaged in the accident and the picture looked like me. The name on the ID, barely readable, was Dr Maria Antonelli. I was transferred to the psychiatric ward that dealt with trauma victims. I was on heavy medication. Days turned to weeks and I was transferred to a special clinic that dealt with amnesia. The medical staff and doctors were convinced that I was Dr Gina Antonelli. My amnesia was turning into a horror movie with me trapped in it.

"My friend, who I had visited was informed that I had died in a car accident. My family went into mourning and cremated the mutilated body of the real Dr Antonelli. I was dead for the world.

"My brother and sister were somehow not convinced that I had died in a car accident and continued to investigate. They spent months in Denver going from hospital to hospital showing my photographs when a nurse remembered that she had seen a patient who resembled the photo. She recalled that I had lost my memory. Finally the police department found that there was a case of mistaken identity when the hospital in Boulder, Colorado where the real Dr Antonelli worked had pressed on with their own investigation. The list of missing persons had my photograph, shown as possibly Dr Antonelli.

"Finally one day, I saw my brother and sister walk into my room in the clinic and my memory was jolted. It took me some weeks before I was able to return home and my memory banks have healed. I think. It was a nightmare of an experience that still gives me the chills."

John, Cathy and Peter sat speechless as they heard Maria talk about her nightmare. Maria looked exhausted and John took her in his arms. "It's all over dear, you will be fine and by golly! Gemini Christmas! We all have a plane to catch."

The foursome sat in the plane to Zurich. Cathy wanted to know more about Maria and learnt that Maria's father was Swiss from Lugano and mother, Italian from Milano. Maria was a software engineer, a graduate of Stanford University. The foursome developed a good chemistry on their flight to Zurich.

Maria had a tearful reunion with her parents and family who had come to receive her at the airport.

It did not take long for Maria to get a job with the Swiss government, working on the Meridian project.

The foursome bonded well together and rented a house in the outskirts of Bern, which had two independent apartments. Their work schedules were hectic but their proximity at home greatly helped enjoying whatever free time they could get.

Life moved on. The Meridian technology was developed for operation with satellites by a joint venture between the Swiss and two U.S. companies working with NASA on various space exploration programs. The Joint venture was able to obtain private funding. This was a text book example of how a segment of the private sector arms industry in the world was working together for peace with a minimum operational intervention or hindrances from world politics. The traditional arms manufacturers were getting the message and diverted their efforts in developing environmental technologies with the assistance of UN and other world programs that were struggling to survive in the business of providing essential needs for humanity. There was a socioeconomic boom in implementing programs and projects to eradicate poverty from the face of earth and it was good for the bottom line. The level of terrorism was subsiding to a historically acceptable level. The economic participation increased reducing poverty, increasing education and hope for people.

The UN special task force program to resolve the Palestinian and Israel problems made considerable headway as the two parties started to lock into programs that improved the economies of both countries. There was a measurable growth of peace and economic development. The start of peace between the factions was giving impetus to the region. The role of control and politics by governments began to fade into the role of cooperation and coordination.

The foursome shared their efforts with pride and humility.

Maria walked in the room where Cathy and Peter were talking about the philosophical Outlooks of life.

Maria hugged the two and said, "I have had the fortune in my lifelong search, for the meaning of life, to meet sages in my limited travels around the world. I have begun to realize the difference between soul and mortal life. I realize how much time I have spent in caring about the welfare of my mortal being, which is in transition, and done little for the caring of my soul, which never dies. This realization alone has been a revelation. I have a strong desire for self realization. The sages I met have helped directing my energies to understanding my soul. I have also seen the insignificance of the word "I", as I realize that the almighty creates life and directs every action in this world, and makes no mistakes. I know that I am on the road to Realization but I am not there yet and need help. In my quest for self realization I have become a happier person. This happiness and peace of mind is so different from the mortal happiness that I cannot describe it. "

Cathy's eyes lit up.

"Where does one find a sage, a teacher that can bring us to the path of Self Realization?"

The following week Maria assisted in giving a seminar, while Peter listened in awe as some of the scientists were digging deeper into human behavioral software programs that the Meridian technology had deployed in diffusing the brain energy waves that equate to violent actions. They had retraced some of the brain wave energy simulating it like the Fantastic Voyage. After all the scientists agreed that, the rate of technical progress was doubling every decade, and the capabilities of specific information technologies were almost doubling every year. The exponential growth is such that the 21st century will have made a rate of progress equal to over twenty thousand years in recent history. Some of the scientists felt that in the next decades, given the speed of growth, the non-biological intelligence would match the human intelligence and perhaps even soar past. A frightening thought for many.

The growth in the robotic technologies was replacing humans, a reality once thought as detrimental to the culture and dynamics of human labor.

The continuing acceleration of the information based technologies, coupled with the ability of robotic machines to share the knowledge at horrific speeds, was opening applications that would help human beings all over the world. For instance biotechnologies and genetic engineering sciences could conceivably slow the human aging process. Nanotechnologies such as the nano-robots could repair cells, tissues and human organs including perhaps the brain, resulting in the increased longevity of human beings.

The Meridian technology was creating a growing team of scientists in Switzerland and overseas who saw that the technology base can be rapidly developed to solve many of the Problems facing a growing humanity.

The scientists from the various countries and backgrounds also shared their concerns with their peers on the growing impact that the fast paced technologies was having on the quality of human behavior and values.

Dr C. Raman from India, was deeply concerned that the technology was enslaving the masses that were becoming human machines with little time left in their very busy career lives, to attend to the nourishment of their souls. Technology and its growing array of products and systems was intoxicating the growing educated class who were becoming oblivious to the real meaning and purpose of life.

Dr Peter Magnuson of Norway was repeatedly pointing out his concerns about the loss of peace of mind in his country or for that matter in the northern European countries that was deteriorating the very fabric of life cherished by their cultures.

Dr G. Mogatu of South Africa was convinced that the technology if not harnessed now with deliberation, would destroy the human being.

Professor Dr Davies showed that technology was one way or the other taking religion out of the lives of humanity except in the poor countries. So the reduction of poverty if done blindly with technology would be like taking human beings from one hell of fire to another. Who was paying attention to the human spirit and the development of its quality? It was most likely the job of religion which was in the process of erosion.

The general consensus among several scientists was that technology was a necessary evil but must be developed in specifically harnessed areas that truly benefit and cures the ills created by the blindly developed technologies that have created more problems such as the environmental fiasco. Technology, after all, created an acceleration of the generation of carbon dioxide, pollution and global warming so the technology of trapping CO_2 and returning it into earth should be rapidly developed and implemented. There was an interesting outcome from one of the studies undertaken by the Meridian research group which showed without doubt the dire necessity to have very capable, knowledgeable, highly motivated and well paid talented teachers in the schools that would stop the steep decline in the standard of education in various countries.

Peter sat sipping his Migros `Excellente` brand of Swiss coffee. How strange, he thought, there was no desire for the cigarette and coffee addictive combination he had enjoyed back in his early working years in New Brunswick. He felt so much better having given up smoking, now mounting up to quite some years. Something inside him said that the special Swiss coffee he had grown to love was also addictive. He smiled remembering that he had taken a bag of ground coffee in his travels around the world with his trusted portable coffee filters so he could brew up his pleasure any where in the world. Drinking good coffee was probably a good healthy habit. It sure beat those coffee blends around the world that were a sad excuse for coffee. He wondered how people drank that stuff and did not die. Why some of the stuff was downright insult to the word "coffee."

He was pleased with how life was unraveling in his desire for peace. There was so much he just did not understand about what people referred to as "inner peace." Cathy and for that matter, Maria were also searching for that inner peace. Goodness gracious! So much of life had passed and the inner peace had evaded them or they just lacked understanding and realization. He felt a surge in the desire to fill this vacuum.

The next few days passed with Peter in a daze. It was embarrassing at times in the meetings when some of his associates made comments like, "Where the hell are you?" No, he was not dreaming, but lacked the desire to be "with it." He looked around the table and wondered if any one knew about inner peace. He could follow the general drift of what was being discussed and then one day it happened. It was a coordination meeting and each participant had a prepared statement or summary that he or she was doing. He had tried to start a discussion going but got strange looks as if he was disturbing their set expectations of the meeting.

Suddenly he heard Wilfred say, "Our intelligence shows that some one is working on technology that could disrupt the Meridian technology." Peter made a sign that he wanted to say something and the meeting flow went silent.

"Well, Peter, what is it you want to say?"

Peter looked thoughtful so the meeting participants looked at him in queried patience.

"Does any one here know anything about 'inner peace'?"

There was a brief pause and at least six voices questioned his sanity. Dr Shiela Meyers who was chairing the meeting burst into laughter. Soon all were laughing.

"Peter, for God's sake, what has 'inner peace' to do with the potential threat to the Meridian technology?" asked Dr Meyers.

"Nothing, I suppose, and yet everything," said Peter.

Dr Meyer's face lit up. "Is there a new software program to combat the anti virus, called 'inner peace'? Do you mind enlightening all of us please?"

"Not a bad idea," said Rolf Shamrock, the software whiz, nodding in approval.

A discussion ensued on the possible algorism. The meeting was dispersing and the chairperson looked frustrated at Peter with words to the effect that he was the cause. Some gave Peter thumbs up as they left. Whew, that was a close call, thought Peter.

Dr Shiela Meyers caught up to him in the hall and nudged him into her office, closing the door and locking it.

"All right, Peter, I want an answer to my question you so cleverly avoided. There is time to be serious and there is time to be funny. Which one is it? Is it funny or serious? Do you realize how embarrassing it is for me that new software is being developed right under my nose and I know nothing about it?"

Peter had posed a question, out of context and spent the next minutes quite perplexed on how people had interpreted him. He had to think fast, to see what he could make out of what he had blurted out at the meeting.

"You folks are super genius at developing all kinds of bio intelligence algorithms. I just wanted to know if some one had developed one for 'inner peace'," Peter said.

"You mean the mortal kind or spiritual kind?" Dr Meyers asked, looking perplexed.

"You are about to lose me," said Peter

"There is a program in the Meridian technology that uses a software on 'mortal peace', I think you, as the early pioneer, must know all about it," Dr Meyer replied.

"No. I meant the spiritual peace or inner peace what ever you want to call it," Peter clarified.

"So, you were indeed pulling my leg. Get serious Peter. The spiritual science is nothing like the material science. Only God knows how to write software in the realm of spiritualism. We are mere mortals," Dr Meyers said, as she relaxed.

Shiela Meyers, by now, was very worried. "Has anyone in the higher ups, like perhaps Dr Stanton, asked for the development of a spiritual algorithm for he is the only one I know mad enough to start something like that?"

"No such thing. I am very interested in understanding the spiritual life. You know there are so many teachings, books, great preachers and what have you, but I am still looking. I am a Catholic so I did Sunday school and the whole nine yards but still very ignorant about spiritualism. Do you know what I am talking about?" Peter sounded as if he was pleading.

"Very much, very much. I have had some deep spiritual experiences, including the one week seminar in the Vatican. I went with my parents to Lourds and once to Fatima and came back with respect for the spiritual soul. My first husband was from Algeria. Well he was Algerian and Lebanonese. So I learned a bit about Islam, but not enough, because of what seemed to me quite some differences with what I understood about religion. I too have had extensive exposure to religion but I am still looking. I have read books about inner peace but they are kind of abstract. So the search continues." Shiela Meyers was enjoying their conversation.

Peter could not help noticing tears in her eyes. She looked sad. Shiela was relaxing and continued.

"How strange that we in the academia and research do not discuss about God. Sometimes I feel that I must be an atheist. Some how God and science are at opposites. How did that happen? You are the first one I am talking about God, after what seems like ages, and that only because you broached the subject. You know I was looking at some statistics the other day which reported that less than 20% of Europeans feel themselves religious except during Christmas which is overwhelmingly a commercial experience. Comparatively, about 50% in the U.S. consider themselves religious. These percentages are about the same when it comes to how charitable folks are on both sides of the pond. Who knows how the statistics are cooked up. So easy to distort the truth what ever that is. I have been to the Vatican to celebrate Pascuas. What an enlightening experience to be in the humungous crowds observing mass given by the Pontiff."

"My wife Cathy and my brother's fiancée, Maria, are also searching for the truth, 'inner peace'. We don't know any social groups, other than the Sunday bible class, where God is mentioned," Peter added sadly.

Just then Shiela's secretary brought her mail. Shiela came alive pulling out an invitation from the stockpile of mail.

"Have you been to the IT/Software Conference in Bangalore? I was one of the guest speakers two years ago but I stayed only a day because of other meetings in Delhi and Mumbai scheduled by my previous employer. Let's look at the list of speakers invited.

You are on the list! And so is Hilfiger! And so is Crazy Dr Stanton!! Wow! Did you know?" Shiela was all excited now.

"No idea! I have to check with the Department Administrator, Cathy," Peter was mildly surprised.

Thirty-Six

Cathy looked up at Peter and smiled as she saw Peter walk in to her office.

"Why if it isn't Dr. Peter Miller."

"Honey! Doc Meyer just informed me that I have been..."

"Yes, dearie, the invitation is on your desk. They may change their mind when they find out that you ain't no doctor." Cathy chuckled.

"Don't look at me; I know nothing about the Conference in Bangalore.
I wonder where they found out about me. Must be a mistake. There is probably a Dr. Miller somewhere." Peter sounded confused.

"This is a Information Technology Conference, darling! They are well connected and know, for sure, all about you, down to the size of your socks. I am very proud of you and you can do is give me that famous confused look."

"All I know about IT is that they are a maze of black hard boxes stuffed with softies that everyone uses and no one knows anything about except some genius who designed it in moments of madness." Peter threw up his hands.

Cathy burst into laughter. "Bravo! What a great one liner! Make it your opening line in the speech."

"Yes, but Cathy..." Peter was trying to protest

"What is the big deal? You have been a guest speaker at a great many conferences including in the United Nations, for Pete's sake! Wait a minute, wait a minute, I know you, and it is not about the IT Conference at all!" said the perceptive wife, Cathy.

"I just had a very interesting discussion with Doc Meyers. Did you know..." Peter failed to get his thought across again.

"Excuse me, but you seem to frequently forget giving me a kiss on each cheek, followed by one on the kisser. Remember no short cuts allowed and only genuine stuff is accepted."

"You know, Cathy, I always meant to ask. Why is it that the man has to initiate the kissy kissy stuff and not the woman, especially now that women are so emancipated, equal rights and all that good stuff?" asked a frustrated Peter.

"This custom was created in the pure macho ages when the man took the lead in most all the initiatives as the head of the family. The woman had a secondary role in life and so was the follower and did not want to appear as easy targets, but I will tell you a secret. It is reassuring for most woman, except the bossy types , when the man takes the initiative and does all she wants. You know, like a well-trained puppet that thinks that he is the absolute boss. It is a hard work for the woman to make it happen. History shows how the man was the superior. Guess who wrote the history books? The reality of history is that the woman was and remains always the brains behind the man. Remember the saying that behind every great man is a great woman. The man was the bread earner in history but the woman was the bread maker..."Cathy replied and had more to say.

"All this crap about kissy, kissy." He got up to leave.

"Don't forget to kiss me before you leave." She laughed and pointed her finger at Peter.

"Nope, I no feel like it. I have a headache and I am the new emancipated puppet man." Peter walked out annoyed.

"Sorry Cathy, I thought Peter was here with you." Miranda handed her a letter and waited to see her reaction.

Cathy looked at a letter on a very expensive stock paper. Her eyes widened in amazement. She looked at Miranda who embraced her with tears of joy. The letter was from the Alfred Nobel Foundation informing Peter that he has been selected with Hilfiger for the Nobel Peace Prize.

The news spread within minutes through the department like wild fire. The media calls started flooding Peter's and Hilfiger's offices and the department personnel feverishly looked for both but they had both vanished.

John and Maria came into Cathy's office hoping for some news and she said, "I saw him about half an hour ago in my office. He was preoccupied and I think I upset him even more."

They rushed to the "human tracking office" with hundreds of high tech machines and zillions of monitors. The experts were trying to trace Peter and Hilfiger and the tracker to their own amazement suddenly went dead. The tracer system showed that both walked out of Hilfiger's office down to the lobby of the department building, out of the building into a taxi, which head towards the Federal Platz (Plaza) and suddenly the tracer went dead. The Police had been immediately alerted and they had set road blocks around the city. The taxi driver who picked up the two rides reported that he was taking his ride to the Federal Platz. The tracer elements were scanning the government offices. In seconds the security officer from the defense ministry reported that Hilfiger and Peter had an appointment to meet the Council member Mr. Johann Peter Pletcher but had not showed up. Their tracer scan, which overlapped the area surrounding the Federal Platz, showed that they were not in the area.

The Meridian main tracer system had lost them when they sat in the taxi and set an alarm which immediately required all taxi call centers to check the locations of all taxis in the immediate area. All taxis were accounted for except for the one being searched. Some external energy had zapped all the communications in the taxi carrying Peter and Hilfiger.

Minutes later reports came in that the Police had found the taxi and the driver who was sitting at the wheel but was not responding because of trauma. The driver was rushed to the hospital and the specialists from the Meridian Department were examining him.

The driver regained conscious and remembered that he suddenly lost control of the taxi and himself. The taxi came to a stop near the exit park to the federal Platz. He remembered that the doors opened and the two gentlemen got out and boarded a strange looking van which vanished seconds later. There were no fresh tire tracks reported by the investigators where the apparent kidnapping took place. The special Meridian stealth Tracers were searching for stealth material but came out negative.

The press reported that perhaps Peter and Hilfiger were on a special security mission and unavailable for comments. All the intelligence agencies around the world were on alert and communicating with each other.

John, Maria, and Cathy sat in the situation room of the Meridian Department, observing and listening to reports coming in. Over six hours had passed without a trace.

John could not contain his composure "This is all like the repeat of the bad kidnapping cycles in the U.S. It is not supposed to happen to us here in Switzerland with the latest state of art tracers in full operation."

Peter was gradually coming to and was lying in a bed. Hilfiger was also coming to and lying in another bed near. They surveyed the room which had no doors no walls and they could hear the evening traffic noise and see the city of Bern lights down under. A holographic text came on.

Welcome to the new space age technology. We hope you are somewhat rested. Please help yourself to the food and drinks on the table.

Hilfiger walked around and said, "Who are you and what do you want from us?"

The holograph text replied;

We are very pleased with all your peace efforts around the world. Keep up the good work. We must warn you, however, that there are evil forces that are working against the peace lovers of the world and may succeed. You know just when you have a great mouse trap someone comes up with a better one. That is how it is. Look around you. The room you are in is set in a different space dimension. It appears as if you are floating over the city. In fact you are. The air temperature around you is controlled for your comfort. Imagine how cold it is outside in the city. Peter looked at his watch. It was over 6 hours since he remembers leaving with Hilfiger for the meeting.

"I am impressed by your technology. Who are you? Why can't we see you? What can we do for you since you also talk of peace? How can we work towards the common cause…?" said Peter.

"Peter," said Hilfiger. "I have been reading your response on this holograph, before you even spoke. This is a far more sophisticated mind reader than the Meridian."

Yes you are right. Your system can read and discern aggressive behavior. We are just faster. We are worried that evil forces are working on a system that will totally control human behavior without the human being even suspecting it. Yes the ultimate nightmare. You must stay ahead otherwise all is lost.

There are different forms of life in the other planets in your solar system, which are observing your world. These different forms of life in these other planets, like yours, have good and bad energies. Your scientists are just beginning to become aware that there are millions of other universes with their own sun etc. We are way ahead of you. Let's say we are wiser. The ultimate forces of all kinds of life are under the control of a power, you call God.

The humans have a power not readily available on other planets. This power is the spiritual energy that was at one time very strong, and is now weak. It is reaching a dangerous level that will make the human being a total slave of the evil energies.

Increase the genuine spirituality in your world. It is the only true powerful protection against your enemies. We cannot help you in the world of spirituality, so we will be watching and trying to learn.

Remember we read your thoughts all the time. We will communicate with you in text as we are doing now. No one else will be able to see the text. We are selecting some more human beings, who are spiritual, to work with you both. You will know them soon.

You will wake up in bed while the world is looking for you.

Peter was just getting his bearings when the bedroom lights came on suddenly blinding him.

"Where the hell have you been, Peter? We have been worried sick! Thank God you are safe. Maria, John and I have spent the last seven hours in the situation room and suddenly received a signal from your transmitter showing you at home. Hilfiger is also at home." Cathy collapsed in his arms and sobbed.

Thirty-six

Cathy was still in bed when Peter left for the office. He called Hilfiger, who was in the office.

"We should coordinate our story about our sudden disappearance, Mr. Hilfiger," Peter said.

Hilfiger shook Peter's hands and looked at him. Destiny had put them through an unrivaled experience. They both stood and shared the moment in silence.

Hilfiger spoke slowly. "Please, call me Hans." He shook Peter's hand.

Peter remembered the Swiss tradition of calling someone by the first name, only after a mutual trust of friendship had been established. It was always the elder of the two who proposed the *per du* (on first names) as they drank a beer, interlocking their arms that held the beer glasses. It is an interesting tradition, slowly fading, as the Swiss enter the world of globalization. Peter recalled how the Swiss in the Swiss company in New Brunswick, felt somewhat uneasy when they were addressed by their first names without the European ceremony. All this fuss about the first name, he thought.

"How about we say that the incident was a malfunction of our personal transmitters. That's it," he said, reassuringly.

"Hans we did not show up for the meeting with Mr. Pletscher. We cannot cook up a story because great minds will drill it with holes. Let us relate our experience at least in a closed session, to a select few in the organization," Peter proposed.

"What about the rest of the Meridian team? They will wonder and guess at first and then write it off as something 'top secret'. Ah! What the hell, let's be open and tell, as we lived it. The main message I got, was that our defense against the aliens is spirituality. It will help in spreading the word." Hans sounded that this was the right thing to do.

"They may not believe us. So what! We do not have to convince any one. Our reputations are not of storytellers. After all, honesty is the best policy. Congratulations on winning the Nobel Peace prize. To tell you the truth, I do not feel that I have achieved anything. I am not happy as people around me are. What do you think is the problem?" Hans sat down as if he was drained of energy.

Peter smiled and said, "No wonder ! You are very spiritual, so the mortal achievements mean little to you." Peter smiled and started to laugh with Hans.

There was excitement in the department that Peter and Hans had not disappeared forever. The technical department brought replacement transmitters for Peter and Hans, unable to explain the mal function. There was a rush of people in the office corridor waiting to see them. Finally Swiss Council President Dr Pletscher walked in to their offices, surprising Peter and Hans.

"Congratulations, you Nobel Laureates from all of us and from a proud nation!"

Hans Hilfiger immediately thanked the Council President while Peter looked on, as he tried to fathom their experience.

There were photo opportunities, speeches and cocktails. Peter could not relate with the celebrations. He was overwhelmed and humbled as the co-recipient of the Noble prize for Peace when there were so many who contributed to making the Meridian a reality. His insides cried as he remembered his granddad who had lost his life, protecting the weapon of peace.

Peter never had a great respect for the founder of the Nobel Foundation. This fellow created dynamite, which created industries for its manufacture and sale all over the world. Peter wondered how many innocent lives have been lost and maimed all over the world. How come the world acknowledged the prize as prestigious? Alfred Nobel earned so many millions, years ago by selling dynamite that he has left a legacy to pay out a million to each great mind for an outstanding achievement/ contribution in areas of science and technology, economics and peace. What a shameful irony and legacy. A possible shamed ego, riddled with guilt, rewarding brilliant achievements every year.

"Hey! Get with it! You are being honored and you are walking around like a zombie! What is the matter with you? You disappeared yesterday and how about an explanation and an apology?" It was John fuming at Peter.

Peter looked at Cathy and Maria who also looked angry at him. He started for the exit door and felt people patting him and shaking his hand as he moved out. He came out to the main office lobby and faced a battery of cameras flashing and reporters wanting him to make a statement or two. He really wanted to run but decided to say and exchange a few pleasantries.

"Can you explain your disappearance with Councilor, Hilfiger?" asked a reporter

"Why, yes indeed!" He started to make a full disclosure of the experience, but could not finish all he wanted to say, because the impatient press and onlookers wanted to ask questions before hearing the full story.

"The taxi driver reported that he was in a state of shock from some energy zap and that you two, he remembers, left in some van…"

"The taxi drivers recollection is correct . We are very proud about the Nobel Peace Prize but I would like to say that this award is for all the people who have been responsible for making the Meridian Peace Weapon become a reality."

"So where did you go in the van and why did you leave the taxi driver alone?" the reporter persisted.

"I am sorry that I cannot expand on my answer because there is national security involved. The whole story will be released to the public, shortly. Thank you." He made a dash out of the crowd. He walked briskly to the basement garage and as he was about to open the car door.

"You are lying through your teeth." The reporter had followed him.

"You are one arrogant and rude reporter, and make sure you print that! Please talk to our press chief."

"No, no. I am sorry. I did not mean to be rude. I am sorry. It is my first major reporting story and I thought that I might get a story by shocking you," said the reporter looking a bit sheepish.

"Did you hear anything I said in my statement earlier? If you think I am lying, then print the truth. There is enough sensational news in what I said." Peter was cool as he faced the reporter, who then decided to leave instead.

Peter shook his head and drove off.

There was a welcoming committee when he got home. Cathy, Maria, and John looked up at him, congratulated and embraced him.

John spoke. "Sorry for my behavior at the party. Hans Hilfiger, took us to the side after the party and told us all what happened to you two." We are not going to discuss this out of our foursome group as requested by Hans, until he releases a statement to the public.

Maria, could not contain herself, "Who do you think they were? Could you see any of the people who talked to you? They probably used a new dimension in the holographic technology. You were probably all in a room and they projected everything into a holograph."

"Great! Let me know when you have figured it out. Sorry, I hate to break the party, but I am going to sleep. I am so tired."

Next morning, Cathy came up to him at breakfast.

"Darling! What is it? You are not your usual self! What did you want to tell me about Dr Meyers the other day when I side tracked you".

"I wanted to tell you that I have the feeling that Dr Meyers knows a lot about 'inner peace'. I find that my thirst for the spiritual knowledge is increasing and frankly I am getting frustrated," Peter said.

"Hey! I almost forgot to tell you that Ram Barua, you remember, from the UN Program on Israel and Palestinians, is in town and will join us all for a Fondue Bourguignon dinner tonight," interrupted Cathy. "Darling you remember him, don't you?" Cathy asked, embracing Peter

"Yes, I do but what does he have to do with 'inner peace'?" Peter sounded miffed

"It should be a sleepy evening for me because Ram only talks shop. I hope he does not bring Ben Sargons with him. That will be a gas!"

Ram was very punctual for the dinner. He pointed out that he had made a special effort since the Swiss are very punctual.

"In India, we are quite terrible about arriving on time. I know that the Latinos and South Americans are not far behind on bad punctuality. Must have something to do with warm, climate, and lethargic behavior. By the way, Greetings from the UN Program team. Ben was sorry that you did not invite him."

Cathy and Peter burst into laughter with Maria and John looking confused.

They all sat down to an evening of Fondue Bourguignon when Ram announced that he was a vegetarian. Cathy was terribly embarrassed and prepared a lavish salad for him instead.

Ram talked about his recent travels to the Middle East and how peace seems to be coming to the region. He was very assertive that the politicians were the main source of the problems and now that it is a people to people initiative, there was real hope for the future.

Cathy suddenly changed the subject. "Hey Ram! What can you enlighten us on the subject of 'inner peace'?"

"What is this? A trick question? No, I guess you are serious."

"Yes, yes," confirmed Peter.

"Inner peace comes from knowledge of God. There is no peace in the material world, especially not 'inner peace'. Yoga and similar exercises do help in calming the mind and balancing the body functions, but the calmness one feels is temporary. The human being comprises of a material body and a soul. The former is material, as we all experience it, and the latter is spiritual. The material part lives a certain period of time and then dies but the soul never dies.

"The human body and the world/Universes around us represents material life which we know is temporary and in transition. The material life therefore starts when we are conceived and then goes on the automatic mode. The human being has no control over the life cycle process and yet the human being makes great efforts to control it. It is the cycle of birth and then death. The human being spends a whole life time totally engrossed, in strangely enough something that is only temporary.

"The soul is a sparkle of God, without which there is no life. Human life starts when the soul enters the body and dies when the soul leaves. It is all according to a timetable set by the Divine.

"The only purpose of life is to focus the soul in search of realization of God. Once on track with pure determination, God guides it through to salvation. The mere realization of the existence of God and his wonders, starts the desire to know him and then as your knowledge of God grows, you fall in love with God. The 'inner peace' is the spiritual peace experienced by the soul which increases with the knowledge of God Realization.

"The human being, by nature, wants to be genuinely happy. Material happiness merely frustrates him. Spiritual happiness, in which you are in the service of God, brings true peace.

"I hope I am making some sense to you!"

Cathy, Peter, Maria and John were impressed and remained absorbed in Ram's discourse.

"Is there a Hand Book for all this knowledge?" enquired John

"Yes, my Hand Book is the Gita, which is the teachings of Lord Krisna to his disciple Arjun. Similarly, it is the Bible for a Christian, Koran for a Muslim, Torah for the Jew and so on."

Peter felt a mild sense of relief; he had not felt in ages. It was as if the dark veil of ignorance was lifting. He smiled.

Ram continued, "Peter, I saw your name on the list of the guest speakers at the IT Conference in Bangalore. I know a very learned scholar who taught Theology at the University. Call on him and he can really get you started. You should read the Gita, before meeting the Scholar, Mr. Gopal Krishnan. I have an extra copy in the hotel and I will send it to you."

Peter was all charged up. Peter read the Gita with Cathy everyday in the mornings and evenings. It was confusing without someone to guide them. The names were very foreign and they were stuck very frequently, but made notes on passages , verses requiring explanations. The conscientious attempts started to reap its reward and they felt that they could understand the teachings. It was surprising that reading the Gita was an eye opener.

Thirty-seven

Bangalore in India was a revelation in itself. The throngs of crowds everywhere, was overwhelming. They settled down in the Hotel Taj which they selected because of its proximity to the Conference.

Peter was one of the early speakers. He spoke about the great strides made in the world to improve communications. The progress was very evident. There was a great variety and substance on the World Wide Web, serving the world community as the super highway. People to people all over the world now communicated, in ever increasing numbers, which is very remarkable.

Peter expressed his concerns at the loss of human-to-human contact. The typical employee sat in front of the monitor and communicated with the world, day after day, reducing physical and eye contacts with fellow employees. The constant deployment of the computer was causing various incidents of physical fatigue. The ailments were more pronounced in employees who were older. The computer was becoming a necessary work tool like a pencil or pen.

The volume of information was getting overwhelming so that it was reducing the thinking and reaction time element required for making decisions. Emailing, very often pressured the employees for fast responses. Peter cited an example of how the computer was able to take the input from its sensors and rapidly spit out results in technical operations but without the human assessment and feelings. The reliance on computers was increasingly so fast that the human being had started to become an absolute slave. The sophisticated software programs, often outwitted the human capabilities. At this rate, unless the IT industry paid attention, the human race would become a slave of the robot computer. All business decisions in the IT industry should consider the value and quality of the human element, in its progress. History, specially the industrial renaissance has shown that a few select leaders blinded by greed and what they considered progress caused irreparable damage to human and other forms of life.

The environment was a classic example of this irresponsible growth.

Peter closed his speech by talking about the sage man in India who was astonished to see the material growth in the country and remarked that there were an increasing number of his fellow countrymen who worked incredibly hard, made a lot of money and then spent money in later years for the bad health.

The speech did not go well with the conference participants. The press made guarded comments that Peter was reflecting on the negative aspects of the IT industry. The only press that picked up Peter's message was the local Times newspaper, which repeated the caution expressed by Peter as a significant factor in the detriment of human behavior and value. Some of the friendly faces he met before making his speech were avoiding eye contact with him. Peter was not surprised because this proved his observation that most of the world had a vast number of followers and just a few leaders with vision who either made human life better or simply increased the linings in their pockets.

The national news media lauded Peter's speech at the Bangalore Conference on IT. They cited that he was a Nobel Laureate and a man with a vision.

"Darling, the IT industry will never invite you again as a guest speaker. I am sure that you touched a nerve deep in the hearts of the great IT leaders you met. You said nothing about the Meridian! How come?" Cathy remarked.

"I do not know the IT language of the Meridian Project. I would leave it to our experts. Some folks did query me about this and that but soon found out that I was quite ignorant. They probably wondered about, who invited me to the IT conference," Peter responded.

Peter called the telephone number of Mr. Gopala Krishnan, Ram had given him. To his chagrin the person who took the call spoke almost no English. He managed to leave his name and hotel Taj as a contact. He felt desperate since Ram did not have the address. Never mind he thought, this country is oozing with great sages and gurus and he was going to find one. The lady at the front desk looked surprised at Peter's request for a guru on the Gita.

"Perhaps I can help you and your wife" sounding confident. She gave simple one liner responses when Peter started reading the questions. The lady, finally, looked at the questionnaire and decided to seek help. The crowd around the front desk in the hotel was getting larger so Peter and Cathy decided to sit in the lounge.

"Excuse me, I am Gopala Krishnan. Are you looking for me? My cousin understood you when you called the other day but he cannot speak English well enough to be understood." Peter and Cathy were thrilled as they stood up to greet.

Peter and Cathy invited Gopala Krishnan to their hotel room to escape the increasing noise level in the lobby and lounge.

Gopala Krishnan was a very humble, simple man and was dressed in the traditional garb. His face was bright and his eyes reflected wisdom and knowledge. He looked in his early sixties and they were surprised when Gopala said that he had just turned 80.

Gopala listened very patiently as Cathy and Peter poured out their desire for spiritual knowledge and suddenly realized that Gopala had not said a word.

"It is wonderful that you seek spiritual knowledge, but why?" He sounded somewhat amused.

"We strongly feel that we have had a very exciting and very eventful life so far but we have always felt empty and it took us years to realize that we had been looking for happiness in the material and not the spiritual world. After we met Ram, we started reading the Gita, as he suggested. It has been very difficult but we are determined. We feel that there is great depth in the teachings of Krishna and we desperately need a teacher to help us through." Said Peter

"Have you read the Holy Bible?" asked Gopala.

"Yes," came their unsure response.

Gopala said, "It is very important to have a good teacher. The knowledge in the Holy Bible is about God. The other day I talked to a holy man whose knowledge of the Holy Koran was truly exemplary. It becomes very simple when one understands the teachings of God. God resides in us but we go looking for him all over. A good teacher is one who is truly a devotee of God and has surrendered to Him. You recall having teachers in school and later in the university who made the subject very interesting and could explain the subject matter in such simple terms and language. You fell in love with subjects you really did not care for, when you started, because the teacher knew the subject very well and had the gift to impart knowledge.

"Remember, while a great teacher was always necessary, you still had to do the hard work. It is the same with the spiritual knowledge. If you are devoted, the Lord takes your hand and guides you through the knowledge of God. Knowledge, by itself, does not satisfy but knowledge with devotion to God brings you eternal peace. After all, God realization is a very clear understanding that God creates and controls the universes and all the forms of life that is created. All what has happened, is happening and will happen is His will. We human beings cannot change His will. He creates and runs the entire show from A to Z. We are instructed to live good, clean lives and He takes care of the results/reactions of our deeds, which are not in our hands anyway. What He does is always good and He never makes any mistakes. So what is it we worry and struggle about in life when we understand that it is all in his hands? So, Spiritual knowledge helps us understand that the only purpose of life is therefore God Realization.

'Seek and ye shall find', as it says in the Holy Bible. The knowledge of God removes the darkness that blinds us from the truth, and we then see Him everywhere which gives us immense happiness and peace."

Gopala suggested that Peter and Cathy live a few days in the *Ashram* where he lived so that they could start by experiencing simple life and attend the lectures by very good teachers. The *Arti,* (praying) and *kirtana* (singing about praises to God) would give them a good base to study the scripture of spiritual science.

The ashram was located on a beautiful, hilly farm land with huts.

"We are almost self sufficient on the farm. We grow our vegetables and grains. We have wells on the farm and we also have a school for the children," Gopala explained, as he gave them a guided tour.

The typical day, started in the morning at 6:00 am, and after washing up, prayers and kirtan followed in a very simple constructed temple. The temple had statues of saints, prophets from all religions with Krishna's statue in the center stage. Breakfast was milk or herbal tea with home made breads and butter. There were plenty of fruits. Lectures on scriptures followed until lunch which was rice, bread, dal (lentil) and two vegetables. The afternoon was for rest, discussions or helping out in the farm. The evening program started with kirtan (singing hyms) followed by puja (prayers), Arti and discourses on the Holy Books.

Peter and Cathy became overwhelmed by the environment and the program. Gopala sat with both of them studying the Gita and answering their questions.

They spent a week and had to return to their 'normal' life in Switzerland. They had a taste of what spiritual peace was all about. John and Maria were anxious to hear about their visit.

Thirty-eight

Peter heard that a learned scholar of the Hindu scriptures was giving a lecture at the college hall in Bern. The word on Cathy and Peter's experience in the Ashram had spread so the turn out at the lecture was a large one with a large contingent from the Meridian Project Department.

The scholar was David Hurschler who was a scientist in Microbiology and after many active years in research and development had given up and made a tour around the world studying scriptures of different religions. Hurschler had an aura of wisdom, like Gopala Krishnan. The auditorium was charged with a wonderful energy. Huschler had become a true disciple of God. Peter and Cathy felt as if their experiences with Gopala Krishnan were about to repeat again. The taste of spirituality was very addictive indeed.

Hurschler spoke. "I have traveled extensively studying the eastern spiritual cultures most specifically Taoism, Buddhism, Jainism and Hinduism. I found that I could relate to Hinduism, because I have always believed in reincarnation of the soul. The Vedas in Hinduism are like a handbook on how life should be lived. The word Veda means, 'the complete knowledge'. The Vedas, it is believed, were written about 5000 years ago. In reality the Vedas are, time immemorial. They are words spoken by God and hence ageless. We know from the scriptures that the teachings, like the Vedas were passed down ages , by a succession of chosen sages, demi Gods, what the scriptures call the *Parampara* system. These chosen sages had achieved God Realization and were exemplary in all respects. These sages taught the true version of the teachings of God and made no changes or interpretations.

"The Vedas were written by the great Vyasadeva, also known as the literary incarnation of God. Vyasadeva also wrote the great epic Mahabharata which is about the battle between the sons of two brothers, Pandava and Kaurava. Lord Krishna, who incarnates himself is a friend of both the brothers and plays the neutral role of the chariot driver of his Pandava friend Arjuna. The Bhagawat Gita is the teaching of God, Lord Krishna to his friend Arjuna before the start of the battle between the sons of Pandavas and Kauravas.

"The concept of interpretations is very important, because it tends to distort from the true, I mean pure, words of God. Each one of us has a unique nature and we behave, act, think etc. according to our nature. We therefore interpret according to our nature, which distorts the purity of the word of God.

"Our nature depends on our past *karmas,* or in other words our past deeds. We improve and build on our nature, by educating ourselves with mortal knowledge to bring happiness into our lives. This happiness, being mortal happiness, is regrettably short lived, by its very definition. We do not know that, so we keep moving ahead in life seeking for happiness over and over again, only to find that it is transitory. We get frustrated and try to seek a better formula so that this happiness lasts forever.

"Those of us, who seek happiness with deliberation, find that there is something wonderful that happens to us when we experience, spirituality. So getting a taste of spirituality, which fills us with an inexplicable wonderful feeling, starts to become a habit. This taste of spirituality is uniquely different from the mortal happiness we experience frequently. Our nature starts to get hooked to spirituality. So we continue our quest for spirituality and seek pure knowledge, becoming aware of our soul and the presence of God everywhere. Our spiritual happiness starts to increase as we progress in the knowledge of God. We observe that our ego fades away and we become detached from the results of our actions, when we concentrate on deeds in the service of God only. The attainment of knowledge of God, makes us realize that God is really everywhere down to the smallest particle, atom, and He is running the show. We become blissful, happy, compassionate all the time and remain in the service of God. The final result is that we do not reincarnate and thus live in the abode of God, when he leaves this mortal body. This is the goal of life.

"The teachings of God in summary say that He is the Creator of the Universes and is always perfect. All events in life happened according to His will. He makes no mistakes. The reincarnation of the souls was dependent on the quality of life the soul had lived. The sole purpose of human life, the most intelligent of all life forms, was to achieve God Realization. God gave the human being the intelligence to discern between good and bad if the human being listened to his or her consciousness. Material life is by definition painful and miserable from birth. The knowledge of God, therefore freed the human being from all the suffering and he or she then lived out the life, never to return. The human being is born with an ingrained nature depending on the deeds of the previous life. This nature if utilized for God Realization frees it from the material world otherwise it recycles or reincarnates again and again until God Realization is achieved.

"I understand that most of you in the audience are scientists. The scriptures I read gave a lot of detail information on the Creation of the Universes. Let me outline, for instance, the earthly and celestial calendars, which give a dimension of time and the age of the current Creation. I hope that it will interest you:

"There are four earthly yugs (ages) in the cycle of civilization.

Satyug has the longest duration in the cycle and is 1,728,000 years long. This cycle is the most pious when peace and prosperity flourishes. Life is tranquil and very spiritual. Most human beings attain an age of about 10000 years or longer.

Tretayug the next longest cycle is 1,296,000 years. The quality of life starts to deteriorate.

Dvarpayug is 864,000 years long and in this age the quality of life continues its downward trend.

Kalayug is the shortest of the four yugs and is 432,000 years long**.** We are living in this yug.

The culprit, that sets the deterioration in the quality of life, is the human ego. This ego diminishes as our knowledge of God increases.

One set of these four earthly yugs is called a Celestial Yug. The measure of time of the celestial is 360 times longer than on the earth. In other words, a day and night of 24 hours of the celestials is equivalent to one terrestrial year. One celestial month consists of 30 earthly months, and 360 earthly years, constitute one celestial year. 12,000 of such celestial years go to form a celestial Yug or one *Mahayug*. Therefore one Mahayug is equal to12,000 x 360 or 4,320,000 human years.

"A 1000 of such celestial yugs make one day (*Kalpa)* in the life of Brahma, or 4,320,000,000 human years. The night (*Pralaya*) of Brahma is of the same length. The day of Brahma is the period of the creation and the night is the period of dissolution.

"30 cycles of such days and nights, make a Brahmic month.
12 such Brahmic months make one Brahmic year.
100 such Brahmic years constitute the span of life of Brahma.

"So the total duration of Brahma's life in terms of human years is:
311 Trillions of human years.

"I read in a recent article on spirituality, that it is estimated that our Creation is about 158 Trillion years old. I would like to give you some more specifics on creation.

"At the time of creation, the Lord spoke the teachings (Vedas) to Brahma, the first mortal living in the universe. Brahma was born from the navel of God and empowered to create everything under the direction of the Lord. Material elements, both subtle and gross were activated and 8,400,000 species of life were created. God created in fact a management team, consisting of Brahma (the creator), Vishnu (the maintainer/preserver) and Shiva (the destroyer)."

In closing his talk on spirituality, David Hurschler said that the teachings of God in the Bhagawat Gita were the nectar of life. Reading and meditating on the teachings in the Gita with the help of a enlightened teacher, would lead to God Realization. He emphasized that knowledge with devotion were essential in the path of Realization.

Peter and Cathy met several who attended the lecture on the Vedas and found that the level of interest and knowledge was extensive. It was very interesting to share their thoughts with many, some of whom taught theology in colleges in Switzerland.

Thirty-nine

Peter found a note on his desk that Hilfiger wanted to see him.

"I have been rethinking about the Peace Prize and I read your comments to the press that the Meridian pioneers and the workforce should be the true recipients. I agree with you wholeheartedly. The Nobel Prize Committee has advised that the award will be shared equally between you and me. I tried to explain about our intention and had the impression that they leave it to us on what we do with the sharing of the award after it is made. The alternative would be we could make the entire sum we receive as a donation on behalf of Meridian to the Swiss charities that care for children all over the world. We can put it to the Meridian Board for approval," Hans proposed.

"I think it is a great idea, Hans," Peter responded.

"By the way the Indian and Pakistani teams negotiating the Kashmir dispute have invited us to discuss the use of the Meridian peace weapon. We tested the system about five times in a border area where terrorists cross the border. The terrorists were shocked and the Pakistani army carried the trouble makers to jail. The terrorists are in the market looking for some weapons to counter the Meridian. Why don't you go instead of John whom we need here on several matters under negotiations?" said Hans. "Hurry back so we can go next week to Oslo for receiving the Nobel Peace Prize." Peter left his office.

John's reaction to the suggestion was luke warm.

"I do not feel that the sides feuding are ready to find a solution. The intelligence the department has is rather negative on any chances of success. The other problem is that India and Pakistan want full operational control of the Meridian weapon and you know that's impossible. The United Nations committee that coordinates the Meridian applications and operations considers any dialogue a wasted effort in the region. Peter, why don't you do an independent investigation on this age old conflict?"

Peter thought a moment and said, "Okay, chief."

Ram Barua at the UN arranged meetings for Peter to test the water.

"I am jealous that you are going to New York which is also my favorite city, but I am overloaded so next time perhaps. Please do not have a great time without me." Peter kissed Cathy before heading to the airport.

Peter had just settled down in the seat when the stewardess asked him if he could exchange his seat so that a couple can travel together. Peter obliged.

The woman sitting next to Peter gazed at him. Peter felt uncomfortable and even smiled at her, but the gaze penetrated.

"Hi, I am..." Peter thought of being polite.

"Yes, I know who you are; Mr. Peter Miller of the Swiss department of defense in the Meridian section."

"Nice to meet you..."Peter was now surprised.

"I am Miranda Mala from the UN security office in Geneva."

Peter decided to cool it and started to read. He felt her repeated gaze in his direction with her piercing large eyes. Peter was on his second drink of the delicious Dole du Valais. One of the group of executives sitting together near Peter looked at Peter and came up to him.

"Mr. Miller, congratulations. It is an honor to travel with you." And the whole section sitting nearby stood up to clap and congratulate Peter. They were all very chatty and Peter saw a chance to escape from the staring eyes. He sat with one of the groups who were going on a medical convention to New York and were in a celebrating mood. Time flew and the flight landed in New York. Peter saw how the lady who sat next to him earlier followed him until he took a cab to the Grand Hyatt Hotel, in New York.

Ram met Peter at the hotel and they went to the bar for a drink. Ram talked about the arrangements he had made with the Indian and Pakistani insiders who could brief Peter. Quite suddenly, Peter caught sight of Miranda Mala staring at him. She was sitting on the opposite side of the U-shaped bar. Peter told Ram about the incident and Ram suggested that he would enquire from the Geneva office on who she really was. Ram had to leave and Peter was tired and decided to call it the day. She crossed his path as he walked to the elevators.

"Yes, I am stalking you. I am sorry to be such a pain. Please give me a few moments of your time. I am a Kashmiri," she said.

So it was back to the bar. Peter was annoyed but did not want to show his emotions. He decided to let her speak and she did.

"Mr. Miller, I work in the United Nations in Geneva. I am part of a group of Indians and Pakistani in the UN in Geneva who are very anxious to find a solution to the Kashmir dispute. The administrations in both the countries have no trust in each other and the stalemate has become worse. There are several Kashmiri concerned citizens who are trying to get the parties to the table but all such attempts have resulted in bitter failure. The people who suffer the most are the Kashmiri whose land has been split by India and Pakistan.

"The so-called terrorists are a mix of genuine freedom fighters and some bad elements. These groups are all Muslims, just as the majority in Kashmir now. The non-Muslims are minorities and afraid of being harassed because they refuse to leave. There are plenty of Kashmiri non-Muslims who moved to India over the years following the partition in 1947. They too long to return to their homeland but have lost hope. It is getting worse since the Muslims on the two sides of the divide are getting into conflicts with each other instead of uniting for the common cause.

"The use of the Meridian weapon gave us all hope of seeing peace in our life time. Both the warring countries are not willing to lose their edge over the other. They have at least agreed to discuss with the Swiss government on feasible solution for peace. Regrettably, both sides, in spite of the good results in keeping terrorists out, want to control the use of the Meridian weapon. So we are heading for a stalemate again because we know that neither the Swiss nor the UN will allow the operation and control in the hands of India or Pakistan. Please help us." Miranda looked exhausted with tears flowing down her cheeks.

"Wow, sister! That is a tough cookie. Do you folks have any ideas of how to reach a breakthrough? Well, OK, will try my best with our very capable team, to come up with some proposals," Peter said, reassuringly.

Forty

Peter met with two senior officials from the legations of Pakistan and India. They were defensive and used the political wobbly-gook language.

He later met a very senior UN official, from India and got a lecture on the history of India and the Kashmir conflict. Peter decided to have another UN official, from Pakistan, to join in the discussions.

Peter listened for about 15 minutes, as both debated and then said, "I can understand the people who represent the interests of their country are defensive but I fail to understand you who represent the UN are no different than the gentlemen I met this morning. Don't tell me that there is no one who can find a solution, with all the brains that are in the two countries. Don't you think that while you sit and debate, forever, the poor citizens of Kashmir who have been separated are dying? What do the Kashmiri want or does anyone even care?

"Let me tell you that all the Kashmiri I met told me that they don't want their land to be split into two regions. They do not want to be a part of Pakistan or of India. They want to develop a country that can trade and live with their Pakistan and Indian neighbors and the international community.

"Apparently no one learns from history, which teaches us, that you cannot rule people against their wishes. How can you forget the British

Raj? Just look at Korea. What a tragedy for the people in the North and South. Did you not learn from the human tragedy of one people divided into two countries after the British finally left?"

The two UN officials listened and shook their heads in agreement.

"So, Mr. Miller, what do you suggest we do?" asked one of them, in a challenging tone.

"You tell me, sir! Help me so that I can help you. I can't understand that there is no genuine resolve, or am I wrong? Are you going to solve the problem or are you part of the problem? Is there no innovation in either country? Is the conflict a chess game with the Kashmiri, the pawns?" Peter responded with some irritation.

The two officials were now clearly disturbed by Peter's comments.

Then one said, "How about if I tell you that the two countries have run out of innovative solutions? The terrible thing is that India does not want any country mediating the dispute."

The other official jumped in, "Who can mediate? It will only complicate the issues by an outsider."

"I have an idea that I would like to explore with you tomorrow. Can we meet in the morning, say 10:00am?" asked Peter, in a tired voice.

Peter strolled back to the hotel, catching a breath of some New York air. He had barely reached the hotel entrance when Miranda grabbed his arm.

"How did it go?" she asked, in a voice full of expectations.

"Well the problem is solved," Peter said, with a wink.

"How? What? What is the solution? Please, please, tell me." Miranda was very excited at the prospects of peace.

"I am just kidding, Miranda, but I have two ideas that could work? Let me test them on you. You don't mind being the guinea pig?" Peter said with a smile.

"No, no, I would rather play the devil's advocate. We consider Pigs a very dirty animal in my country," she responded, almost insulted.

The two sat in the lounge with a drink. Peter collected his thoughts and spoke.

"Numero Uno proposal, is that both countries open the dividing border in Kashmir so that the Kashmiri people can once again be united as one. Both Pakistan and India should infuse aid, to build the infrastructure and develop the region. The Kashmiri people would be allowed to move freely into Pakistan and India. No time table should be set for a final solution on Kashmir. Let the Kashmiri people build their own form of government and move freely. I feel that the problem will go away after some years without the pressure from either Pakistan or India. A Win-win solution for all peace loving people. The Swiss, under the UN flag, will help with the Meridian technology to keep any insurgents from destroying the peace."

Miranda was thoughtful and then said, "As a Devil's advocate, I love the idea."

They both laughed, and Peter somewhat nervously.

"What is the second proposal?" Miranda enquired.

"Let the UN randomly pick ten young men and women from Pakistan and India, who are in their teens or so. Let the Kashmiri likewise select randomly twenty of their youth. The UN then creates a work area for small workshops for all the youth to meet and organize there agendas and come up with a solution or two, acceptable to the thirty youth participants. The workshop should be in some remote area of Kashmir. Let the youth decide their future and then put it to vote in Kashmir. The results would then be binding to all parties. How you like them apples, kiddo?" Peter said with a good feeling about his ideas. Miranda's deeply thoughtful facial expression gradually turned to a broad smile.

"You are every bit what I heard and read about. You are hope. We are so involved in the problem that we have become a part of the problem itself. I will collect the underground peace seekers. You present the two ideas to them tomorrow evening. I will pick you up at the hotel at 6:00 pm. Sorry to keep you working. I am desperately, hopelessly selfish about finding peace in my beautiful country."

Forty-one

Peter entered the conference room in the UN secretariat with Ram Barua. There was a large group instead of the two he had met the day before.

One of the UN officials he had met opened the meeting.

"I hope you are not surprised at a large turnout. We discussed amongst ourselves what you scolded us about yesterday. We were shook up but are grateful for your frankness. We felt that you spoke your mind to help us. So the collection of heads you see here are Pakistani, Indians and Kashmiris. I must say that Miranda Mala who is very much part of this group told us last night about the two peace concepts. We feel that they are innovative to say the least."

Peter observed that more people were pouring into the large conference room. There was a sudden excitement and Peter saw the UN Secretary General enter the conference room. He greeted Peter and remembered him from the UN special program, meetings on Israel and Palestinian peace efforts. The Secretary General spoke

"My executives for the far eastern affairs briefed me this morning about your two ideas/concepts to bring peace to the disputed Kashmir. We would, first, all like to congratulate you and your well deserving Swiss Meridian team on the Nobel Peace prize, before we get started. Perhaps you can elaborate on your proposals for peace in Kashmir."

Peter felt somewhat unprepared but he was going to wing it like in the good old days.

"I am honored at this august gathering and your presence. Thank you for your kind wishes on the Nobel Peace Prize. I would like to give you some of my formulating thoughts behind the two alternates which are not mutually exclusive. These alternates are really street smart logic. We all suffer from a very salient omission in our human behavior. We don't speak our mind openly for job insecurity, job protection and other strangely unjustifiable reasons. The formality or show kills our insides and so we end up playing the verbal chess game. One of the culprits, perhaps, that make a complete mess in finding simple, fast solutions, is our inability to really know each other's mind. Sometimes we think we do, but the truth is we guess most of the time. Add to this, the lack of a burning desire for peace, and a deep compassion for the multitude of human suffering, and what you end up is a status quo.

"We end up forming groups and circles with people who so called `think like us'.

Progressive and innovative management rewards resolution of problems by their employees, but large governmental type organizations, has decision makers who because of their own political agenda choke simple solutions, and ideas. Commonsense solutions are very often found by the average person on the street. Our organizations, our lives, which are complicatedly wrapped up in confusion, become oblivious to what the person on the street, says or thinks.

"The Kashmir dispute cannot be solved with the present constellation of political parties on all sides, in my opinion. The ongoing debate and decisions are made by elected individuals who have a history to grind and are choking the future of the youth in Kashmir, Pakistan and India.

"What good are we to humanity if we cannot stop the suffering? The poor humanity anxiously waits for improvement in the quality, of their miserable lives after electing people, only to be terribly disappointed, as they have been for years. The elected leaders, who get elected promising to help the poor and neglected lives, lose contact of reality, once elected. The poor masses do not stand a chance. Sometimes acute desperation, forces the militant citizens to take arms against the establishments. They are stamped as trouble makers and terrorists. No one does the obvious, which is to talk to them, until many lives, usually innocent ones, are lost.

"The human beings that are poor in material wealth, the masses, are held hostage by the very system that is supposed to protect their interests.

"The Swiss government sent me to New York to feel the pulse of the disputing parties on their willingness to resolve this age-old problem. We have received an invitation by the Governments of India and Pakistan to attend a meeting on the deployment of the Meridian Peace weapon, knowing that both disputing factions want to exercise direct control on the Meridian peace weapon. I take it that neither India nor Pakistan trust the Swiss and their proven commitment to Neutrality. The Swiss government is therefore about to decline the invitation.

I would like to make an appeal to all the peace loving human beings to join hands and bring peace to Kashmir because the politics will not do so. Thank you."

The UN Secretary General agreed to open a special session and invite Kashmiri, Pakistani and Indian youth to discuss the two alternates and any others they wish with the objective of implementing it on a people to people basis. This was a bold decision because it circumvented the elected governments. As expected the governments reacted adversely.

Peter sat with Ram and Miranda for a late lunch. Miranda had cancelled the meeting with the underground peace seekers group because the circumstances turned for the better.

Forty-two

"Hi, Dearie! What are you up to? The wire services have given your speech at the UN thumbs up. John and Hans are enjoying having leashed their Peter weapon. The India and Pakistan negotiating committee has just gracefully withdrawn the invitation to the Swiss government. Hans has agreed that I join the entourage to Oslo next week for the Nobel Peace Prize ceremonies. You should visit mom and dad this evening since I see from your schedule that you will fly back tomorrow," said Cathy on the phone.

"How is business? Is it turning routine for you?" Peter enquired.

"Basically, yes. We have an increasing problem in Rigistan who had requested a Meridian team with a drone to control conflicts at their border in the north. Our team is on location and now held hostage by the Rigistan government and the warring faction from the north. The UN has protested and the UN envoy will try to get our team released. That is the only hot spot right now. Please, darling, don't go to Rigistan to solve the impasse. I told John but he just smiles. Other than that, it is all swell here." Cathy reported.

Peter called his mom and decided to spend the evening with them in New Brunswick. He was about to leave the hotel for New Brunswick when his phone rang "Hi, Peter. This is General Strong. We have just learnt that you may be in harms way. We have you on the tracking system and have alerted the Swiss intelligence. I am dispatching a U.S. army car with a MP bodyguard to take you wherever you want. They will stay with you 'til you fly back tomorrow. Love to see ya in DC when you can."

There was a knock at the door just as Peter was planning to leave his hotel room and someone hit him and covered his mouth with chloroform.

Peter came to in a small room. It appeared to be morning. His head and body ached and he felt very groggy. His hands and feet were tied and he had a tape over his mouth. There was a hooded man with a large knife and a pistol sitting near the door. The man who was snoozing immediately woke up when he saw Peter trying to move. He yelled at Peter in a unfamiliar language and ended his sentence with, "I keeel you!" Peter's body ached all over. The unconscious state, he thought, was better.

The door swung open and Peter briefly caught a glimpse of two men also wearing hoods. One came in and removed Peter's tape from his mouth. He came close and started to feed a hamburger to Peter. Peter welcomed food since he was famished. His thoughts began to dream of his mom's delicious Italian food.

"Don't get any ideas. One wrong move and you will die," said the stinking hooded man. He had a Jersey accent, Peter thought.

Some time lapsed and another hooded man walked up to Peter and pointed the pistol to Peter's head. "Listen Mr., you tell your people to give us the drone weapon and we will let you live."

He dialed a number on his cell phone, with a voice scrambler and held it near to Peter. The number was busy. He kept trying to call and the number was busy.

Peter could see the growing frustration on the man's face as he kept swearing. More time lapsed and finally the call went through.

"Hello? Hello?" came a heavy accented voice at the other end. The man thrust the pistol at Peter's face and said, "Tell them."

"Hello, I am Peter Miller. Please give the drone weapon to whoever these guys are," said Peter, strictly following the instructions.

The man at the other end did not understand and kept saying hello and some words that Peter could not understand. So Peter repeated the sentence and again got the same response.

The hooded man cursed and spoke in broken English, muffled through the hood he was wearing, asking for Hilfiger repeatedly. He paced about trying in his broken English, cursing and suddenly stopped, as if he understood the response and then threw the phone on the ground saying

"God damn it! Damn it! Wrong number." He stormed out of the room. He quickly returned and showed Peter the telephone number of the Meridian Department office in Bern. Peter shook his head affirmative.

Peter wanted to laugh but his body hurt badly and so he stayed calm. He saw from the small window in the toilet, that he was in a high rise apartment building. His captors came back with apparently a new number to call but were unsuccessful. The situation was beginning to amuse Peter. Who were his captors trying to call now? He wondered why his surveillance team had not tracked him down. What were they waiting for?

Finally his captors came back and asked Peter for his office number in Switzerland. They compared it with the number they had, and it matched. Peter gave the number from Cathy and they looked then decided not to call the number Peter gave.

Peter wondered if they did not call the number he gave because that could give away their location.

A few days passed and Peter waited for an opportune moment and addressed the masked man who had a Jersey accent.

"Who are yous guys? What is all this about?

The man observed him and said, "Where dya get the jersey accent?"

I am from New Jersey, that's where," Peter replied.

"No shit man, that's funny, it sure is. I no notin man, I am doin my job, that's all. Where from jersey are you?"

"New Brunswick," Peter replied.

The masked man went into an uncontrollable laughter, "No shit? How about that, ain't that a gas!" His loud laughter brought the attention of four masked men who came in the room and started to kick the jersey boy and Peter, repeatedly, "shoo, shoo, shut, shut, no noise, we keel you."

The jersey boy was hurt bad like Peter and removed his mask when the others left.

Peter thought the face looked familiar. "Hey, you Joe Malone's son"?

"And so what's it to ya? You got me into real trouble, look at me, I am a mess."

Peter quickly replied, "I went to Brunswick High with Charlie Malone, that's what , you piece of…."

The unruly gang came in again and seeing the Jersey boy without a hood, gave him and Peter another round of beating, leaving them both unconscious.

When Peter came to, he saw that the jersey boy was also tied up and lay in a pool of blood.

Peter reckoned that he had spent four days in captivity. He was fed every day a hamburger and allowed two supervised visits to the toilet in twenty four hours. Peter could barely walk because of the pain all over his body.

His left calf muscle was very sore. He realized that it was an open wound and then was awakened to the fact that his implanted transmitter had been removed. Hours went by and it was getting dark. He heard the jersey boy moan.

"Boy! I am hurt some real bad. I am going to kill these bastards," he moaned

"Save your strength," Peter said.

"See if you can reach my knife in the left pocket. Minutes passed as Peter wiggled into a position to get both his tied hands in the jersey boy's pocket. He pulled the knife out and lay on it when he heard the door open. Two of the hoods looked in and then shut the door again. Peter did not hear them locking the door this time. He waited and then tried to cut the rope that tied his feet but the pain in his body was excruciating. He then tried to cut the tape tying the jersey boy's hands and succeeded. The jersey boy reacted and took the knife, cutting himself free.

"Lie still, I'll be back for ya," he whispered to Peter.

The jersey boy opened the door slowly and drove the knife into the guy on guard outside the door. There was a muffling of noises and struggle followed by two gunshots and then two or three more. The gunshots woke up the neighbors and Peter heard sirens. Then he heard doors opening and banging close. Then sounds of people running. Suddenly the door kicked open and a police man aimed his pistol at Peter. The policeman flashed his light at Peter and saw someone tied up and beaten. The cavalry arrived and the ambulance rushed Peter to the hospital.

Peter opened his eyes to see the room he lay in filled with cops. The nurse pushed all the visitors out of the room and came up to Peter.

"See what happens when you leave home?"

Peter was all bandaged up and hooked to all kinds of IVs. He managed to say, "Where am I ?"

"You are in Brunswick General Hospital, in New Brunswick. Welcome back home. You have been out cold for two days. Your mom and dad are anxious to see ya. Your wife had fainted and is under observation. You are very much alive and the paparazzis can't wait to take your pictures and the reporters have held a vigil outside the hospital. You are one famous guy. Oh, yes, and you are very much alive and my name is Phyllis and what else do you want to know, my phone number perhaps…"

Two doctors came in and took his vital signs. "You will be fine soon. You were real lucky that the cops got to you in time. How the hell did you manage to get in this mess?"

Peter faded away for another couple of days. His injuries were serious.

Peter opened his eyes and got a glimpse of Cathy and his mom sitting at his bed side. His dad, John and Maria stood nearby. He felt extremely weak and then slipped into a coma. He was gaining conscious, but in a zone where he could hear people talking but could not move or speak. He wondered if he was dead. He could feel life coming back slowly. It felt like eternity, and finally he spoke

"I am fine honey," he said, with all the energy he could muster. "Don't you give up on me; you hear?"

The gloom in the hospital room turned into one of celebration with nurses trying to keep the noise level down.

Peter had been over four weeks in the hospital and was now finally on the road to recovery. The doctors insisted that he should stay in the hospital for another week.

He had missed out on so much in the four weeks. His room was filled with messages from well wishers and his room looked like a flower shop.

Peter could recall his last conscience moments as a hostage, but it was somewhat blurred. He recalled and wondered what happened to the jersey boy who turned into a savior from a kidnapper? Yes the police wanted answers too.

Joe Malone came to see Peter.

"Gee, Peter, I sure am glad you are getting better. Frank, you remember, the guy who saved you is still in coma from a head wound and multiple knife wounds in the neck. Frank is my youngest and is a cop, but the police and we have questions about what he was doing there. The other kidnappers were all killed in the gun battle".

The New Brunswick police chief walked into Peter's room, before Peter could answer. Cathy was sitting next to him and it felt that a mystery question needed an answer. Peter thought and said

"I recognized the similarity of your face when I saw Frank's face and it occurred to me that he was Joe's son. I think that got him in trouble with the kidnappers and they beat him and me to pulp. Frank must have been working undercover. I recall that he took the kidnappers on his own, in spite of the serious injuries. He had lost quite some blood. He is a hero in my books."

"I can't understand why he worked, undercover without informing the department. We found a hood cover in Frank's pocket which confirms your recollection that Frank was working undercover. There were five kidnappers, we found all shot to death by the cops who answered an anonymous 911 call. These guys all entered the country illegally. Do you know who they might have been?" asked the police chief.

"The kidnappers demanded that the drones sent to Rigistan by the Swiss government on assignment, to assist them, should be turned over to the Rigistan government. They were unable to make a contact after many frustrated attempts," said Peter trying hard to recall.

"We checked the home made phone contraption, the kidnappers used. It was for local calls only. The kidnappers had an arsenal of weapons but strangely all the firing pins were diffused in a way that the weapons were beyond repair. It worked out for the better otherwise we would have had a bigger blood bath. We have some unanswered questions, such as who made the anonymous 911 call and who disabled the firing mechanisms of the weapons in the possession of the kidnappers," said the chief, looking puzzled.

"The government of Rigistan denied any attempt to kidnap Peter when confronted but continued to repeat their request for taking possession of the drones. The UN envoy sent to Rigistan to get the drones back, had a very trying time. However as soon as the news on the kidnapping of Peter hit the press alleging that Rigistan may have something to do with it, the Rigistan government denied but immediately released the drone with a hastily worded apology to the UN. I am very sure that the government had a hand in Peter's kidnapping" filled in Cathy.

Later, there was a hush in the room as Peter saw Hans Hilfiger and Dieter walk in. They both carefully gave Peter a hug.

Hans spoke, "My God!, Peter you have had a life time share of kidnappings and injuries. Thank God that you made it alive from the terrible ordeal. Here is your Nobel Prize and the check that I accepted on your behalf. The atmosphere was very solemn at the ceremony, and the award committee was deeply concerned about your safety. We learnt about your sudden disappearance from the hotel after you were missing a day, about the same time your parents called Cathy. We sent the Mirage with the drones to locate you. The U.S. Secretary of Security personally joined us in the search. We were puzzled that there was no trace of you. The drones located the blood stained RFID planted in your leg, immediately, in a empty apartment in Hoboken. We knew the problem was very serious. The Swiss government issued an ultimatum to the government of Rigistan, for the immediate release of our team and the drones. Rigistan was for days, insisting that we transfer one drone free of charge so that they could fight the insurgency in the north of Rigistan, but the UN and we suspected their motives. We suspected that they had a hand in your disappearance. The UN issued an ultimatum to Rigistan also. I prayed for you in our Cathedral in Bern with the Meridian Project group.

"Peter! The hologram suddenly appeared at the alter as I prayed. The text said that you were held captive in New Brunswick, and the exact location. The text also said that all the weapons with the kidnappers had been diffused. The text after I had alerted the U.S. Authorities, read that they called the Emergency 911 telephone number, since we were too slow. Peter, I am a converted man. The Lord answered my prayers."

Peter felt tired and the visitors left.

Peter opened his eyes to see the large glaring eyes of Miranda. She would have kissed Peter had it not been for the watchful eyes of Cathy.

'Thank God, you are better. Your kidnapping broke nearly a war of words between India and Pakistan, each suspecting the other for having kidnapped you. You will be glad to know that the rival governments have accepted your alternate solutions for peace and are implementing them with the watchful eyes of the UN. The people of Kashmir have a great deal to thank you for all your assistance. The citizens of Srinagar in Indian Kashmir have decided to mount your statue in one of the main squares in the city, in your honor." She broke down in grateful tears.

Cathy was anxious to bring Peter up to date but in small doses as advised by the doctors. She had prepared a file, full of newspaper cuttings about Peter including the Nobel Prize ceremonies that Peter was unable to attend. She had not left Peter all the time he was in the hospital. Peter's mom and Dad visited him everyday.

The last week in the hospital gave Peter a chance to collect his thoughts. So much had happened. Some of which he would rather not recall. Peter restarted the meditation and the breathing exercises; his friend Gopala Krishnan had taught him in Bangalore.

Forty-three

Cathy looked at him with loving eyes. "Darling, are you ready for the best news of your life? We will have a baby! I am in the third month of pregnancy."

The news really hit Peter with emotions, he never experienced before. Suddenly his drifting thoughts took a consolidated direction. He was terribly in love with Cathy and with his baby, on his way. Cathy had told him that it was a boy. He could now feel that his family was becoming complete.

His parents made sure that the flow of visitors stayed to a minimum to give Peter time to convalesce.

His old friend Joe came in and told him that he had visited the hospital several times only to be told that he was still unconscious. It was a reunion of two really good friends.

Joe started to talk about what he was doing.

"I did get my Masters in education from Rutgers. I got thinking about teaching at the Brunswick High and felt real bad about the state of education in the country after I went to the teacher's convention in Atlantic City. We were an unruly bunch, you remember, but this is a whole new ball game. It is a, 'I don't give a damn' generation. Guess who is at fault? We are. The teachers are very badly paid to begin with. Frankly, Pete, I found most of the teachers are scared of the students.

Some of the teachers took a beating, which I found was not uncommon. Jesus Christ! Pete, what the hell is goin' on?

"I studied and reflected on the misery of the state of education in our town and learnt that the condition prevailed in plenty of public schools in the country. I then sat the tough guys and gals I knew, you know the hard core ones, and talked to them.

"These kids told me that neither the teachers nor the education system motivated them. They felt rebellious and no one really talked to them. They were treated like crap at home and in the school with only threats. They really saw no discipline because there was no one they respected in the school or for that matter at home. The only role models were the tough cookies so they followed them. It was a rebellion against the system. Most of them saw themselves victims trying to survive. The neighborhoods they came from were tough, and rough, teaching them the survival of the fittest. They hated the smart kids because they were unable to learn because of their learning deficiencies. They suffered from mental blocks since kindergarten and were immediately treated as waste. They never saw love nor felt it at home. I asked them if they had heard about God. Most of them had no concept of God the Creator. They thought I was talking rubbish when I mentioned God. Most of them said that they never believed in God, if there was such a guy. Pete, I can't help feeling that our generation has failed in bringing up the next generation.

"You remember how little we knew about world geography, history, international awareness, mathematics, and other subjects? Well let me tell you, it's still the same. The problem now is that the country is going global whether we like or not and these kids are lost. I see how smart the kids of the new immigrants are, and they may be our salvation. In short our public education system must be revamped or we will head down making our future generations misfits in the world."

Joe looked dejected and yet showed that inner strength he always had to make a difference or as he always said, 'give a damn'.

"Guess what, Pete," Joe continued. "I was depressed every day when I went to the school to teach. I looked for an analyst, you know, a head-shrinker. Did not find one that could calm me. Then by chance I met the old Prof Jim Marconi and let me tell you. This guy was on the ball. He had all the answers. Remember Prof Marconi who taught us literature and poetry and how we really enjoyed his class. The Prof is now in his eighties and has studied all the major religions of the world. He summarized to me what life was all about. He said that life was meant for finding God and seeing how we are part of His creation. He sang the old song *'He is Got the whole world in His hands , He is got you and me brother in His hands , He is got you and me sister in His hands, He is got the whole world in His hands'.* You remember that song don't ya? The old Prof explained to me about Karmic law, *as you sow, so shall you reap.*"

Peter and Cathy were so impressed by what Joe said that they all decided to pay the old Prof a visit.

The Prof had a glow about him. He talked very calmly with a remarkable simple explanation about life. They recalled how enjoyable his classes were on literature and poetry.

"Teaching any subject is very tough. The teacher must know the subject extremely well and be able to teach in simple words with love and passion. They have dropped poetry from the school curriculum. Can you imagine that? Literature and poetry are the heart of a good sound education. What I have been teaching is the correction in our history books that make us whites look great and the red Indians the bad guys. We took their land and they now live in desperation in reservations. There is very little in the history books in the schools about the blacks. I read some books written by blacks on their tragedy. We should teach our kids how the white man made black human beings their slaves. How can a growing and developing young mind even begin to appreciate the tragedy we inflicted on the Indians and the blacks. We should understand the contributions they made to our history. Our education system in the public schools dehumanized races so the young minds have no respect for humanity just because they were not taught to relate to it, understand and respect human dignity.

"History is full of mad men whom the people followed blindly out of fright or whatever their reasons were, which brought their nation to ruin. Remember how we talked about the holocaust in your class. Does one have to be Jewish to feel the pain of over six millions annihilated by a mad man? We do not learn from history and so history repeats itself. Leaders have no statesmanship or vision. How can they make valuable contributions to the quality of human life? They are simply too interested in lining their pockets. Have we made the generations insensitive to atrocities? Just see the amount of crime in society. We encourage it in our young minds with indifference and then pay lip service to any correction to resolve the problem. Our school systems and parents pay little attention in the civilized development of our young generations and then wonder what went wrong. Discipline, compassion, love, religion, humility, and God are now meaningless words. The communists took God out of the lives of the people and left a society without a soul, lost in every sense of the word.

"Ah! You did not come to discuss about the tragedy of life but about the celebration of life. We are required to simply do our best and leave the rest to the Almighty. He is the one who makes it all happen. We must dissolve the 'I' in us. We must study the scriptures with devotion. The increasing love of God becomes our salvation. We should become detached from the material and live in the spiritual self. We really enjoy life when we serve God with a single devoted purpose. Our inside fills with love and genuine peace. We break the Karmic cycle and eliminate the misery of life and death. It is the inner peace that we all seek all our lives, since it sustains and is not temporary. Divine knowledge of God brings us the peace we seek all our life. This requires good Realized souls. Where are they? We owe it to ourselves not to waste this life and when we reach God realization to teach and help others out of their misery.

"Each human being suffers or enjoys in different degrees depending on the past Karmas. We are reincarnated into better or worse life depending on the extent we obeyed and lived according to the teachings of the Lord. What happens to us in our next life depends on what we do in this life. This cycle of life and death and then rebirth can be stopped by knowing God and serving Him, which is God Realization. It is not difficult to understand and love God with devotion. All you need is the unflinching desire to escape from the miseries of life and death. The bliss enjoyed in devotional love of God is intoxicating and the desire to enjoy the material life completely vanishes. After all who in his right mind would not want to be in complete bliss? Quite simple, my dear Watson!" He smiled in devotion.

Peter listened with great joy, the nectar that flowed out of the message from the great Prof Marconi. "Are you familiar with the teachings in the Gita? What have you learnt from the holy Bible?"

The Prof said, "The Gita is very deep by any standards. It is not complicated. You should study with love and Devotion for God. Let me read to you the *Gita Saar,* which is the nectar of the Gita." He read with a glow in his face and tears of devotion.

"What are you worried about? Who are you afraid of?
Who can kill you? The soul is neither born nor ever dies.

"What happened was good. What is happening in the present is good, and what will happen in the future will also be good.
Do not worry about the Past, Present or Future.

"What have you lost, that you are crying about?
What did you bring that is lost?
What did you create that is destroyed?
You never brought anything with you, when you were born.
Whatever you received was here in this world.
Whatever you gave,you gave here
Whatever you received, you received from God.
Whatever you gave, you gave to God, knowingly or unknowingly.
You came empty handed and will go empty handed.
What is yours today, belonged to someone else once and tomorrow will belong to some one else.
You are taking pride in the ownership of something that does not belong to you
This very happiness is the source of your misery.

"Changes are the law of nature
What you consider death is in fact real life
You became rich in one moment and poor in the next moment
Remove from your heart and thought the concept of yours, mine, big, small, ours, theirs
It is all yours and you belong to all

"This material body is not yours, nor are you the body
The body is made of fire, water, air, earth, sky and will return to these elements
But the soul is ever present, so who are you?
Surrender yourself to God
He is the sole and ultimate support and course of life
The one who understands this is always free of fear, worry and sorrow.
Offer everything you do to God as you go on in life
You will always enjoy the bliss of salvation in your life with this understanding

Forty-four

Peter and Cathy were overwhelmed with the depth of spiritual knowledge of Prof Jim Marconi. What a great soul. They learnt that the learned, God Realized people were all over the world. Peter was thrilled that such a sage lived in New Brunswick. They also remembered the words of Gopala Krishnan in Bangalore , that there was no need to go looking for God , because He lived in every living being, was everywhere, and helped those who seek Him.

The world now looked very different and so much for the better. Peter saw his parents ageing and so loving to Cathy that he had a strong urge to settle down in the town of his birth. He wanted time from now on so he could devote to the study of the scriptures and the family which was soon going to have a new member.

John and Maria had gotten married in Basel, Switzerland. John wanted to spend time with Maria and his father. He had had a very active and eventful life that he no longer cared for and so he got a teaching job in the University of Basel. He did not want to run around any more.

The Rutgers University, Peter's Alma mater, offered him a job to teach International Relations. Peter expressed his concerns at the interview about a Godless society. Peter suggested that the University offer a course on 'Inner Peace' starting with the freshman year all through the four or five year university degree as a part of the regular curriculum for a bachelors' degree. There were several lengthy sessions with the

Board of Trustees of the University and the faculty over teaching 'Inner Peace' as a subject . At each session Peter won the hearts of the faculty and Board members who had strongly opposed that religion be kept out of the curriculum. He appealed to their contemplative souls that education without a spiritual awakening would be a waste, since the most important course in life was knowledge of God.

Peter prepared the courses for five or optional four year curriculum with inspirational lectures, debates and discussions. He included guest speakers, who had achieved God Realization, from all walks of life including clergy, rabbis, Hindu gurus, Buddhist monks, and Islamic scholars etc. Spiritual music/singing/prayers sessions were also scheduled in the curriculum.

Peter had assigned the 'Inner Peace' Course for one credit in the Freshman year, two credits in the Sophomore year , three credits in the Junior year and four credits in the Senior year. The exams at the end of each semester were written essays by each student on what they had learnt. The emphasis was not on testing but on learning. The goal of the 'inner peace' courses at graduation was to make the University educational experience complete in material and spiritual aspects of human life.

Peter wanted that each graduating student should get a good education, balanced with the power of spirituality.

The University finally agreed to start with the freshman year course as a test. The course was a resounding success and the attendance increased in leaps and bounds. Students in the second, third and fourth years started to also attend the class.

The Dean and faculty extended the courses as requested by Peter, initially. Peter felt a greater sense of satisfaction than he had ever felt in his successful campaigns for Peace. Teaching a large class of faces eager to absorb what he and his guest speakers said was very rewarding and he felt spiritually rewarded.

Soon the press took it on as a story and there were many editorials appearing in various news papers and magazines around the country.

Hans Hilfiger had also retired from his tenure with the Swiss government and become a Professor at the University of Zurich. Hans invited Peter to give seminars during the summer semesters in

Zurich. Peter also gave lectures at the University in Basel. His role now as a teacher was expanding with invitations coming from around the world. Peter was very content, busy like the old days minus the type of excitement he really did not miss.

"Darling, I have never seen you so happy. Our family is complete with our son Franz. Now that we are back to the United States and getting some routine in our lives, I am grateful to God that we live in a country where we are free, well all right relatively free. There are millions of people in so many parts of the world where the word 'freedom' does not exist. How sad," Cathy said.

"You know, darling! I don't miss the excitement of my job in DC or in Switzerland. I am glad we quit. I came real close to getting killed. There is something I learnt after all what I went through. Life, liberty, opportunity and the freedom to follow your desires are so very precious and must not be taken for granted. I sure have lots to be thankful for. Are you glad we quit? "said Peter, sounding content.

"Yes, but, you always forget to kiss my cheeks before giving me one on the smacker."

"There is a lot of room for improvement, darling. I will work on it!" He gave Cathy a kiss that took her breath away.

About the Author

Ken Mathur was born November 22, 1937 in New Delhi, India. His school years in New Delhi, Simla, Bombay and Calcutta gave him an early taste for a variety of cultures in India.

He traveled to the Unites States in 1956 for a B.S.M.E(Mechanical Engineering) degree from the Stevens Institute of Technology 60', Hoboken N.J. He was one of the first students from India in the Institute that had only a hand full of foreign students in 1956. The Dean of Men, having failed to pronounce his name, Kanwal, called him 'Ken'instead.

He started his career in Switzerland with Brown Boveri Co.(now Asea Brown Boveri) as a project engineer in the Electric power generation Division, and traveled in Europe and India. He was fascinated by the tremendous variety of technical, business and human challenges, working with diverse cultures. His desire to absorb and enjoy the multiculturalism, continued after a short business tenure in India, Switzerland, Canada before returning to New Jersey.

He became a Vice President and left the corporate culture of Brown Boveri Corp in North Brunswick, New Jersey after eighteen years, entering the world of Consulting with trouble shooting assignments, which took him to the far corners of the world. He found people fascinating, very different and yet very much the same in their desire to interact with other people around the world. A vast majority of people he met seek peace, harmony, freedom, opportunities to work and make a decent living. He feels like a citizen of the world, blessed and grateful for his upbringing and the variety of education and experience he continues to receive in the world. He can speak and mumble in a few languages. He found that people are so much friendlier when they feel that you understand and respect their culture and make an effort to speak their language.

He has retired from the business world at the age of 68 and shuttles with his wife, visiting his three children and a grandson in Switzerland, Miami, and Spain.

The *Peace Lover* is a reflection of his hope and desire for mortal and spiritual peace in the world.

BOOK Summary

The principal character; Peter Miller, a regular Jersey kid, a second generation Swiss, working his way through life in New Brunswick, New Jersey, spurned by his attraction to the world of internationalism.

His patriotism, challenged by 9/11, spur him into working for the Intelligence Agency where he encounters forces he could never have imagined. Living through kidnappings and attempts on his life, he stays focused in solving and defusing problems with simple and direct solutions; his very nature. His first task of stopping the sale of Swiss arms to insurgents takes him to Switzerland. He learns about the world of weapons and arms trade with its desire to increase the bottom line with little regard to human life. He learns about the unsolved mysterious death of his grandfather by chance and enters the intrigue of a highly sophisticated Swiss weapon, developed to disable insurgents. He shuttles between Switzerland, the United States, and the United Nations, trying to make the special interest forces return to becoming human beings in order to resolve conflicts around the world, while applying the Swiss weapon of peace, to diffuse the criminal warring factions.

He meets the love of his life, an American of Swiss origin, during his life of suspense and thrilling adventure.

Peter Miller remains unfulfilled after helping develop a sense of relative sanity in the world scene. He looks for a deeper meaning of life and searches for spirituality, spurned by his desire to seek inner peace.

He finally settles down in his home town, New Jersey, after suffering serious wounds when kidnapped.

He realizes the importance of spirituality and turns his life in the pursuit of learning and teaching inner peace to the new generation.